"OUR LADY WITH THE FIERY EYES"
Nuestra Señora Con Los Ojos Ardientes
Copyright 2019, Gary Parker

ISBN…9781091040854

with

Sea Dunes Publishing House

All rights reserved. No part of this book may be printed, scanned or reproduced without prior written permission from the author and publisher, except in the case of brief quotations used in critical articles and reviews.

Cover Art…Seajay Milner
Edit Assistance…Sam Milner

ACKNOWLEDGEMENTS

I want to thank my Mom and Dad for the guidance I got as a child…a teenager…a young adult and even to this very day. My folks were strict growing up especially my Dad. My parents were strict because they loved me. It took me having my own children to figure that out. I was taught to respect others and most importantly, the value of a hard day's work. I was also taught that not even the sky is a limit when we want something bad enough and are willing to work hard and take a few chances to fulfill our dreams.

I want to also acknowledge my wife Missy. She has globe trotted with me over the years to keep me happy by allowing me to chase what she thought then as an elusive dream. I know it's not been easy leaving good jobs, relocating to another area and then starting over with a new job. Over the years she has herself been bitten by the allure of treasure and loves to hunt artifacts. How could I have gotten a better life partner than her? I love her and this book should lay testament to just how strong that love is.

I want to thank my buddy, Captain Fizz, whom I hooked up with too late in my life. He has inspired me and unselfishly pulled me into his world of treasure stories and treasure salvage. Wish I had found you years ago, dude!!

I also want to acknowledge Sam Milner and his wife Seajay. I met these folks on a memorial cruise for the world's greatest treasure finder, Black Jack Haskins. After being introduced to Sam as a writer, editor and publisher, I was convinced by my wife Missy to blow the dust off the manuscript of this book which had been in the making for years. Sam read through the manuscript and gave me the inspiration and guidance to finally bring it to fruition. Thank you Sam for getting me off dead center!

It's amazing the number of great people you meet on life's trail. Some are family...some are wonderful acquaintances... friends who help us not to fail. Help them when they need a hand...show them love when things are rough. We're all just one big family but struggle to admit it... or show it enough.

The Author

DEDICATION

This book is dedicated to my Mother, Nan Parker (Cardinal), who is fighting hard to beat ovarian cancer as this book is being completed. Mom was always my "go to parent" when life gave me trouble and heartache. I loved my Dad but Mom seemed to be able to make everything better.

Nan Parker Cardinal

Joshua Robert Parker

I also dedicate this book to the wonderful and comical Son that we lost too early, Joshua Robert Parker. Josh could keep you in stitches with his great personality and sense of humor. It was Josh who actually gave me the inspiration to write this book. He was riding to work one day with his Mom and a song came across the radio. The title of the song was, *I Would Die For You*. Josh looked at his Mom and said, "That's Dad…he would die for you."

CHAPTERS

1…Treasure Dreams and the Boogeyman

2…Back to Fort Myers, Florida and…
   "X" Marks the Spot

3…Back To Jamaica and On The High Seas

4…On The Scatter Debris Trail

5…Ben Makes A Deal With The Little Big-Man

6…Treasure And Trouble

7…Do We Have An Accord?

8…Black Hands At Last

9…Rough Seas Ahead And More Trouble

10…The Unveiling and Broken Heart

11…Back On The Pile Of Gold

12…Ben Shakes Hands With The Boogeyman

13…When Death We Don't Part

"OUR LADY WITH THE FIERY EYES"
Nuestra Señora Con Los Ojos Ardientes

PROLOGUE

Late in the year 1669 a flotilla of four Spanish galleons sailed up the west coast of South America loaded with gold, silver and emeralds, all plundered from different regions and indigenous inhabitants of that continent. Their destination was Panama City where the treasure was offloaded and transported across the isthmus of Panama by mule train to Portobelo, a principal Spanish port located on the Caribbean Coast. There, the treasure would be stored and await the arrival of Spain's Terra Firma Fleet which had been loaded with European goods that the Spanish colonies could not otherwise obtain. After unloading those goods, the fleet would take on those treasures that had arrived from the South American region. From Portobelo, the Terra Firma Fleet would rendezvous with the New Spain Fleet in Havana where the two fleets would make their way up the East Coast of Florida and eventually cross the Atlantic Ocean returning to Spain.

On August 3rd, 1670; the Capitana, *Nuestra Señora Con Los Ojos Ardientes*, "Our Lady With The Fiery Eyes", and eleven other ships were loaded with the awaiting South American treasure. The heavily armed Capitana was loaded with the lion's share of the treasure. Once loading was complete, on August 5th the fleet fired their cannons for good luck and weighed anchor setting sail during the height of hurricane season. This was done against Captain Bonito De Santana's better judgement. However, King Charles II, whom was the seated King of Spain from 1665 to 1700 desperately needed the delivery of this treasure fleet in order to help fund the war effort, was willing to run the risk of the possible loss of the fleet. He demanded that the flotilla set sail for Havana immediately upon completion of loading the treasure and other provisions.

The flotilla set sail for Havana, Cuba as ordered. On the third day of their voyage they began to experience heavy seas and increasingly steady winds. The captains and crew members could feel an ill wind about to overtake them. Too late to turn back, the Capitana was passing off the western most tip of Jamaica on the evening of August 10th, 1670. The storm that had been menacing them was now on top of them in full fury and blowing with hurricane force. The Capitana and three other supply ships that had been sailing in sight of one another were slowly and helplessly blown onto the treacherous reefs off the western fringe of Jamaica.

The Capitana's manifest and passenger list, along with other documents found in the archives, revealed that she was carrying 300 souls which were all lost to the raging waters. The ship had been loaded with 200,000 pesos of silver and gold coinage, 300 silver bars, 200 gold bars, a large quantity of emeralds and two chests full of worked silver and gold jewelry. Also on board would have been a large amount of contraband treasure which would have escaped being recorded by the board of trades agent as it was being loaded. This practice was implemented so that the ship's owner could smuggle a portion of treasure back to Spain for himself, without having to pay the "King's Fifth" or twenty percent of the treasure as required by law. This contraband was typically hidden amongst the ballast stones in the ship's hull. The hulls of the tall, wooden ships of those days were weighted down with stones called "ballast" in order to keep the ship in an upright position while sailing on the water.

Most interesting, but not recorded on the ship's manifest, the ship was allegedly carrying a solid gold altar weighing several hundred pounds which had been fashioned by the Indian goldsmiths of Peru under the direct supervision of Spanish architect, Hernando Montessori, famous for his design and construction of Catholic churches in Spain. This golden altar was to be a gift to King Charles from Hernando in hopes that the King might see fit to authorize and fund Hernando in the building of the first Catholic church in the "New World". Also on board would have been a vast amount of personal wealth carried by the ship's passengers.

Although the golden altar was not noted on the ship's manifest, Ben had come across some unofficial documents years earlier that alluded to this magnificent story. He'd also come across other documents in his years of research that mentioned the name of the architect, Hernando Montessori, from the same period. Ben was well aware of the fact that even if the altar did not exist, the documented treasure aboard, as well as the contraband treasure and personal wealth of the passengers, would make this one of the most valuable wrecks ever located in the Caribbean waters.

Eight of the twelve ships that left Portobelo on that August morning were never heard from again. The four vessels that did manage to keep their keels off the reef were badly damaged and limped into Havana several days later reporting the loss of the fleet. When word reached Spain of the tragedy, King Charles immediately ordered four ships to set sail from Havana in search of the lost ships, any possible survivors and most importantly…to salvage what they could from the remaining treasure. The four ships searched the area eight days and nights and found nothing but some floating wreckage. The exact location of the Capitana would remain a mystery for the next 340 years.

CHAPTER 1

Treasure Dreams And... The Boogeyman

It was a Saturday afternoon a mile offshore the west coast of Jamaica. Another day of diving was about to come to an end as the sun began to sink in the western sky. One last magnetometer hit was left to be investigated before the group called it a day. The crew had been pulling the instrument back and forth for three weeks, systematically searching the ocean floor for signs of metal that might indicate the remains of a shipwreck. The dive season was about over for the crew when a signal came across on the control box indicating the signs of ferrous metal below. Crew member, Troy Mann who was monitoring the equipment, slapped the captain on the back. Then, he pulled the captain's headset off his head, something which the man wore constantly as he listened to classic country music for hours on end. "Pull back on the engine...throw a marker...and drop the anchor! We've got a hit, mon!" Troy shouted.

 Using their annual three week vacation from their otherwise boring jobs, the group had been searching every summer for the past three years for the wreck of a 200-ton Spanish galleon. Documents declared that the galleon met its end during a hurricane in the summer of 1670. The diving-group consisted of self-taught shipwreck historian Ben Carson, and his long time friend, diving companion and treasure-hunting buddy, Troy Mann, both from Fort Myers, Florida. Their boat captain is a country-music listening and singing islander, Simon Role, whom Ben and Troy affectionately refer to as...Marley, because of his dreadlocks. Marley had been a part of the group every summer and was originally hired for the use of his boat, his knowledge of the waters, understanding of the local folklore, and because of his connections on the island. Marley often entertains the crew with his rendition of Johnny Cash's song, *Ring Of Fire,* and several other classic country hits. Marley is an atrocious singer, although Ben and Troy never hint the fact to him. They are actually entertained by Marley's lack of singing ability, and besides...it helped to pass the time of the tedious task at hand. The fact that Marley believes that he is an aspiring singer makes the entertainment that much more comical. Ben and Troy simply clap and continue with their work after every song Marley entertains them with. Afterward, Marley stands up at the helm of the boat and bows.

"No worries, mon!" he laughs.

****

Based on documents which Ben had dusted off in the Archives of the Indies in Seville, Spain; the ship was the Capitana, or lead ship of the flotilla, *Nuestra Señora Con Los Ojos Ardientes, "Our Lady with the Fiery Eyes".*

The dive team's second year's search had resulted in the finding of several scattered brass spikes and old rigging. None of what the team had found this season could be proven to have belonged to a sailing vessel from the 1600's, let alone having belonged to the ship in which they were searching for. However, late into the third year of searching, the team discovered a large storm anchor on the western fringe of the reef. One of the large flukes of the anchor was dug deep into the sea floor where it had rested for years. The long shaft and eye of the anchor were pointing almost due east which told the crew a lot about the ship that had broken free of this anchor. It told them that the vessel would have been a ship equivalent to the size of the Capitana and would almost certainly have been blown on an eastward course. All Spanish ships of that era carried several anchors of different sizes for various uses. The storm anchor was the largest of the anchors carried and would have been used during events in heavy seas. The anchor that was found was definitely of Spanish origin and could be traced to the 1600's by its design and construction. Also found in the immediate area were two large iron cannons which were also of the right origin and construction for a 1600's era Spanish vessel.

From the information Ben had gathered from the Archives of the Indies in Spain, this was his explanation of the way it happened...

"On the eve of the ship's sinking, I imagine the wind was blowing the rain horizontally. The big ship would have come off the crest of the waves crashing down in the troughs between the waves. Sails, rigging, spars and masts were being ripped and snapped off like toothpicks as cargo that was tied down on the upper decks tore loose from their tie-down rings and strewn across the reefs. Most likely, some of the crew had been busy working to keep the decks cleared of wreckage while other crew members might have been chopping down what masts remained in an effort to stabilize the big ship. Meanwhile, passengers huddled below decks with rosary beads in hand praying for a miracle. There would be no miracles, and in a last attempt to keep the big ship off the reef, a storm anchor was deployed. Cannons, along with anything of weight and no value was jettisoned in hopes of lightening the load so that the ship might float higher in the water avoiding the jagged coral heads below. When the big anchor hooked the bottom, the huge rope snapped and whipped back to the deck like the tentacle of a giant octopus, knocking sailors off the deck like rag dolls and into the raging seas. At that point, the big ship was doomed. Her hull would have grounded onto the reef while the bottom was ripped open, spilling the contents of the precious cargo and scattering the King's fortune and future all over the reef. During the break up the upper deck portion most likely sheared-off from the hull thus scattering wreckage, passengers and sailors for miles somewhere west of Jamaica near the Pedro Banks."

Marley's eyes were as big as pieces of eight as he listened to Ben tell the story of the ship.

The discovery of the anchor was a major clue for the team because it told them that this location defined the western edge of the search-area and that the ship and its remains should rest due east of this location...somewhere between the anchor and shoreline, thus reducing the search area tremendously. There was also a real possibility that these finds could belong to one of a number of the one-hundred documented wrecks in these waters.

As Ben made his way over the stern of the boat to take a look at one last mag-hit before wrapping up the season, he made a comment under his breath.

"We haven't found the kitchen sink yet and I sure had hoped we'd make it a perfect season!" Then, he pulled his full-mask over his face which provided communication between himself and crew members on the boat. He grabbed his metal-detector, took a giant step off the back of the boat, let the air out of his buoyancy compensator and disappeared beneath the waves to have a look at what the magnetometer had alerted them of.

When Ben touched bottom in about twenty-five feet of water, he had a quick look around the scene to see if he could locate anything obvious before starting the metal-detector search. There were a few scattered ballast stones strewn all over the area from centuries of shipping, something to only get a little excited about. However, a pile of ballast stones *could* indicate the debris field of a vessel that was breaking apart...something worth writing home about. Ben also saw a familiar barracuda that always seemed to be hanging out under the boat, along with the usual schools of reef fish that were busy darting in and out of the colorful sea growth, and the occasional curious reef shark that would get just close enough to make a diver a little uncomfortable.

"So far...nothing but a scattering of ballast stones," Ben said, letting the crew aboard the boat know what he was encountering. Then, he switched on the metal-detector and began the tedious process of swinging it back and forth while systematically covering the sandy bottom around the marker-buoy weight and in between the coral heads.

About thirty minutes into the process, Ben picked up something metallic on the instrument. He ran the detector over the length of the object and determined that it must be about two feet in length. He began to fan the sand away with his hand and soon uncovered a large, old, iron spike that could have come from just about anything. Ben placed the old spike by the marker float weight to take it back to the boat with him when he surfaced. This was done to remove the item from the search area so if the area needed to be surveyed more thoroughly at a later date, the trash item would not be detected again and more time wasted. He quickly began his search again, moving the detector back and forth laterally. Soon, he got another screech in his ear indicating metal beneath the detectors search-coil. He fanned sand away for several minutes until he uncovered a small, black conglomerate that appeared to be made of silver. When silver has been in saltwater for an extended period of time, it turns black and develops a thick, black coating over it. Ben put the clump in a mesh bag which he carried on his side and continued his search. It wasn't long before the detector screeched again and again. After fanning a hole in the sand about one foot deep, he recovered a small, blackened, box-shaped object about the size of a match box, most likely made of silver.

Ben's heart pounds with excitement as he realizes that finding this item may possibly have put them in the debris-trail of more personal items, most likely...in the path a ship had taken while breaking up. He felt more confident than ever that the group was on the verge of finding some significant artifacts, albeit not the main treasure, since these items could have come from one of the supply ships. Ben also had a hunch that if they took the GPS coordinates from the anchor, along with the GPS coordinates of this latest find, the crew should be able to draw a straight line on the charts between the two points and have a very precise path that the ship took while breaking apart, if indeed these items had come from the target ship. The line over the chart should also lead the crew to the final resting-spot of the main portion of the treasure and hopefully...the golden altar!

As Ben continued to search, the thought ran through his mind about being at the end of the dive season and not being able to continue the search for another year. Knowing how treasure can change the perspective of practically any man, he made the decision not to share the find with Marley in fear that he might decide to spill-the-beans to some local yahoos and continue the search without himself and Troy. At this point in the game, Ben only had an "Electronic Survey Permit" from the Jamaican Government which did not give him the rights to anything that may be found, only the rights to look for it. The next required steps would be to identify and then request a

"Salvage Permit" which would give the permit holder the right to lawfully harvest their find under close supervision. This step by step process is by design for admiralty-laws in most countries and is in place to tip-off bureaucrats that something of value or interest must have been found so that more red tape, cost and litigation could be put in place in order to detour the rightful finders, who have spent all their own money at this point, from staking their claim. At this point, the treasure is still up for grabs.

Ben searched around the base of the coral head for a few minutes more. The sun overhead was starting to sink and visibility underwater was starting to decrease as a result. Once again the detector chirped and Ben fanned and dug in the sand anxiously in anticipation of what may lie below. Suddenly, there before his eyes...lay a gleaming gold coin on the hard rock bottom! The coin was definitely of Spanish origin. The coin was large and most likely an eight escudo, of which the Capitana was carrying chests full of this denomination in both gold and silver.

Ben tucked his treasures and mystery conglomerate into his wetsuit and ascended to the surface. He kept a wary eye on the menacing looking barracuda that seemed to be perpetually suspended lazily beneath the boat. Ben thought to himself as he passed the fish... *"This creature must be a sentinel for King Neptune, guarding the riches that the sea has harvested over the centuries."*

Once he was back on the boat, Ben instructed Marley to mark the spot on the GPS so the group would know where to continue their search next season. Ben also made a note of the coordinates in his dive ledger and then secretly removed the items from his wetsuit and tucked them away in his dive bag. He was eager to share the finds with Troy but he thought he'd better not let Marley in on the excitement just yet. That, meant sharing the find with Troy would have to wait as well. Ben felt as if he was going to explode keeping the information to himself, but knew that it was necessary not to reveal "the finds" at this point.

"Okay, cowboy...it's a wrap for this season..." Ben said with a sigh... "Weigh the anchor and let's get under way".

Marley pulled the anchor, fired up the diesel engine and turned the boat toward the dock in Freetown for the last time this season. On the way back to Freetown Bay the group always passed an island with a high hill on it rising nearly a hundred feet above sea level. At the top of the hill was a large old mansion, which by the looks of the architecture, appeared to have been built long ago. At the water's edge in a protected lagoon were two docks with a boat tied to one dock that never seemed to move.

"Hey Marley...what's up with the island and the old mansion?" Ben asked.

Marley replied, "Strange things take place on that island...things that are not to be talked about by the good folks of Freetown."

"Come on, Marley...give us some details about some of the strange happenings that you're privy to."

Marley replied, "You know...voodoo...black-magic, and witchcraft kinds of happenings. The old surgeon from the East, which the townspeople call, the *Boogeyman*, he lives in the mansion. Rumor has it that he steals peoples body parts and then sells them to people who are in need of 'em. I've heard..." Marley continued... "that he gets as much as five million dollars from rich Americans for a liver, or a heart. Those are just stories, though. I don't know if there's truth to those stories, but...it kinda' makes ya' wonder," Marley pondered aloud. "You *do* know...that the only time you see another boat at the dock is late at night after somebody from nearby seems to disappear on that night…Coincidence, you might say? I don't know, but I'd appreciate it if this conversation didn't go no further and stayed right here on this boat."

"Oh, come on now, Marley," Troy resounded "It sounds like ghosts and goblins to me.

"But, I *have* heard stories of people waking up in a bathtub full of ice with some of their parts missing…" Marley continued.

"Surely, Marley...if you know of these stories, then...why wouldn't the local officials know about them as well, and then...go out there and bust the old butcher," Troy asked.

"Troy…Troy...Troy, mon! You telling me that you've not witnessed enough around here these last three years to not know that local officials are corrupt and most likely take kickbacks from everything that is allowed to happen around here? This is why the towns people keep their mouths shut. They don't want their children or loved one's to be the next to disappear!"

As the boat pulled up alongside the dock Marley cut the engines. Ben commented, "You know...*I've* heard these stories of people waking up iced-down, as well. There *could* be some truth to it, so...I say we steer clear of that island, boys. By the way, Marley...nice ghost story," Ben remarked. "And...it's gonna' stay right here in the boat. Right, Troy?"

"Yeah, I'm not saying anything!" he replied, rolling his eyes. Glancing back over his shoulder at the old mansion, he comments under his breath... *"But...given our luck, that pile of treasure is gonna' be laying right at the foot of that dang hill!"*

Having to fly out early in the morning and return to Florida, Ben and Troy shook Marley's hand and hugged his wife, Tanya, who from time to time came there to meet them at the dock at the end of the day.

Ben handed Marley a wad of money with his left hand and put his right hand on the man's shoulder. "Marley, mon...this, should square things up between us. Wha-da-ya' think?"

While Marley counted the money, Troy spoke. "Thank you both. We look forward to seeing you when we return."

Marley, Tanya, and their two young sons of eleven and twelve years of age live in a very poor area in the harbor village of Freetown. Marley works at odd jobs and fishes to make ends meet while Tanya takes care of the house, the two young boys, and makes baskets and other items from palm fronds, selling them to the tourists who visit the resorts located at the more affluent part of the island. Marley always welcomes Ben and Troy and looks forward to the three weeks a year when he has a steady income from renting his boat and sharing his knowledge with the pair of wreck divers.

Tonya shouts as Ben and Troy turn to begin carrying their supplies down the long dock. "Next time you come, you boys need to bring your lovely wives with you to keep me company while you boys are off playing like a band of pirates searching for booty."

Marley laughed. "This is the only booty I need," slapping Tanya on the backside. "Get in the boat, girl...and I will allow you to ride back to our castle with me, *if*...you act right," he added.

Ben assured Tanya that the girls wouldn't miss out on the next trip. The wreck-diver's wives had always accompanied Ben and Troy in the past and had become closely attached to Marley, Tanya, and the boys. However, this season...Lindsay, Ben's wife, had started a new job and was unable to take the time off to come along. Darlene, Troy's wife, decided to stay in Florida with Lindsay to keep her company while the guys were in Jamaica. As Ben turned away, he couldn't help but grin and think to himself... *"Given the circumstances this time around, there's no way those girls are gonna' miss out on the next trip!"*

Back at the motel, Ben stashed the items away in his luggage for safe keeping and hoped they'd make it through security without a random luggage check which occasionally takes place. Having to keep the items hidden, Ben had not yet had a good opportunity to take a closer look at the items. He'd also decided not to tell Troy about the items until they were safe back in Fort Myers. No need in two people looking paranoid and drawing unwanted attention at the airport!

The next morning, Ben and Troy caught a cab to the small airport where they checked their luggage for loading. Ben was "sweating bullets" in fear that his luggage might be searched and the items found. That, kind of situation certainly would have landed the pair in front of some corrupt officials with a thousand questions, while Troy...with no knowledge of the items, would be clueless to what was even happening. *"What a mess that would be!"* Ben imagined.

Ben had a ten dollar bill in his hand ready to tip the luggage handler, making certain it was visible before the handler picked up the men's luggage in hopes that the sight of the bill might entice the handler to hurry along. The handler picked up the pair's luggage, threw it on the cart for loading, and stuck out his hand. Ben watched as other bags were loaded on top of theirs and the cart was pushed to the airplane for loading.

As the small commuter plane left the short runway, it soared what seemed to be straight up in order to clear a mountainous region while heading south. As the plane made a right bank to initiate the turn north, both men stared out the windows at the turquoise, blue Caribbean waters below in silence and thought to themselves... *"The next trip will reveal the mother-load!"* ...just as they'd thought every time before. However, this time Ben had the feeling that the next trip would begin paying for their expenses and was pondering on whether the pair should start the "Salvaging Permit" process with the Jamaican Government, or simply bring the stuff up secretly and move it through the blackmarket. The sad part about the blackmarket angle would be the fact that the golden altar, if it *did* actually exist, would possibly be melted for the sake of the gold and the altar would be lost forever in modern jewelry. This is happening more and more as governments broaden regulations and laws that prohibit the private sector from doing what the private sector does best...recover treasure at their own time and expense! Ben and Troy have much planning and many decisions to make before next diving season.

CHAPTER 2

Back to Fort Myers, Florida…and "X" Marks the Spot

The small commuter plane landed at Southwest International Airport in Fort Myers at approximately two o'clock Sunday afternoon. Lindsay and Darlene were there in Ben's big red Ford F-250 awaiting Ben's and Troy's arrival. After hugs, kisses and pleasantries were exchanged, the girls immediately began questioning them about their trip; were they any closer to finding the wreck, and…how Marley and his family were doing?

At that time, Troy was still not aware of the "finds" Ben had made on his last trip below the surface to the reef.

"I wish I had more exciting news for you girls, but…the trip produced the same old junk, you know…washers, dryers, and…we even found the kitchen sink this time around," Troy said half-heartedly. "The good news is… that we've reduced the search-area by another twenty or so square miles, which puts us closer to finding the wreck."

Ben, who was about to bust wide-open at the seams, had only one thing on his mind. "Crew…the sun's well over the yardarm. I say, let's head for Mullet Creek Marina and get us a few cold drinks. Then, Troy and I can reflect back on the trip and fill you girls in a bit."

The marina Ben mentioned is a popular "watering-hole" for locals conveniently located near both couples neighborhoods. Characters such as: Mullet Dan, Painter Mike, Plumber Dave, Candyman and Harley Charlie…just to name a few, are frequent clientele. If you're a local, no one is called by their first name. Everybody at the marina has a nickname. Troy's nickname is simply, "Troy boy" which was a play on Troy's last name, Mann. Ben's nickname is, "Pig Iron". Ben got his nickname while diving on the 1715 fleet. He had found what he thought was a silver bar that was attached to the rock bottom from hundreds of years of encrustation. Ben chipped, chiseled and pried for over an hour to free the item from its resting place while communicating to the crew on the boat that he had a silver bar. The bar finally gave up its grip on the bottom and Ben carried it to the boat. When the bar was placed on the back of the boat one of the more seasoned crew members laughed and shouted "Pig Iron!" Ships started carrying iron ballast bars called "pigs" during the 1800's as opposed to stone ballast. From that day on, Ben was known as "Pig Iron" to the treasure hunting community.

The marina also draws its share of "Snowbirds" during the winter months, especially on Sundays when Sonny...a local entertainer sets up his P.A. and sound-equipment for folks to try their hand at karaoke. Some participants are really quite good, while others...let's just say they're in the same league with Marley. No matter how good or how bad the talent, everybody claps anyway.

Ben had in mind that the marina would be a good place to retrieve the recovered items from his luggage and share the excitement of their good fortune with the rest of the gang. So, the group settled down at a table somewhat distant from the main portion of the crowd and ordered drinks.

Smiling and bubbling, as usual...Mama Di was waiting tables that afternoon. Mama Di and her husband, Big John, are the gracious proprietors of the marina. Mama Di is always dressed in a fanciful outfit, complete with pink rubber boots. Big John is a big man who also sports a big smile and is always interested in what the group of treasure hunters are up to.

Ben stood up from his chair, walked over to his truck, removed the items from his luggage, and then walked back to the table where Mama had the first round of drinks set up on the table.

After taking a big swallow of beer, Ben said, "Listen-up guys. This year's trip was anything but, a normal-run. I've got somethin' to show you all!"

Troy looked at Ben with a confused, but excited look on his face. "Whatcha' talkin' about?"

When Ben unwrapped the items from the cloth he'd wrapped them in for transport, the group could hardly believe what they was looking at. There, in Ben's hand was the silver pill box, the gold coin, and the encrusted mystery-conglomerate, or E.O. which some treasure-salvors refer to encrusted-objects. The girls shrieked with excitement as Troy took the items from Ben's hand to examine them closer, himself. Up to this point, Ben hadn't even had the opportunity to examine them closely.

Troy quickly pointed out the date on the coin he held in his hand. "Wow…1668 vintage! And, it has a Lima mint-mark on it, which certainly could have come from our shipwreck," he added. "When a gold coin is recovered, it looks as shiny as the day it went down," he explained to the others. "Even after 300 years in the saltwater it requires little, if any cleaning."

The silver pillbox was lightly coated with sulfide and had what appeared to be initials inscribed on the lid, which couldn't quite be distinguished. The blackened conglomerate seemed to be of little interest to anybody, but Ben knew that this encrusted object *could* have nice artifacts on the inside, such as…rings, or maybe even coins. The E.O. would have to be X-rayed in order to determine what it may hold inside its mass.

Michelle, or "Mick"…as she prefers to be called, is a close friend of the group and just happens to be an X-ray Technician which has worked out well for Ben over the years. On occasion, Ben had asked Mick to sneak E.O.'s in to her workplace and run them through the X-ray machine, which she had reluctantly agreed to do. She didn't know it yet, but Ben was going to ask her the same favor on this latest find.

When the excitement diminished somewhat, Troy looked at Ben. "Hey…why didn't you tell me about what you found on the reef before now?"

"Troy…it's like this…" Ben began as he explained the reasoning for his actions.

After listening to Ben's explanation, Troy replied, "Given the circumstances…I would've probably done the same thing."

"Thanks, Troy, I was afraid you might be hurt that I didn't feel like I could share that pertinent information at that particular moment. I just couldn't run the risk of Marley letting some local yahoos in on *the find*".

"Nope. All is good, Ben," Troy reassured him.

"Now, let's get this pill box to your place and get it in the reverse-electrolysis tank for cleaning so we can make out the inscription on it. If we're lucky, it might be a clue to the whereabouts of our wreck. First thing tomorrow morning I'm gonna' give Captain Fizz a call and then e-mail him a couple of photos of the coin and pill box. I can count on him to give me some credible information on what we've found."

"This Fizz character I always hear you and Lindsey talking about…you'd think I would have been introduced to him by now. When am I gonna' meet this dude?"

"Troy, I'm thinking very soon. Now that we've found something of interest…I think I can convince Fizz to break away from his busy schedule to come have a look at what we've found. You know…Fizz learned a lot of what he knows from two of the finest treasure hunters who ever lived. One was Art McKee, the proverbial father of treasure hunting. The other was Jack Haskins. I was reading about these guys years before I ever met Fizz. Jack "Blackjack" Haskins has probably directed expeditions to more treasure than any other person in the business. Jack taught himself how to read the old Spanish language from the ships manifests in the Archives of the Indies and spent days on end reading and deciphering the passages in order to find clues to the locations of possible treasure producing shipwrecks," Ben concluded.

After helping some novice boater tie-off his skiff to the dock, Big John made his way over to the group before they could get away. With impeccable timing…he appeared holding a choice of poison in hand and a huge smile on his face. "Well, treasure-hunters…any luck this year?"

Troy quickly replied…"Nothing this year, John. But, we're gettin' closer. And besides, if we *did* tell you we found treasure, then…we'd have to kill you…and, Mama needs you too much!"

John smiled ever wider as he turned to help Mama Di serve several patrons. He announced loudly, "Well… there's always next year, guys. Keep lookin'! When you get filthy rich, I expect you guys to buy this dump from me so Mama and I can retire, ha…ha!"

John is a trustworthy man, but both Ben and Troy knew that the word of a possible "treasure-find" is almost impossible to keep quiet, even for the tightest of lips. As the saying goes, *"Loose lips, sink ships!"* No need in letting too many folks in on this, just yet.

The group left Mullet Creek Marina and went to Ben and Lindsay's. There, in order to clean the pill box, they immersed the object into the small reverse-electrolysis tank where the item is suspended in the solution with a piece of wire from a stainless-steel rod stretching the length of the tank. A low-voltage electrical current is then run through the water with a battery charger. This process is used to remove the sulfide from the silver without doing damage to the artifact itself. Aware that this process was very slow and would take days to complete, they parted ways for the evening and settled in preparing to get back to their normal routines. At this point in their lives, their boring jobs seemed to be more of an inconvenience than a necessity.

The normal routine for Ben and Lindsay began with Ben traveling to Ocala, Florida every Monday morning where he was the Vice President of Operations at a mining company. Since the trip was close to 225 miles from home, he stayed in Ocala during the week and traveled back to Fort Myers on Fridays. Lindsay is an M.R.I. Technician and works in Naples, a short distance south of their home.

The normal Monday through Friday routine for Troy and Darlene is managing a flooring installation business which they both worked throughout the week. The couple was originally from Georgia where Troy ran his own trucking business. Darlene was quite the country gal and managed a Waffle House Restaurant along Interstate-75. Troy happened to wheel into that particular Waffle House one morning for breakfast and it was love at first sight. The couple married and moved to Florida. Troy sold the trucking business and started the flooring business so that he could stay home with Darlene.

Most every weekend, the group rendezvous' on Ben's pontoon boat exploring the many islands and keys in the area. One island in particular which they'd discovered had an old Indian mound on it which was eroding away by the waves in the Caloosahatchee River outfall. The island is steeped in history beginning with the Calusa Indians, an early 1600's Spanish mission, conquistador history, and ending with a Second Seminole Indian War fort which was active on the island in the 1830s. The group had also discovered a fresh water spring in the interior of the island which explains the hub of activity that took place there through the centuries. There, treasure and archaeological finds varied greatly in age and were for the most part, worthless. Nonetheless…Ben and Troy enjoyed collecting the items anyway. You never know when something of value might be found. Hunting the island and surrounding areas for artifacts also gave them an opportunity to pass the time until their next trip to Jamaica could be made.

On Friday evenings the group meets at the Mullet Creek Marina for a few drinks and to plan out the weekend's activities which always included treasure-hunting for some kind of artifacts, or bits of junk, as the girls put it.

When Ben arrived home from Ocala on this particular Friday, the first thing he did was to check on the progress of the pill box cleaning. He shut off the electrical current which had been running through the solution and then pulled the pill box out for a look. He was pleasantly surprised to see the pill box gleaming and looking practically new. He could clearly make out the initials, P.A.F., and a small Spanish coat-of-arms beneath the initials…something that had been totally obscured by the sulfide layer. He wiped the box clean of the solution, wrapped it in a paper towel and then called Troy in order to set up the usual get together at the marina. He also asked

Lindsay to make certain that Mick was going to be there, as well. He, had a favor to ask of her.

Ben put the pill box in his shirt pocket, wrapped the conglomerate in a fresh paper towel and then grabbed the copy of the passenger list of the Capitana which had been discovered in the Archives. Hopefully, they could look through it and match the initials on the pill box to a name on the passenger list. Next, he and Lindsay hopped into his truck and headed for the marina to meet up with the rest of the gang.

Passing by Troy and Darlene's home on the way to the marina, they made a quick stop, picked them up and continued driving the short distance to their destination. On the way, Ben pulls the pill box from his shirt pocket and shows Troy. Taking the item in his hand, he marvels.

"Holy mackerel! *You*, look as beautiful as the day the silversmith made you. After all these years of looking… *this*, is without a doubt, the coolest thing we've ever found. Ben, I feel like our luck is getting ready to change for the better."

When the four treasure-hunters arrived at the marina, they joined the group of characters who were always gathered on Friday evenings for a drink. After ordering a round of drinks for themselves, they seated themselves at a table some distance away from the main crowd so they wouldn't attract too much attention. Then, they began looking through the passenger list of the Capitana. They'd just about gone through the 300 names on the list without a single match. Their hopes were dwindling of making a match, when…the next name on the list was, Pedro Antonio Fernandez. The group stared across the table at one another in disbelief. With the exception of Ben, they all stood up, high-five'd each other and shouted, "We've got her!"

Ben remained seated, calmly staring at the initials on the pill box comparing them to the name on the passenger list while going over in his mind the fact that he had to tie this man, Pedro Antonio Fernandez, to the wreck which they were looking for. He needed something more than just a set of initials, which could well be coincidental. He'd also noticed that the patrons and staff of the marina had turned and were looking at the group as if they were crazy. Ben quickly tried to cover for the outburst by saying aloud… "Practical joke! We're gonna' play a practical joke on Mick...you know…we'll get her goat, but good! All is good folks, now…don't 'chu all go tellin' her nothin…" he said assuringly.

As the patrons and staff turned their attention away from the group, Ben said to his crew… "You all trying to hide something…because…if you are, you really suck at it!" Ben, being the thorough kind of person that he is, continued…"Let's grab one more brew and then head to the house to look up this Pedro guy on the internet. I just wanna' be certain that he was conducting some kind of business on our ship before we celebrate him too much. Lindsay, call Mick and tell her to meet us at our house".

Troy, being the spokesperson for the rest of the group, commented…"Come on Ben. It would be *way* too much of a coincidence for two guys with the same initials to have been on two separate ships that wrecked in that area."

"Listen Troy," Ben replied. "It shouldn't take too long to come up with something on this guy, and then…I'll be satisfied that we're in the scatter-trail of our ship and not *one* of those supply ships that went down, sinking with the same flotilla. Lindsay, call Mick and tell her to meet us at the house," he repeated.

Once they were back at the house, Ben sat down in front of the computer and began his search while the rest of the group, satisfied with the fact that they had their ship, uncorked a bottle of champagne and began celebrating around the pool behind the house. Ben had been searching for about an hour when Mick entered through the side door of the house and walked into the room where he was conducting his search. Mick is the kind of person who's always wearing a smile on her face, thankful that it was Friday.

"Alright Ben, what's so important that we're meeting here instead of at the marina where I could be drinking a beer?"

Without as much as a, "How do you do?" Ben pulled the conglomerate out of his shirt pocket, unwrapped it and laid the object on the computer desk.

Immediately, Mick shouted…"Oh! Now I know. *You,* want me to take that *thing* in to work with me and take a picture of what's inside of it…knowing, that if I get caught…I could lose my job…or even worse. Is that what you're wanting, Ben?" Mick asked jokingly while smiling ear to ear, and continued on her roll, adding… "I could've been at the marina where some tall, dark and handsome man would have most likely bought me a drink by now, but instead…here I am with *you*, without a *beer*, and… looking at what appears to be some *clump-of-crap*."

Ben stopped her in her tracks and said, "We just left the marina, Mick, and believe me…there's no man down there who fits the description of, *tall, dark and handsome*. There *were* a few short, balding, paunchy and pale guys hanging around. But no tall, dark and handsome ones. Sorry." Ben continued… "However, there's plenty of beer in the fridge and it just happens to be *your* brand…free and cold!" he jested, poking fun at her frugality.

"Oh well…" Mick teasingly resigned. "I guess I'll do it. But, it may cost you more than *one* beer, Ben."

"Great!" Ben roared. "Now…put this in your car so you don't forget it," he said, handing Mick the conglomerate. "Drink three beers and call me Monday, once you've had an opportunity to see what's inside.

"Yes, Doctor Ben," Mick said, turning and making her way out on the pool deck. There, she was told by the others why the celebration was a bit more than usual.

Ben looked back at the computer screen speaking aloud, "Come on now, Pedro. I need to know what ship you were on, dude."

After two more hours of searching, Ben had still come up with nothing on Pedro Antonio Fernandez. He finally gave up on the internet search and called a good friend in Spain who'd helped him find the original documentation on the shipwreck.

Maria Preciado is a middle-aged Spanish woman who works at the Archives of the Indies in Seville, Spain. Her position there is in the document restoration lab and is well trained on researching the thousands upon thousands of bundles of ancient records or "legajos" in the archives. If anybody could find something on Pedro, it would be Maria.

The documents in the archives were hand-written by scribes who were onboard every ship of every flotilla spanning 350 years of shipping treasure from the "New World" back to Spain. During this period of Spain's history, all seated kings demanded that hour-by-hour and day-by-day documentation be kept in order to protect the King's interests and to possibly aid in the recovery of lost riches, should they disappear. Documents were written in triplicate and were transferred from ship to ship when weather and seas allowed, in case a ship was lost. Typically, the Capitana, the Almiranta, or the ship that was positioned last in the flotilla, and a smaller, faster and more maneuverable supply ship, would have a copy of the documents onboard. The documents were written in ancient Spanish Castilian writing and took someone like Maria who had training in order to translate them.

After pleasantries were exchanged and some small-talk with Maria about how she and her family were getting along, Ben got straight to the point. He told her that he might be on to some leads about the shipwreck on which they had discovered documents three years ago, and once again needed her help researching a man's name who might have been on the ship. After Maria's normal tasks in the restoration lab are completed, she is allowed to perform independent research for people in the evenings. Maria charges a minimal amount for her efforts and told Ben that she'd be happy to help. Maria also told Ben that since he'd last been in the archives, they'd started to catalogue a lot of information in the documents onto a computer database which could possibly make the search much quicker and easier.

"Now, what is it exactly, that I'll be looking for, Ben?"

"Maria, I found a silver pill box which has the initials P.A.F on the lid. I searched through the passenger list that you and I ran across in the archives and found the name, Pedro Antonio Fernandez. I need to know who this guy was and if *he* has any connection with, *Our Lady With The Fiery Eyes*. If you can find something out for me, I promise that when our ship comes in, you'll never have to look at another one of those old musty papers ever again!"

Maria replied, laughingly. "I'll hold you to *that*, Ben. And, if your ship *does* come in, I'll even deduct what you've already paid me from my share of whatever you find. I'll get started Monday evening, Ben. I'll e-mail you if anything comes up."

"*You*, are a true Spanish angel, Maria," Ben replied. "I'll look forward to hearing from you soon."

Meanwhile, back on the pool deck where festivities were well under way, Troy had grilled some burgers for supper…with all the trimmings. Ben walked out and addressed the group,

"I've given up on finding Pedro tonight. I've got Maria, my secret weapon in Spain, looking for him. Maria's like a bloodhound looking through those old documents. I think we oughta' go look for some domestic treasure tomorrow and take our minds off this stuff we brought back from the reef for a little while. After all, it's gonna' be another year before we can make another run at it, and…we've got a lot to discuss. I always said that if I hadn't chosen to work for a living, most likely…I'd have already been rich," Ben concluded.

The whole group agreed and decided they'd go to Mission Key the next morning and look for artifacts around the old Indian middens mound that had been washing away in the surf.

The plan was to meet at the marina in the morning around seven o'clock and make the one hour ride out to Mission Key where they'd hunt artifacts, grill lunch on the boat, and then start making the plans for the next trip to Jamaica during the process.

The next day, Ben backed his boat down the narrow old ramp, splashing into Mullet Creek and prepared the boat for the day's outing. The girls were always a half hour or so behind the guys. Actually, this arrangement worked out well for the guys, giving them time to get the coolers loaded and iced-down, and to fill the boat with gas. As usual, Lindsay, Darlene and Mick all showed up after the chores were complete and stepped onto the boat for a day in the sun.

The pontoon boat slipped away from the fueling dock around 8:00 a.m. as the crew waved good-bye to the locals who'd already begun seating themselves at the outside bar for morning beverages. The ride out to Mission Key was always relaxing with plenty of wildlife to enjoy while making your way through the mangrove passages. Occasionally, if you were lucky, you might spot a manatee or a bald eagle. There are always plenty of bottlenose dolphins, otters and a myriad of bird species available for viewing. The scenery is breathtaking at this time of the morning.

The boat passed by Mound Key on the way to Mission Key. Mound Key was a major Calusa Indian village-site with several man-made mounds on it. The tallest mound rises thirty-two feet above sea level and is constructed entirely of shells…the highest point in that part of Florida. This would have been the temple-mound where the cacique, or king of the tribe would have lived. The state of Florida had recently purchased the island making it a State Park. Searching *that* island for artifacts will land you behind bars. Any items of historical interest that are present on *that* site will simply have to remain lost forever for no one to learn from or enjoy.

The boat reached its destination at 9:00 a.m. straight up. Troy set the anchors in knee-deep water and commented on how much more of the mound had washed away since they were last out there. Then, Ben and Troy busied themselves getting the floating sieves into the water where they could shovel material from the mound into them for processing. The girls remained on the bow of the boat slathering-up with lotion and getting floats deployed where they would watch the boys look for bits-of-junk.

The whole time Ben and Troy were working, they were discussing the next plan of attack in Jamaica…such as, what additional equipment they'd need for the salvage; should they go to the Jamaican government for a salvage-permit once something of significance is found; how they'd get the treasure out of the country if they decided to choose the way of the black-market, etc.

Ben finally said, "Well…damn, Troy. You'd think we'd be getting to the exciting part of the adventure with this treasure business, but instead…it seems to have just gotten more complicated."

"You're right…" Troy commented. "I recall a book I read sometime back about treasure and the trouble it creates for the finders. Let's just enjoy the day and let our brains vegetate for awhile. All this research and thinking is enough to give a man a headache. Besides, we have plenty of time to work these things out."

The pair had been working for about three hours when the girls started talking about how hungry they were getting. The guys took the hint and stopped what they were doing in order to start working on some lunch. They'd added several things to their collection of artifacts. They'd found three Venetian glass beads, which the Spaniards would have brought over from Europe to trade the native people out of something of more value. They also found one rock plummet, or net weight, and a bone needle.

"Pretty good haul for the day," Troy remarked. "Its not taking the place of silver and gold, but it'll have to do, for now." Working over the sieves was back breaking work so the guys were happy to start grilling some burgers and dogs for lunch.

After lunch, the group simply relaxed for the next few hours of their day and talked about Jamaica. Soon, storm clouds were beginning to build, as they generally do in Southwest Florida in the afternoon. So, the group decided to weigh anchor and take a leisurely boat ride back to Mullet Creek instead of waiting longer and having to race back in order to avoid being caught in the inevitable downpour.

As they were getting underway, Lindsay sat down on Ben's lap at the helm and said, "Ya' know…while you and Troy were discussing your options and plans for the next trip to Jamaica…I was thinking."

"Well…*that's*, never good…" Ben teased. "And what were you thinking?"

"Well, you know…*we've* always dreamed of owning our own yacht someday."

"Yeah, we've discussed it. Go on…" Ben coaxed.

"Well…if we had that yacht, we could take it to Jamaica and have a way to bring the treasure back that you boys are gonna' find."

"Damn! Ya' know…*that's,* the reason I love you so much, Lindsay. *Someone's* gotta' be an out-of-the-box thinker instead of always being a practical thinker, like I'm plagued with being. Hey, Troy…" Ben shouted over the sound of the outboard engine…"some of the questions in our previous discussion may have just gotten answered!" Turning his attention back to his wife, he said, "Let's discuss this in more detail later, Lindsay. This may be an opportunity to make two dreams come true at the same time."

At about the same time Ben picked Lindsay up to give her a big kiss, his cell phone rang. He gently set Lindsay back down on the deck and picked up his phone from the helm. Looking at the number on the Caller-I.D. he said, "Well, I'll be…it's Maria. I wonder why she's calling on a Saturday?" Ben answered the phone but could only hear crackling. After making several attempts of conversing with her, he said, "Maria, I'm on the water and have poor cell-service. If you can hear me, I'll call you back as soon as I get in to an area with better service." Ben closed the phone, tossed it on the helm and said, "Okay guys, this leisurely boat ride's over. Maria's found something…I'll bet my life on it! We've gotta' get to the marina where we have some phone service."

   Ben pushed the throttle handle completely forward on the boat and had the 150 horsepower outboard engine giving everything it had. He was pressing his luck speeding through idle zones and narrow mangrove passages. Other boaters were shaking their fist at him, and worse…but he kept the vessel at full-throttle until approaching the ramp at the marina. At the marina, he docked the boat, jumped off and immediately dialed Maria's number.

   "Hello, Maria…you got something for me, darling?"

   "Yes, I do. Remember all that song-and-dance about your ship coming in?" Maria said.

   Ben interrupted and said, "Yeah, yeah, yeah…I remember Maria. Now, tell me what you've come up with."

   Maria began by saying, "I decided to go back into the Archives today and have a quick look through the computer database that I was telling you about. In no more than about five minutes…I had your guy looking me straight in the face. It turns out that Pedro was the Viceroy of Peru under King Charles II between the years of 1667 and 1672. He was returning to Spain under the King's orders to report to the King on his interests and affairs in Peru. He left Portobelo on a flotilla in 1670 which was mostly lost to a hurricane. Ben, this *has* to be your man. It's too much of a coincidence not to be!" Maria exclaimed.

"Maria, I own you *big time!*" Ben replied excitedly. "And, I promise…you won't be forgotten when it comes time to divide the treasure. Now…I've gotta' go and share this with the rest of the gang. Good-bye for now, Maria. You'll be hearing from me again…hopefully soon!"

Ben turned to the rest of the group who were waiting impatiently to hear what Maria had to say. He walked over, high-five'd Troy and said, "Okay, gang! Now… even *I'm* satisfied that we're on the trail of the *Lady With The Fiery Eyes."*

After Ben filled them in on the details he'd just received from Maria, Lindsay asked, "But, how do we know that this man, Pedro Fernandez, wasn't on one of the supply ships?"

Ben replied with confidence, "Honey, there's no way in the world that the Viceroy to the King of Spain would've been a passenger on a ship full of hogs, chickens and toothless sailors! He, would've been on the Capitana. Troy, let's get this boat loaded up, buy a round on us, get back to the house and get the charts out. We've got some plotting to do. I can flush the outboard and cover the boat tomorrow."

The boat was loaded on the trailer. Then, the group walked up to the little outside bar where Big John was tending bar. "John, how 'bout serving a round to the house…on us!" Ben offered.

Big John looked at the crew and said, "Big day, treasure-hunters?" Troy replied, "John, you have no idea. And…you already know what I'd have to do if I told you…"

John smiled and shouted, "Round for the house on the treasure-hunters! I guess maybe they found a doubloon or two today!"

The "crew" left the marina and went to Ben's place where he pulled the charts out that they always carry with them to Jamaica. The location of the anchor and cannons had already been plotted on the chart. Ben took the coordinates from the dive book that he'd secretly recorded the day he found the pill box, and plotted them on the chart. Using a thin pencil and a straight-edge, he carefully joined the coordinates. Both Ben and Troy stood back looking at the line which ran almost due east…just as they'd expected from the clue that the anchor had given them. "

"We have the path she took during her break-up. Somewhere on that path is, X-marks-the-spot," Ben remarked.

They both smiled with satisfaction as Troy added, "Ben, next season is gonna' really be big. But there's one thing that troubles me."

Ben quickly responded. "What could possibly be troubling you right now, dude? We've narrowed our search down to within the debris-field of our targeted vessel and are gonna' be finding treasure beyond our wildest desires next season…and you have an issue?"

Troy pointed to the chart, shook his head and said," If you continue our path further east, it runs right smack dab into the Boogeyman's Island, just as I had feared in my wildest of nightmares!"

Ben laughed and replied, "Well, I'll be damned. Troy, you're absolutely right. But, we're not scared of the Boogeyman, are we?" Then, Ben picked up his parallel-ruler, laid it on the line that he'd just drawn, and walked it back to the compass rose on the chart. "There's our course, Troy…just north of due east at 86 degrees." Next, he wrote the compass-heading down on the chart, looked at Troy and continued speaking…"Next year, we're all gonna' be rich beyond our most fabulous dreams, Troy. I can feel it."

Ben and Troy spent the rest of the evening making plans and discussing when they should let Marley in on the information. The girl's, on the other hand, were discussing how big of a yacht they were going to buy and how they'd spend the rest of their lives motoring around the Caribbean and Bahamas.

Ben winked at Lindsay and said, "Come on girls…get your heads outta' the clouds now. We've got a lot of work to do before you have to worry about *that*. I think I'm gonna' call it an evening, gang. Tomorrow, I'm just gonna' relax before I have to head back to Ocala on Monday morning."

"Sounds good, Ben" Troy agreed "I'm kinda' beat myself. I could use a break, too. We'll see you next week."

After Troy and Darlene went home, Mick pouted, "Well…I guess I'll go home, too…if everyone's gonna' be party-pooper's."

"Don't forget to X-ray the conglomerate," Ben reminded.

"Got 'cha covered, Ben. But, it may cost you a trip to Jamaica next year," she remarked as she walked out the lanai door.

"Bye, Mick!" Ben and Lindsay shouted. "Have a good week and we'll see you next weekend."

After their company had gone, Ben and Lindsay sat together on the lanai. All of a sudden, Ben looked at Lindsay and said, "You know…I think we should go ahead and do it."

"Do what?" she asked.

Ben looked her in the eyes and replied, "Begin looking for a yacht."

Lindsay sprang to her feet, threw her arms around Ben and said, "Now, you're talking, Captain! Ben…this, could be the beginning of our next adventure, and it's going to be a grand one!" Immediately after the words came from Lindsay's mouth, the pair looked at each other and almost simultaneously said, "*Next Adventure…*that*, has* to be her name."

"I can swing financing the yacht for the time being. Then, when we come back with the treasure we're gonna' recover, we can pay the balance of the loan and have clear sailing." Ben's mind had been working overtime ever since the plane left the ground in Jamaica. Figures were tumbling around in his head like a pair of dice bouncing off the board on a gambling table.

Bright and early Sunday morning Ben and Lindsay were setting in front of the computer looking at yachts and day-dreaming. They decided on one with three state-rooms, each with its own "head". They wanted at least a 60-footer with an enclosed flybridge, and Ben wanted it loaded with all the latest in electronics.

With those decisions made, Ben said, "I'll contact a yacht broker tomorrow. I'm ready to get this dream of ours moving and make it a reality. Once the treasure is found and recovered, it will keep us from being slaves to bankers for the remainder of our lives and we'll be able to do as we please from then on. I think I'm gonna' go down to the marina, flush the boat engine, cover it up, and maybe stop to B.S. with Troy a bit. After that, I'm thinking that maybe you and I'll just sit around the pool for the rest of the day and veg." Then, Ben leaned over close to Lindsay and said softly, "How 'bout you going and getting all beautiful, put on a tiny bikini, or nothing at all…and I'll be back in little while."

"Get out of here, ya' perv…" Lindsay said pushing Ben away.

"How about *you* going and taking care of the boat, skip the B.S. session with Troy, and get on back here to your loving wife where she just *might* have a little surprise waiting for you when you get back."

"Oh, hell yeah…mama!" Ben shouted as he rushed out the lanai door. *"This, could quite possibly be a new world's record for flushing and covering a boat,"* he thought to himself.

Monday morning, the members of the group each settled-in to their individual, mundane routines while dreaming of treasure and riches.

Monday evening, Ben was staring at the calendar in his office trying to plan his next vacation, when his phone rang. Ben picked up the phone thinking that the call pertained to business. "Ben Carson…how can I help you?" he said.

"Oh, skip that professional crap, Ben…it's Mick?" the voice replied. "I've got your clump-of-crap under the X-ray," she whispered. "All I can make out are several small, flat, odd, irregular shapes."

"I'll be damned! Just as I had thought…Cobbs," Ben said.

"What the heck are, Cobbs?" Mick whispered.

Ben quickly responded, "Cobbs, are irregular-shaped coins. Before the screw-press was invented, Spanish coins were cut with shears in order to cut them into the desired weights. Mick, I need you to run that clump-of-crap, as you refer to it, by my house tonight. I'll have Troy come over to pick it up so that he can put it into the reverse-electrolysis tank for cleaning. Thanks a million,

Mick. You may as well help yourself to a couple of beers while you're there. I know you will anyway."

"Okay, Ben…if you're going to twist my arm, I'll get there straight after work," she replied with a chuckle.

There, in Ocala…the work-week dragged on slower than normal for Ben. On Friday afternoon as soon as he got home, he went to the lanai where the cleaning-tank was set up. Troy and the girls were already there putting the finishing touches on the coins. There were fifteen coins in all, and all were of two reales denomination. Troy had the coins gleaming as if they were brand new. The coins were in fairly good shape, plus the mint-marks could be made out on a few of them. They were minted in Lima, Peru just like the gold coin, but they couldn't distinguish the dates.

Troy stared at the gleaming silver coins and said, "It's hard to imagine that this is just the tip of the iceberg."

Ben added, "These coins were probably the property of a Spanish sailor and were most likely carried in a canvas bag in his pocket or tied to his belt. When the canvas eventually rotted away, the coins had already stuck together, there…waiting for me to pick them up. Tomorrow, let's set a date for our next trip to Jamaica. Troy, I think we should wait until we arrive in Jamaica before saying anything to Marley. He, may be able to tell us what our best option will be." Troy agreed and the group decided to meet at the marina Saturday afternoon to set a date.

The next evening, Ben and Lindsay were getting ready to leave for the marina when Lindsay brought up the fact that she wasn't feeling well.

"Ben…I think I'm going to stay home and rest. I think I've had a little too much adventure and excitement. I think you're wearing me down."

"Come on, you light-weight," he replied. "We've got a lifetime of adventure that's just gettin' started. Now, you get all prettied-up so you can whip those local boys at the marina into a frenzy, and let's get going."

"No…you go ahead, Ben, I'm going to rest. Whatever you guys come up with will work for me."

Ben rarely left Lindsay's side on the weekends, especially since he's gone all week long, but…plans had to be made and set in stone. Ben kissed Lindsay and asked if she needed anything before he left.

"I won't be long, dear," he promised. "Just long enough to set a date so we can let Marley know to get the cobwebs out of that old boat of his and keep those weeks available to us."

Ben met Troy and Darlene at the marina. After telling them that Lindsay was tired and at home resting, the three of them looked at a calendar and decided on the weeks of October 10, thru the 31.

Ben looked at Troy and stated with a slight grin. "The fact that we'll be there on Halloween should make it even more interesting, Troy. Maybe we'll even see the Boogeyman," he laughed. "Those dates should also be good since the hurricane season should be winding-down by then," he added.

"Alright. It's a date!" Troy reaffirmed. "Now, let's have a few beers and call it a night."

"No thanks…I think I'm gonna' have to pass and head back home to Lindsay."

"Well…then be that way, Ben. I was gonna' buy you a drink!" Troy said emphatically.

"Nothing personal, guys. But I need to head out of town late tomorrow for an early Monday morning meeting and I want to spend the evening with Lindsay."

"Just teasing there, buddy. We understand. We'll see ya' next weekend."

"Oh…by the way, guys. We'll be going to Jamaica in style next year." Ben added.

"Wha-da-ya' mean?" Troy asked.

"Lindsay and I have decided to buy that yacht we've always dreamed of."

"Are you crazy?" Troy replied.

"Yeah…probably. But we're gonna' do it anyway. We're looking for something around 60-feet long that'll have accommodations for all of us to be comfortable. We've discussed it and have decided to move forward with the plan. No time like the present."

"Well…you're right about *that,*" Troy replied "I just hope you've thought everything through."

"You know me, Troy. I wouldn't be doing it if I hadn't given it a lot of thought. It'll be fine. Plus, it's also the answer to how we're gonna' get some of that treasure back here to the States, that is…if Marley thinks the black-market's the way to go."

"Yeah…you've got a point there, Ben" Troy said, thinking aloud. "Alright. Now, get on home to your little darlin' and we'll see ya' later."

When Ben returned home, Lindsay was sound asleep. He kissed her good night as he climbed into bed with her and said softly, "I'll see you in the morning, dear."

The next morning Ben's internal alarm clock woke him at 6 a.m. He climbed out of bed so as not to disturb Lindsey and walked into the kitchen and started a pot of coffee for her just like he always did on Sunday mornings. He let her sleep for a while longer before waking her.

"Good morning, dear," he finally spoke. "How are you doing this morning?"

Lindsay yawned and answered. "Other than the fact that I was sleeping like a log…I'm feeling fine. I was simply exhausted and needed some rest. Sorry about last night, dear."

The remainder of the summer went pretty much the same every week. The group collected themselves on the water most every weekend hunting artifacts and enjoying life. The weeks and months went by quickly. October 10, was quickly approaching, the date which the group was scheduled to start their return to Jamaica for another season of shipwreck hunting and adventure.

CHAPTER 3

Back To Jamaica …On The High Seas

Saturday, the first day of September was Ben's fiftieth birthday. At Ben's request the group rendezvoused at Mullet Creek Marina for a "low key" get together in celebration of their good fortune up to this point. They still had a lot of final preparations to make before leaving for Jamaica and he wanted to keep a clear mind.

At this time, Ben and Lindsay were closing a deal on a 60-foot Viking which their broker had found for them on nearby Marco Island. The group had planned to go down to Marco Island on Sunday morning to seal the deal, get a few quick lessons on the operation of the vessel and then bring her back to the marina where she'd remain moored until setting a course for Jamaica. The marina had hook-ups for power and water which would give Ben and Lindsay all the comforts of home while living aboard the boat from time to time.

The trip from Marco Island to the marina was quite interesting although a bit unnerving at times. Ben had been around boats most all his life and had obtained a master captain's license, but he'd never navigated anything of this size in the narrow and sometimes shallow water passages leading through the mangroves to the marina. They were successful in their trip from Marco to the marina and arrived with no mishaps, tying-up to the dock around four-thirty in the afternoon. Afterward, with Big John's assistance, the boat was hooked-up to marina power and water. Then, the group settled down on the bow of the boat for a few drinks to unwind.

During the next month when they weren't working; Darlene, Lindsey and Mick busied themselves choosing the clothing and shoe selection they'd need for the trip. By this time, Mick had also decided to join the group.

   On their free time, Ben and Troy kept busy making modifications to the boat in order to hide treasure and artifacts just in case Marley gave them the word that black-market was the group's only option. They wanted to have a plan in place to hide the booty should they be boarded by either the Jamaican authorities on the exit from Jamaica, or the U.S. Coast Guard on their return to Florida waters. The two men decided they'd mount an electric air-compressor in the engine room which was equipped with a thirty gallon tank, giving them plenty of room inside it to hide a substantial amount of treasure. Ben also took a small plasma-cutter and welder from his garage and mounted it on the workbench in the engine room of the Viking. The plan was to cut one end out of the tank, fill it full of gold and silver, weld the end back on, and then repaint the tank in order to cover the freshly welded seam. After completion of their treasure hiding place, they'd simply "deep six" the plasma-cutter and welder. In the event that they'd be asked to turn the air-compressor on, it would still function…even if it were filled with treasure. They both agreed that this precaution should make it past even the most thorough of searches, short of tearing the boat apart piece by piece which has been known to be done if officials suspected drug smuggling. Both Ben and Troy had squeaky clean pasts, therefore neither of them should be suspect for drug smuggling if officials called for a background check. They were both aware of the fact that this small tank wouldn't come close to holding all the treasure they were anticipating to find, but they also knew that they couldn't be too greedy or they might run the chance of getting caught if indeed the black-market ended up being their only choice. Besides, filling the tank full of gold and silver would equate to millions of dollars and make both of them very comfy for the remainder of their lives.

    The two of them also discussed their plan of attack once they resumed following the debris-trail. They'd decided not to take a lot of heavy duty excavation equipment such as prop-wash blowers and air-lifts, equipment that would definitely draw attention to their activity. Rather, this time around they decided to simply take what could easily be gleaned off the ocean floor and be satisfied with that. They also decided that the money made from the finds this season would help pay for the more expensive and in-depth salvage next season. In order to move large quantities of sand quickly, they'd take electric dive scooters which are prop-propelled hand-held devices that are made to move a diver through the water faster and easier than swimming with fins alone. When a positive signal is received by the metal-detector, the scooter's prop can be pointed downward in the sand enabling them to move a lot of sand very quickly. It's not unusual to see a sport diver using a dive scooter thus making this method less conspicuous. Ben and Troy had used this method when diving on the east coast of Florida working the Spanish 1715 shipwreck locations with another group for fun on weekends. The 1715 wrecks litter Florida's coastline between Sebastian inlet and Fort Pierce.

    With the modifications made and all necessary equipment and provisions loaded, the treasure-hunters were ready to set a course for Jamaica early the next morning. *Next Adventure* would cruise at 25 knots, or just under 29 miles per hour. Ben had calculated the distance on a navigational chart and determined that barring any rough seas or trouble, they should be able to make the 1,000 mile journey in approximately 40 hours on one tank of fuel.

The evening before getting underway, the group went through the list of equipment and provisions checking it once, twice, and even a third time to be certain that everything was aboard to cover any situation that might come up while at sea, as well as checking the equipment needed for this next phase of the treasure hunt and salvage. Ben also stashed his 9-millimeter handgun on the boat saying, "You can never be too safe. We could run into yacht-hijacking pirates out there."

Following that comment…Mick quickly replied, "Well, as long as the pirate's not a winch, he has all of his teeth, and…he looks like Captain Jack…I'm not gonna' resist, too much."

"Only you, Mick…" Ben sighed. "Now, let's settle in and get some rest. I wanna' be on the water and underway at first light. Troy, can you give Marley a call and let he and Tanya know that the girls are coming with us on this trip? Also, tell him we're traveling aboard a 60-foot yacht and that we'll need a dock that will accommodate us with at least 30-amp power service and water, though 50-amp power would be better. If I have it figured right, we should see him at the docks Sunday night around 10 p.m."

"Roger that, Captain," Troy replied "I got cha' covered."

"Thanks," Ben acknowledged. "I'm gonna' program the autopilot to the GPS for our trip and then get some rest. See you all first light."

The next morning at 6 a.m. sharp, the group rendezvoused at the dock and boarded *Next Adventure*.

Ben stood on the bridge and shouted, "Okay, mates…I've checked the weather and tides. It looks like smooth sailing all the way to Jamaica!"

Troy directed his attention to the girls. "Just for sanity's sake, let's run through that check list one last time before we untie and get underway. Now, I'm not talking about swimsuits, purses and shoes. Besides, there aren't any nightclubs where we're gonna' be."

As the girls and Troy were going over the list one last time, Ben was below deck checking to be certain all the systems were ready for the trip when he happened to look at the air-compressor he and Troy had mounted to the work bench. Immediately, he made his way back to the salon area of the yacht where the rest of the group was completing their list.

"I think we've forgotten something."

"I can't imagine what it would be, Ben?" Troy reassured. "We've been over this list four times now and every item on it is stowed away on here somewhere."

"Spray paint," replied Ben. "Spray paint to repaint the compressor after we've welded it back up."

Troy smiled and shouted to the crew, "Prepare to shove off…time's a wastin'!"

"Paint!" Ben repeated.

"I told ya' last night, dude…I got cha' covered. There are four cans of spray paint in one of my bags. I happened to think of it last night and had to make a late run to Wal Mart. It's onboard…don't worry."

"*You da' man*, Troy," Ben said grinning. "Now, let's get this party started!"

Satisfied that the vessel and crew were ready to go, Ben shouted, "Everybody got their passports?"

"Affirmative, Captain…" came the crew's reply.

"Okay, Troy…let's lose our grasp from land for a bit and get goin'," Ben said, firing-up the diesel engines. Troy untied the last line from the dock, jumped aboard *Next Adventure,* and the five treasure hunters were underway.

As Ben cleared Matanzas Pass on the northern tip of Fort Myers Beach, he turned the vessel south. After steering well clear of other vessels and getting into deeper water, Ben switched the vessel to auto pilot. The auto-pilot would maintain the pre-programmed heading and pretty well steer the vessel to Jamaica itself. They would always maintain a lookout perched on the fly-bridge monitoring the electronics and systems to be certain they were functioning properly, and…of course…to keep an eye out for other vessels. Ben pushed the throttle controls completely forward, turned on the synchronizer so both engines would be running at the same speed, and *Next Adventure* jumped-up "on plane" with ease.

The cruise would take them along the easternmost edge of the Dry Tortugas, down around the westernmost tip of Cuba…being very careful to steer clear of the Cuban territorial waters. From there, they'd continue south cruising past Grand Cayman Islands on the windward side and then on to Jamaica.

The water was like glass. The GPS informed Ben that they should be rounding the Dry Tortugas in approximately five hours, if the water remained calm and Ben could maintain top speed. There was a slight nip in the air for an October morning so the girls were below deck in the galley making coffee to help ward-off the chill. Ben and Troy were comfortable inside the enclosed fly-bridge busy monitoring the instrumentation and having a discussion on how to approach Marley with their proposition. Ben knew that it had always been Marley's dream to escape the poverty of Freetown and relocate his family to the United States where they could have access to opportunities that would never be available for them in Jamaica. If he and Troy can convince Marley that he will be a rich man when the treasure is found, his dream can come true. Ben and Troy would help him with the formalities of becoming a U.S. citizen. But, should Marley deceive them, his dream would never become a reality.

"Hey you girls…" Ben shouted. "How 'bout some of that coffee! It's gonna' be blazing hot up here soon, and then I'll be lookin' for a beer."

"Sorry, ole buddy," Troy said shaking his head. "But…with you being captain of the boat, and all…you'll have to wait until we tie-up in Jamaica before you can enjoy a cold one."

Ben came back with… "Yeah…well, you being the co-pilot and all, I guess you'd better stick with coffee, too."

Soon, the girls were up on the flybridge with a hot pot of coffee for the guys. The group had been underway for about an hour and the sun was well above the horizon to the port side, warming the air and making for a beautiful day at sea.

Approximately four hours later, around eleven-thirty, Ben spotted the Dry Tortugas Island chain on the horizon off the starboard side. The girls were watching bottlenose dolphins jumping out of the water and swimming ahead of the boat as if they were leading the way. If *Next Adventure* continued her current course for another 292 miles, approximately 10 hours, the vessel and crew would remain about 80 miles off the coast of Cuba and well out of territorial waters. Then, the vessel would need to take a more southeastern heading for another 389 miles before making a turn due east in order to make the last leg of the trip to Freetown's harbor in Jamaica.

Around 10 p.m., Ben was aware that their vessel was getting close to the point where the auto-pilot would start making the turn to a south-by-southeast heading and that they were as close to Cuban territorial waters as they were going to get.

"Troy, keep an eye on the radar. If a vessel motors-up on us quickly, we need to pull back on the throttle and let 'em board us. I don't think we'll have any trouble, but… you never know." As captain of the boat, Ben felt the responsibility of the well-being of everyone aboard.

Next Adventure began the south-by-southeast turn at approximately 10:30 p.m. The way Ben figured it, they were a half-hour behind schedule.

The next part of the trip would keep the treasure-hunters on this new course for another twelve hours before making the due-east turn and the final leg of the journey. The night was uneventful as the guys watched the sun begin to rise over the eastern horizon Sunday morning around 6:30 a.m.

With a groggy look on her face and one eye barely open, Mick came up to the flybridge with a pot of coffee in hand. "Where are we, guys?"

Troy being the quicker witted of the two men replied, "Welcome to the Caribbean, Love."

"Very funny, Troy," Mick yawned. "So…I guess I'm not going to meet a dashing buccaneer, am I?"

"Mmmm…I reckon Ben and I are gonna' have to do, Love…" Troy replied with a piratical accent in his voice."

"You guys are taken. And besides…you're not quite what I'd envisioned as a buccaneer, anyway," Mick muttered softly.

Ben and Troy turned immediately toward Mick and simultaneously shouted, "Yaargh!"

"Ha…ha…you pirate *wanna be's…*" Mick laughed. "Now…one more time, where are we, guys?"

"Well, Mick…the way I got it figured, we're about four hours short of viewing the Grand Cayman Islands. About an hour after that, this ole girl's gonna' make a due-east turn which will put us at Freetown harbor another twelve hours after *that*," Ben explained. Then, he turned to his co-pilot. "Troy…I've gotta' get some sleep. Wake me up when you see Grand Cayman and then, *you* can get some rest."

Ben went below deck to the master state-room and crawled beneath a pile of covers with Lindsay. "Darlin'… did you have a good night's rest?"

"Not really," Lindsay answered. "I felt a little dizzy last night when I turned in. I've laid here all night long, freezing," she replied with a shutter. "Perhaps it's just the wine and a bit of sea-sickness. I don't know."

"Well, I guess that explains all the blankets. As soon as we return home, you're gonna' see your doctor."

"Oh…I'm fine," she replied, trying to reassure Ben. "I'm just going through *the change*."

"You're going to the Doc…" Ben said sternly. "Now…don't argue with me. As for right now…I've gotta' get some sleep. Troy's gonna' wake me up when he sees the Grand Caymans in about three hours. Here… come cuddle up with me, dear. I'll keep you warm," Ben whispered closing his eyes for some much needed rest.

At 10:30 a.m., Troy sent Mick down below to wake Ben and let him know that the Grand Caymans were visible on the horizon off their port bow. Ben came up to the flybridge, studied the horizon, looked at the instrumentation and remarked, "Wow…right on schedule,

Troy boy. Good work! Now, it's your turn to go below and get some rest. We should be in Freetown harbor in about thirteen hours."

Troy obliged and went below deck while Lindsay and Darlene were in the galley trying to wake themselves up and get breakfast on the stove. Darlene, being the Georgia Southern Belle that she is…as well as the best cook of the crew, quickly accepted the responsibility of preparing meals during the trip, as long as the others jumped in to help with the clean up afterwards.

Ben watched the Global Positioning System for the next hour and waited patiently for the auto-pilot system to initiate the due-east turn. Right on schedule, the vessel made the turn to port and lined itself up for the final leg of the journey.

"It's all over but the shouting now, girls…" Ben laughed. "We'll be at our final destination around ten o'clock tonight. We'll give Marley a call around eight so as not to wake him from his beauty sleep. If we're still on schedule at that point, we can let him know our estimated time of arrival so that he can get the boat slip ready for us and have the proper paperwork from the Dock Master in order to register the vessel for our stay. We'll all need to go to the magistrate's office early tomorrow morning in order to clear customs."

The last leg of the trip was uneventful. Ben called Marley at eight o'clock that evening in order to make preparations for their arrival. Sure enough, at 10 p.m., *Next Adventure* was easing-up to the dock where it would remain moored for the next three weeks. At least, *that* was the plan for the time being.

As the vessel pulled alongside the dock, Ben swung the spotlight around to help him negotiate the big vessel into place. He could see Marley and Tanya standing on the dock. Marley was wearing his cowboy boots and shorts, as usual. Ben laughed, "Well…nothing's changed with our buddy, Marley. He's still the stylish islander he's always been."

When the vessel gently bumped against the old rickety dock with its moldy, sun-baked rubber fenders, Ben threw Marley a line and prepared to lower the gang plank. Once the vessel was somewhat secured, he made his way down the gangplank to the dock, kneeled down and kissed the dock. Then, he looked up at Marley. "Mon…you're a sight for sore eyes!" he said as he stood to give Marley a big bear hug.

Marley's response was…"Mon…you need to get the girls down here! You think I set all this up just to see you and Troy's old ugly behinds?"

Troy had spent the entire last twelve hours of the trip sleeping, but now…he and the girls were making their way off the vessel eager to stand on solid ground for the first time in forty hours. The group all exchanged hugs, kisses and pleasantries before introducing Mick to Marley and Tanya. Immediately, the girls all began conversing with Tanya about how she'd been since they'd last seen her and if the boys were doing well.

Once the introductions and pleasantries were out of the way, Marley said, "Look mon…you all need to get back aboard the boat and stay for tonight. The Jamaican guard will be here in the morning to inspect your vessel. I'm sure they're goin' to get you registered and check your paperwork at that time."

"What's up with all that?" Ben asked. "We've never had the full-prostate-exam before."

"Ben, mon…" Marley said shaking his head and laughing. "You come boating into Freetown harbor, of all places…with a big fancy yacht like yours…something like you'd see on the television show, *Lifestyles of the Rich and Famous*, and you're asking why the prostate-exam? Not to worry…I think everything will be cool, mon. Just play the game with them. They're also goin' to post a man at the end of the pier tonight to see that you all stay on the boat, you can bet on that! Have you got anything on the boat that you shouldn't have?"

"I have a handgun stashed away, but it's registered," Ben replied.

"Well…if they ask…you need to give it up, mon, and hope that you get it back when you goin' to leave Jamaica. But, don't count on it. Once, I was acquainted with a boat captain who was hired to take the owner to Cuba in order to fish in the Hemingway Tournament. After it was over, the owner of the boat told the captain to take the boat to Mexico and that he was goin' home for a business meeting. He also told the captain that he was bringing his family down to Mexico for a vacation and that they would meet him there. The captain took the boat over to Mexico and when it was inspected by the Mexican Immigration Authorities, they found a pistol hidden beneath a mattress. The captain was placed under arrest and the boat was seized. The Mexican Authorities kept the captain *and* the boat for almost two years before they let the captain loose after a great deal of argument and intervention with the U.S. State Department. The whole incident happened simply because the captain had no papers for the gun and didn't declare it to the officials when the boat was inspected, even though the owner of the boat *did* have a permit. The owner of the boat hadn't informed the captain about the gun that was hidden under the mattress. So, what I'm sayin' is…even though you have a permit for your gun. Remember…you're in another country now…"

"Thanks for the tip, Marley. A word to the wise is sufficient."

The group told Marley and Tanya to have a good evening and climbed back aboard the boat.

"Get some sleep my friends," Marley shouted over his shoulder as he and Tanya walked away.

"Sleep, hell!" Troy replied. "I've been sleeping for the past twelve hours!"

"Sorry 'bout your luck, pal," Ben told him. "I'm gonna' get some sleep and be ready for tomorrow's B.S. with the guard. You can stay up and watch for the Boogeyman."

"Oh yeah, very funny," Troy remarked. "And, thanks for reminding me. By the way…wha-da-ya' think this search Marley's concerned with is all about?"

"Can't say that I rightly know," Ben pondered, scratching his head. "Probably, some new formality. Whatever, I'm sure glad we decided not to bring a bunch of heavy duty equipment with us. I'm not gonna' concern myself with it until I need to. All the paperwork's in order, so…I don't know of anything they could find that would keep us from doing what we've come here to do." Ben yawned. "I'm beat, and I'm gonna' turn in. See you in the morning, partner."

"Alright Ben, but I'm grabbing a six-pack of beer and do me a little star-gazing, I reckon."

"Knock yourself out, dude," Ben replied as he turned to go below. "Oh yeah…" Ben grinned as he turned back to look at Troy. *"Beware of the Boogeyman."*

"Damnit, Ben…you're always messin' with me," Troy thought to himself as he grabbed a six-pack of beer out of the galley and went to the flybridge. There, he sat in the captain's seat staring out across the harbor at the lights from the Boogeyman's mansion wondering what evil

deeds might be going on. The more he let his imagination wander, the creepier he felt. Finally, as a chill ran down his spine, he thought to himself … *"If that treasure ends up being anywhere around that Boogeyman's creep show, I'm gonna' let Ben have it all."* After finishing off the six pack of beer, Troy made his way down to his stateroom, crawled into bed with Darlene and fell asleep.

An unpleasant wake-up-call came around six o'clock Monday morning when the crew of *Next Adventure* heard the sound of stomping boots at a synchronized rate and speed tromping across the sun-bleached cracked boards that make up the rickety dock. Ben and Troy both jumped out of bed simultaneously. They heard the sound continue up the gangway and onto the aft deck of the vessel. Before the guard was able to make their way to the salon door, Ben and Troy unlocked the door and slid it open to greet their unwanted, but expected guests.

There were four members of the guard in all, armed with what looked to be military issued 45-caliber sidearms. The shortest of the four, who was clearly the highest ranking member of the guard, asked for everyone to come topside so that he could check their passports. Troy disappeared below deck to the staterooms in order to roust the girls out of bed.

"Grab your passports, girls! We've got company on deck…the local guard that Marley warned us about." As the girls tried to make themselves decent while grabbing their paperwork, Troy started back up to the salon deck where Ben was standing with the guardsmen. By this time, the short man in charge was checking Ben's passport and asking what business the group has in Jamaica. Ben explained to the man that this would be the fourth year in a row that they'd come to Freetown in search of a 1670 shipwreck. Ben also handed the man the signed permit from the Jamaican government granting him the right to look for the shipwreck. The guard looked at the permit with a crooked grin and raising eyebrow and commented… "Soooo…you're treasure hunters, are you?"

"Yes," Ben stated firmly. "Not necessarily very good treasure hunters, but…we're persistent at any rate."

The little big-man looked at Ben with a curious smirk and said, "Good luck. I'll be verifying this permit with the magistrate."

Ben wiped the sweat from his brow as the little man continued his duty by looking at the rest of the group's paperwork while the other three guardsmen helped themselves to searching *Next Adventure*. Once the passports had all been verified, the little man told Ben to register his vessel with the consulate and then walked to the aft deck. Meanwhile, the crew could easily hear the sound of opening storage areas and rummaging through the ships stores below deck. The search continued for close to two hours while the crew stood nervously watching the little big man pace back and forth on the aft deck talking to someone on his radio. Finally, with the three guardsman satisfied that everything was kosher, they reported back to their leader on the aft deck.

"All is in order, sir!" One of the guardsmen gave his superior the word he'd been waiting for. Next, the pint-sized guard came back into the salon where the crew of *Next Adventure* was waiting and told them that everything had checked out and that they were free to conduct their business, however…they *could* certainly expect another search before leaving the dock and heading back to the States.

Ben replied affirmatively…"Not a problem, sir. I'll have the vessel registered, ASAP!"

As the guardsmen left the vessel in single file, down the dock and away from *Next Adventure*, Troy looked at Ben. "Now what? We don't dare bring anything back to the boat."

"I don't know, Troy," Ben muttered. "But, we'll think of something. We always do."

Troy had a bewildered look on his face. "Hey, Ben… where in the heck did you stash that gun?"

Ben looked at Troy and smiled. "As they say in today's military, *'Don't ask, Don't tell.'* Now, I'm gonna' go get the paperwork filed on the vessel while you give Marley a call. Have him meet us here at the dock around noon with his boat. Hopefully, I'll be back by then and we can get this program underway."

It was close to four hours later when Ben arrived back from the Consulate's Office where he'd registered the vessel and given the Consulate all the pertinent information, including the date of departure. Ben looked at Marley, who'd shown up as requested. "Well, you weren't jokin', ole buddy. We got *that* visit this morning."

"Yah, mon," Marley smiled. "Don't ever think I'm jokin' around about something like *that*. Did everything go alright?"

"Yeah…I suppose," Ben replied. "Now, let's the three of us take a boat ride and have a little talk."

The guys jumped into Marley's boat and headed offshore about two miles when Ben told Marley to cut-the-engine. Marley did as Ben requested and the boat come to a slow stop. "Okay, guys. What's so important that we had to come all the way out here to chat?" Marley asked.

"Well…" Ben started. "You know that dream of yours of taking your family to the States where you could break away from the poverty of Freetown, and where your boys could get a decent education?"

"Yah, mon…" Marley answered. "What about it?"

"Well…what would you say if I told you that Troy and I are gonna' make that dream of yours come true?" Ben said smiling.

Marley's face lit-up with a smile that reached from ear to ear. "And, tell me…just how you plan to make that happen?" he asked.

"Last year, on the last day of diving…" Ben started out…"I found a small silver box, fifteen silver coins and one gold coin."

"Get outta' town!" Marley exclaimed.

"No joking. It's the truth…and…Troy and I think we've solved this puzzle about where the treasure is located and are thinkin' that we might just strike-it-rich this season." Ben continued his line of talk sharing all the details with Marley in order to convince him that they were onto something. "Now, Marley…here's the deal. We'll make you rich beyond your wildest ganja-induced dreams and help you with all the red tape for you and your family to become United States citizens. But, you have to work with us and keep your mouth shut. Betray us in any way…" Ben continued…"and all deals are off!"

Marley looked at Ben. "I am greatly offended that you would think that I might betray you guys. We have become too close over the years and besides, Tanya and I feel that we are all family. How would you think that I would betray you to those thieves and crooks?"

Ben looked down at the deck of the boat as if he was heavy-hearted. Then, he looked back up at Marley.

"Look, buddy. Don't take it personal. There's a lot ridin' on this trip and we felt that we *had* to have this conversation with you. Where there's treasure…there's trouble. It's just a given fact. I've seen men turn against their own brother where treasure was involved. I'm sorry if I insulted you. Do we have your word on the deal?"

"Yah, mon. You have a deal!" Marley said firmly. "Now, let's get to work."

"One more thing we need to discuss," Ben added. "In your opinion, should we apply for the salvage-permit with the government, or should we sneak the treasure out bit-by-bit and sell it to private collectors in the States?"

"You will *never* be granted a permit to legally get anything out of here," Marley replied. "These crooks would *never* allow anything of any value to slip through their greedy hands."

"So, wha-da-you suggest?" Troy asked.

"Sneak it out little by little on your boat," Marley suggested. "And, if we find too much, I have a place where it can be hidden where no one would ever find it".

"That's kinda' what we thought. Do ya' think we'll be getting any special attention from the guard while we're out here?" Ben wondered aloud.

"Mon, I don't know anymore. It seems as though they've tightened-down on security around here for some reason, and they *really* seem to be interested in what you guys are doing. So, we need to be careful."

Next, Ben went into detail with Marley about the air-compressor and how they planned to cut the end out of it, hide treasure inside, weld the end back on and then repaint it.

"Wow…pretty original idea, guys. *That*, just might work," Marley said. "And, I have an underwater cave that I stumbled upon a few years back while lobstering. We can stash the overflow there for safe keeping."

Ben thought for a bit before speaking. "Well, the treasure's been hiding pretty well for the past 350 years.

Maybe we take what we can and leave the rest in place until next year. We can discuss *that,* when the time comes. As for now, let's get back in and load up the equipment so we can get out early in the morning. Time's a wastin'!"

The group made their way back to the dock and began the task of loading up the dive gear and electronics. Before the loading was completed, Ben loaded up a milk crate which he'd brought along with some lengths of rope inside of it. "Hey guys…if we find anything down below, we may need this. I have a plan on how we can transport the treasure without bringing it up on the deck of the boat for prying-eyes to see."

"That's, what I like about you, Ben…" Troy said, "…always thinking. Sometimes, not real clear, but…always thinking anyway."

Ben took inventory of the equipment that was loaded on Marley's boat and felt satisfied that they'd not forgotten anything. "Marley, let's get out of here at first light in the morning. I've got a hunch that we're gonna' be busy men tomorrow. Oh yeah, one more thing, guys…" Ben added. "Let's not tell the girls about the Boogeyman. Troy's already freaked-out enough over this tall tale. We don't need to give the girls the willies, too."

"Aye aye, Captain Ben," Marley said jumping onto his boat to head homeward. "Oh yeah, mon…one more thing!" Marley shouted before firing-up the engine. "I don't smoke ganja. Tried it once, and just look what it done to my hair!"

CHAPTER 4

On The Scatter Debris Trail

Ben's alarm went off early at five o'clock, sharp. He showered, dressed and made his way up to the salon deck of the boat where Troy was already working on loading up a cooler with some food and water. "Did you get the girls goin', Ben?"

"They *know* what time we're leavin'. I'm not gonna' pry them out of bed *every* morning. If they don't get up… then, they miss the boat."

Troy laughed, "Oh yeah, you *know* they'll have our backsides if we run off without them."

"I suppose you're right," Ben grumbled after giving it some thought. "Tell ya' what…you put some coffee on, and I'll go awake the sleeping beauties and let 'em know the rules going forward".

An hour and a half later, Troy went out onto the aft deck with a cup of coffee in his hand. He could hear Marley's boat approaching in the distance. The morning was calm and you could barely see the sun peaking over the island. Troy stood there looking at the distant sky thinking to himself… *"This…is gonna' be a good day to get rich!"*

As Marley was tying-up to the dock behind *Next Adventure,* the girls came stumbling up the stairs looking for coffee. Troy shouted. "Our ride's here, girls…you'd better get movin' or the boat's gonna' leave without you. We got work to do!"

The guys busied themselves loading provisions, double checking equipment and making certain that everything was loaded onto the boat that they'd need for the day. Ben grabbed the chart at 6:45 just as the island was bathed in daylight. Everybody was on the boat and ready to shove-off. Marley untied the boat while Ben pushed it away from the dock and then jumped aboard. Marley cut the wheel to the left, throttled-up the diesel engines and they were underway.

"Okay, guys…what's the plan?" Marley inquired. Ben unrolled the chart and entered the coordinates for the anchor site and the pill box site into the GPS.

"I think we should go halfway between the anchor and the site in which the pill box and coins were found. Then, we need to start working our way toward the pill box site on an 86 degree heading. I don't think we need to spend a lot of time between these two sites, but I do think we should cover that area somewhat. What's your thoughts, Troy?"

"I'm with you on that one, Ben. I think when we find something major…it's gonna' be beyond the pill box site. If not, then we can cover the area between those two sites more thorough later."

"Okay Marley, *that's* the plan," Ben said. "Go to the anchor. From there, maintain the 86 degree heading for about a quarter mile…then, we'll get serious, guys."

Marley looked at the GPS which had now collected enough satellite information to get a fix on their immediate location, and the location of the anchor. Then, he turned the boat in the direction of the anchor, pushed the throttle forward wide open, and started closing the gap between themselves and the 350 year old anchor.

After about twenty-five minutes of running wide open, the GPS gave the signal that the boat was approaching the anchor site. Marley slowed the boat and eased forward until they heard the *beeping* of the GPS letting them know they'd arrived over their destination. Marley slowly turned the boat while maintaining the anchor coordinates. Next, he lined his compass up on 86 degrees and set up a line on the GPS screen between the two sites while easing forward and maintaining that course. Ben and Troy were busy getting the magnetometer ready to deploy and awaiting Marley's signal telling them that they were approximately a quarter mile away from the anchor site, just as Ben had suggested. Ben instructed Marley that he wanted him to run a loose zig-zag pattern back and forth across the line until they reached the pill box site. Then, they'd tighten the zig-zag over the unexplored ocean bottom so that they'd be covering the area more thoroughly. The sophisticated equipment left a path on the screen called a "snail trail" which showed them where they'd been over the line between the points. That way, Marley could maintain a fairly consistent pattern. Ben had also instructed Marley to mark the spot on the GPS where the magnetometer would be deployed so they could return back to the same exact spot and restart their search in the opposite direction, if necessary.

 A quarter mile into the course Marley gave the signal and marked the point on GPS. Ben tossed the magnetometer over the side, let it trail-off a short distance behind the boat and then tied the umbilical to a cleat on the side of the boat. Troy put the headset on in order to listen for a signal from the equipment. Simultaneously, Marley put his headset on in order to listen to some old Johnny Cash music.

 They had a half mile of ocean to cover to the pill box site. With the tedious back-and-forth movement, it would take most of the day to cover the distance. Troy was listening intently for a hit while Ben was watching the GPS screen making certain that Marley was staying on course.

Meanwhile, the girls had come out of their jackets and were lying on the bow of the boat covering their bodies with sunscreen and working on their tans.

Hour after hour went by without the equipment giving them any signal of passing over anything metallic. From time to time Ben would lightly flip Troy on the shoulder to make certain he was awake. Troy responded by raising his finger and shaking his head to assure Ben that he was awake and on top of his game. Marley was entertaining the girls with his rendition of Johnny Cash's tunes, *Ring of Fire* and *I Walk The Line.*

Another hour passed when suddenly, around 2:30 in the afternoon, Troy jumped up and pulled the headset from Marley's head. "Stop the engines and mark the spot! We got a hit!" Ben tossed the marker-buoy overboard and Marley marked the spot on the GPS while shutting down the engines.

"About time!" Ben shouted. "I thought we were gonna' be skunked today. We're within a couple hundred yards of the pill box site."

Once the spot was marked and the anchor was deployed, Ben and Troy did their usual game of rock, paper and scissors to see which one would make the first dive of the season. Troy won the honor of the first dive and began to pull his dive gear off the rack while Ben busied himself getting the surface-supplied air equipment ready for the dive. Once suited up, Troy jumped off the back of the boat, resurfacing long enough to grab the hand-held metal-detector from Ben. With detector now in hand Troy quickly slipped below the surface to have a look. The water depth was about twenty feet and the visibility excellent. When Troy touched down on the bottom he took a quick look around, as he always did, and then reported to the boat that nothing obvious was visible. Then, he began the search with the handheld detector. While moving the detector from side to side, and being careful to cover every square inch of the sandy bottom, he worked his way toward the lead weight and rope that was holding the marker in place while making circles around the marker, each larger than the one before.

About an hour into the search Ben keyed-up the mic and said, "Hey dude…don't keep us in suspense up here. Have you found anything, yet?"

"Nothing yet…" Troy replied…"but, when I do…you'll be the first to know." Troy had no more than got the words out of his mouth when the detector chirped loudly. "Hold on there! I just got a hit!"

"Well, I'll be, Troy. I must be your good-luck charm," Ben responded.

"Yeah…whatever. There's been no good luck involved in this search so far. We've worked our butts off for the little bit we've found." Troy began hand-fanning the sand away from the target as he'd done so many times before, but quickly…he could tell that the target was covered too deep and that he'd need some help. He communicated to Ben. "Get one of the scooters ready. I'm gonna' surface and bring it back down with me so that I'll have some help removing some of this sand and shell."

Troy surfaced, grabbed the scooter and quickly returned to his target. Once he was back on the target he turned the scooter backwards and blasted the water propulsion straight down on the target, quickly blowing a hole in the sand two feet deep and three feet around but he still couldn't see the target. He worked at it feverishly for another half hour creating a hole about four feet deep and six feet around. Suddenly, he got a glimpse of something other than sand and shell. Troy gently removed another two to three inches of sand by hand-fanning enabling him to now see his target. He quickly finished the excavation by digging with his hands and was able to remove the heavy object from the hole before the wave action could fill it back in, which only takes a brief moment. Once the object was removed from the hole, Troy checked the hole again with the detector to make certain that nothing more was in the hole.

"Well, guys…" Troy laughed, as his voice echoed through the radio. "Nothing but a piece of junk. It looks like maybe some old keel-spikes that are all rusted together. It's not even worth hauling up other than just getting it out of the search area so we don't find it again."

Marley grabbed the mic from Ben's hand. "Bring it up, mon…we'll take it back to the dock. If the guard comes to see if you have found anything, it should give them a good laugh and maybe they'll soon lose interest in what we're doing."

"Good thinking, Marley," Troy replied. "I'm gonna' tie the marker rope around it. It's too heavy to haul up on my own." Troy tied the rope around the object. "Okay, Marley…haul it to the surface and load it on the boat. We need to have a closer look at it on the way back in." Marley hauled the object up and laid the piece of iron on back of the boat.

Once Troy was back on the surface, Ben remarked, "Well guys, once we get things squared away and back to the dock, it's gonna' be gettin' late and we need to get the equipment cleaned up and ready for tomorrow. We'll be over the pill box site early tomorrow and hopefully, our luck will improve." Troy climbed back onto the deck of the boat and removed his equipment. Marley pulled the boat anchor off the bottom, fired-up the engines and headed back to the dock.

On the return trip, Ben and Troy inspected their find and determined that it was indeed a bundle of keel-spikes that would have been carried in ships stores in a wooden crate for making repairs during the careening process. A wooden ship of that period would have to be careened, or turned over on its side in shallow water from time to time in order to clean the barnacles and growth from its hull. Other repairs would also have been made, if needed…such as replacing the spikes that held two giant timbers together which formed the ship's keel.

Once the group was back at the dock, the iron object was heaved onto the dock for all to see. Then, the group started unloading the equipment so that it could be rinsed clean with freshwater and loaded back onto Marley's boat for tomorrow's trip. The group had just completed the task when Troy said under his breath, "Don't look now…but, here comes the Gestapo, just as we'd expected."

The short guardsman was accompanied by his usual entourage. After marching up to the group, the short stocky man with a cocky grin on his face spoke. "Well, treasure hunters, any luck today!" Ben quickly spoke up, pointing at the rusty iron.

"Yes, sir! We *did* have some great luck today. We found this really old piece of iron that we feel could be some sort of good-luck omen. I'm not certain of what it is, but it's kind of neat…don't you think?" The little man looked down at the iron, and then…he looked back up at Ben.

"Looks like a piece of junk to me," he said, obviously unimpressed with their find.

Ben quickly responded. "Well, sir…with all due respect, one man's junk is another man's treasure, and…I just happen to think that this is a real treasure." While the little man was still staring at Ben with a look of amusement on his face, he ordered his men to check Marley's boat.

Once he was satisfied there was nothing of any value onboard, the little man laughed. As he turned to walk away he said, "Have all *that* junk you want, treasure hunters. There's plenty out there…" The little man walked away with his goons filing-in behind him as they made their way back up the dock.

"Marley…" Ben stated…"your idea of bringing that piece of metal back to the dock was nothing short of genius!"

"Yeah, mon. I know you think I'm just another pretty face here, mon…but I have some good ideas. We'll bring back some junk for them to look at everyday, and then, like I said…maybe pretty soon they'll lose interest in what we're doing. But, don't let your guard down too much. It's goin' to cost you somethin' before you get out of here. They figure that if you've got enough money to have a big boat like this, then…you oughta' be able to grease a palm or two before you get out of here."

Ben knew that Marley was right. One doesn't just motor into the harbor in a boat the size of theirs without drawing attention to themselves from not only the other boaters, but also from the authorities who oversee the harbor.

After the group settled-in for the evening, and they all had libations in hand, Ben began telling the crew one of Captain Fizz's treasure hunting stories…

"I know you've all heard me talk about Lindsey's and my treasure-diving friend and diving-guru, Captain Fizz. Well, once upon a time…Fizz told me a story about finding treasure on a shipwreck-site that I wanna' share with you. He and his diving-partner were salvaging the site of the *San Jose* of the 1733 Fleet down off Lower

73

Matecombe Key. The actual wreck-site was mostly ballast rocks and some old timbers. However, they had learned that there was a 12 foot cannon located on a bounce-spot. A bounce-spot is a location where you can imagine twenty-foot hurricane surges tossing a ship up and down and where on occasion, one of those ships hit the reef. Well, when a ship bounced off the reef, the bottom of the ship would open up and spill the contents of the ship's hold onto the ocean floor. First of all...when a Spanish galleon encountered a hurricane, they locked all of the passengers below deck. That's where the term, *batten down the hatches,* comes from. All those poor souls were locked below deck. I can tell you now that the passengers were horribly miserable. It's absolutely the worst place to be seasick. I think all of us have experienced the hell of being seasick at one time or another."

"You can say that again!" Troy interrupted. "The first time I got seasick, I felt so bad that I was wishin' God would take me right then and there!"

"That's the feelin', dude. Anyway, as I was saying...the passengers were locked below deck with the animals and cargo. One could easily be crushed by either the cargo or an animal sliding around all over the place, for that matter. You can imagine all of the puke and poop...burrrrp...I'm making myself sick just talking about it! Now…on the deck of the ship the crew members are doing all they can to keep the ship upright and afloat, but with the cannons all coming loose from their ports and placements, they'd go rolling around, and in some cases, they'd be flying all over the deck, depending on how large the surge was. *Boom*...the cannons go rolling across the deck at a hundred miles and hour. *Boom*...suddenly, the cannon's in mid-air when the ship drops from the top of the wave to the bottom of the trough between waves. *Loose cannons*! That's where the term *loose-cannons* comes from. That site, is where the cannon either went through the gunnels or over the side when the tidal-surge pushed the ship beyond its limits. A lot of other stuff falls out of the ship at a bounce-spot too, which means you wanna' take your metal-detector out there and see if you can find what other stuff fell out."

"Ben, maybe a bounce-spot is where you found the small pill box," Lindsey suggested.

"That's, entirely possible. Oh, one more point. When Captain Fizz and Jack Haskins were diving on the 1715 Plate Fleet wreck-sites, they got a hit on something made out of iron. It turned out to be a cannon. First, they put flotation-straps on it and with the help of a prybar, they were able to turn it over. Beneath the cannon they found two-hundred eight reales coins! Two-hundred pieces of eight! They were stuck to the bottom of that cannon. All of the coins were in excellent condition only because iron oxidizes faster than silver. If all those coins had been laying around on the ocean floor unprotected, there wouldn't have been crap left of them. They would have oxidized. The cannon protected the coins. So...what I'm saying is this...that when we get a ping on the metal-detector, it's always possible that there's something hidden below what may look like a piece of junk, and that sometimes there may be treasure found not only at the shipwreck-site, but also at a bounce-spot where the ship bottomed-out on the reef."

"Great story, Ben," Darlene remarked. "I can't wait for the rest of us to meet Captain Fizz."

"When we all get back to Fort Myers, I'm gonna' throw a little party for all of us and Fizz will be the first name on the guest list."

The next morning went pretty much like the previous one with Troy waking to get provisions ready, making coffee and urging the girls to put some hustle in their movement. By 6:30 the group was on the water heading for where they'd left off the previous day. On the ride out to their diving location Ben explained his intentions to Marley.

"I want us to start a little west of where we found the keel-spikes and deploy the magnetometer there. I want us to sweep the area again and be certain that the keel-spikes were the only thing in the area.

Marley gave the signal when the boat arrived just west of the spike-site, as Ben had requested. Troy threw the mag overboard, let it trail back a bit and then tied-it-off to the cleat. This time it was Ben's turn to take the monotonous job of wearing the headset and listening for a hit. Today, he'd be making the first dive as well. Marley settled onto the course and began the zig-zag pattern across the line as before, then…put on his headset to listen to the country music that he so dearly loved.

The GPS gave the signal when the boat passed over the spot where Troy had found the keel-spikes, however… no other metal objects were detected. The boat continued the back and forth movement across the course line for the next hour and a half. Now, the waypoint mark for the pill box site could be seen on the screen but was still approximately a hundred yards away. Suddenly, it was like a replay from the previous day. Ben ripped off his headset. Then…he ripped Marley's headset off and shouted, "Toss the anchor and mark the spot! We've got a hit!" Troy had already thrown the marker-buoy overboard before Ben could get the words out of his mouth. Marley slowed the boat, turned back toward the marker and threw out the anchor.

As Ben was getting his dive gear on, he joked, "Well folks…I'm entering the water as an average man, but…I'm gonna' come up a filthy rich one." He took a giant step off the back of the boat and quickly resurfaced to grab the metal-detector from Troy. Then, he sank out of sight.

Once he was on the bottom Ben had a quick look around, spotting something that appeared to be out of place just behind the boat's starboard position. The object lay between a couple of good sized coral heads that reached to within four feet of the surface. As he was making his way to the object, he radioed to Troy. "If my eyes aren't deceiving me, Troy boy, I believe we have a fairly good sized pile of ballast stone down here." A few second later, as Ben finned his way closer to the object and the visibility improved from the shorter distance, he spoke with excitement in his voice. "Oh *yeah…*we've got a pile of stones, gang!"

"Can you see anything else, Ben?" Troy asked.

"Nope, nothin' else. Just the ballast pile about ten yards wide and maybe *that* long again, and…a couple of feet above the sand." Ben muttered quietly in his face mask to himself, *"Here's where her bottom began ripping-out, but…there has to be a much bigger pile further east."*

Troy keyed-up the mic on the radio and said, "I'm gearin' up to come down and give you a hand, Ben. We need to tear that ballast pile apart, stone by stone."

"Well, there's gotta' be something metal down here somewhere. It's safe to say these rocks didn't create the signal," Ben announced.

Troy was geared-up and in the water in record time. He joined Ben on the ballast pile giving him a "thumbs up" as the pair went to work. They systematically ran the metal-detector over the pile of stones and then removed the layers of stone one by one. Most of the stones weighed around ten to fifteen pounds each, so work was not too terribly difficult, simply time consuming. The process began first with Ben running the detector over the entire pile, being careful to cover every inch. At one end of the pile he got a really strong hit on the detector but nothing else on the remainder of the pile. Then, the pair began the process of removing stones. After clearing a layer of stones about four feet in circumference, Ben ran the detector over the spot again to be certain they'd cleared the right area. The detector rang louder than before, but still …nothing was visible. Next, another layer of stone was removed which revealed the origin of the hit on the detector. It appeared to be a large iron-pin which most likely was holding the portion of the ship together which the jagged coral had ripped from the bottom, thus allowing the ballast stones to spill out. Ben laid the large pin off to the side in order to carry it back for "show and tell" with the little guardsman. The next task was the painstaking process of removing an entire layer of stone. The pair began the daunting task which took nearly an hour. Now that a layer had been removed, Ben picked up the detector and began swinging the instrument back over the remains of the pile. There was nothing. No sign of a signal was heard on the detector. This process was repeated four times with no results other than making the pile smaller.

    Ben looked at Troy and gave the finger-across-the-throat sign. Troy radioed to Ben and said, "What…are you giving it up?"

    Ben shook his head from side to side indicating "No" and then pointed to the surface. Ben made his way to where the big pin was lying and picked it up to haul back to the surface with him.

    The pair took a quick break on the surface while Marley refueled the engine for the surface-supplied air system. While he was topside, Ben grabbed a scooter to help move sand. Then, they once again dropped back down and immediately resumed their work.

Again, another layer was removed from the pile. This time they also had to blow the sand away from the edges of the pile so as to reveal the portion of the pile that was covered beneath the sand. The pile was much larger than it had appeared above the sand line, but Ben was still confident that this was only a small portion of the ballast that had spilled out at this location when the ship ground-in to the nearby coral heads. With another layer of stones removed and the sand blown away from the edge of the pile, Troy picked up the metal-detector and swam across the pile swinging the detector back and forth. About midway on the pile, Troy stopped and began concentrating and listening intently on one area.

"I've got a faint signal here, dude." Troy said. "Let's remove some stones from this area and see if the signal gets any stronger."

The pair began removing stones until they had another layer removed from the area which Troy had received the signal. Again, Troy swung the detector over the spot and received a much stronger signal this time. Troy looked at Ben nodding his head "Yes" as they started removing more rock from a much more concentrated area. This time, they kept a keen eye on the voids between the stones for something metallic. Another layer was removed. When the current carried the sediments away, Troy reached down into the hole, fanned away some more sand and caught a glimpse of something that nearly made his heart burst from his chest. After digging a bit more with his hand and fanning more sand and silt away, he removed a small six-inch by one-inch by half-inch gold bar from its 350 year resting place. On board Marley's boat, an eruption of excitement emitted from the radio receiver with the guys sudden release of testosterone.

"We da' men! Yeah…we da' men!" they exclaimed.

Marley picked up the mic in response. "Hey mon, you jokers mind lettin' us in on the excitement?"

"We're on our way up, guys! You gotta' *see* this!" Troy roared. As Troy broke the surface of the water behind the boat, he held the gold bar above him so that the first thing they saw from the boat was the gold bar gleaming as if it had been newly poured. Marley sat back in his seat with a bewildered look on his face while the girls were jumping around, dancing and screaming like a bunch of out of control high school girls at a rock concert. Marley jumped back to his feet, grabbed the gold bar from Troy and began helping the two men with their equipment as they climbed back aboard the boat. Once the two divers were standing on deck again, the rest of the group stood around them with disbelief in their eyes and dollar signs in their heads as they stared at the small gold bar.

Ben looked at Marley. "I *know* you've got a fish scale somewhere on this boat. How 'bout grabbin' it and we'll see what this baby weighs."

Marley jumped up and grabbed the fish scale from the cuddy area of the boat. He took a short piece of fishing line and tied around the bar and suspended it from the hook on the scales. All eyes were fixed on the little indicator that lined-up with the corresponding number that matched the weight of the bar. The indicator lined-up just over eight pounds. Ben quickly began muttering to himself as he paced back and forth on the deck doing the math in his head. As the figures became more clear to him, and his calculations more precise, his voice began to rise in volume until his crew-mates could hear and understand every word. "Eight pounds…sixteen ounces to a pound…

convert that to troy ounces that's, 117 troy ounces. Gold is around twelve-hundred dollars per ounce right now which makes our little treasure worth roughly…140 grand, at current spot-price value. Consider the artifact value and shipwreck story that goes along with it, I figure to a rich private collector, this bar should fetch something around a hundred-grand!"

The group stood in silence trying to let what had just happened to them soak in when suddenly…Ben thought aloud. "The guard! What the hell we gonna' do about them bastards?"

Marley laughed. "It's one little gold bar, mon. Surely, we can hide *it* from *them*. I guess it does look like we're goin' to need a plan to move this treasure after all. I thought you guys were full of B.S. all these years. Tell ya' what I'll do. I'll take this bar down below and hide it where they'll never think to look for it." Marley took the gold bar, went below deck, and then returned with a smile. "There! They'll never find it where I stashed it. But, *that* hiding place won't hold much. We need a plan."

It was now about three-thirty in the afternoon when the group decided to call it a day and to return to this spot tomorrow and search more thoroughly before moving along to find the main pile. The marker-buoy was pulled into the boat so as not to reveal the area and Marley fired-up the engines and headed back to the dock.

After returning to the dock the group began their usual daily ritual of unloading equipment and rinsing it off so as not to draw any attention to themselves. Like clockwork, here came the little man with his entourage. Ben said, under his breath, "Okay everybody, here comes the goon-platoon. Marley, I hope you've got that bar hidden *real good*."

"Not to worry, mon," Marley reassured Ben. "Nobody gonna' find that bar where I got it stashed."

The little man and his platoon walked up the dock and straight to the boat. "How did we do today, treasure hunters?" Then, pointing his finger at one of his men, he signaled for the soldier to search the boat.

Ben quickly spoke up. "Well, sir…if you'd given us time, we would've had the treasure we found today on the dock for you to view. We have nothing to hide from you, and no reason to hide it."

The little big-man cocked his head to the side and replied, "So…you found something, yes?"

"Yes," Ben replied. And, if one of your associates would be so kind as to look in the aft starboard bait-well, he'll find it."

The little man looked at his man on the boat who'd overheard the conversation and pointed to the direction of the bait-well. The man on the boat opened the bait-well door and removed the rusted pin. He handed it to another of the guardsman who was standing on the dock, who in turn laid the piece of iron on the wooden dock for the little man to inspect. The little man looked down at the rusty piece of iron. Then, he looked back up at Ben. "Men… check through all these bags of equipment, too."

Ben reacted quickly. "Look…we just wanna' finish cleaning our equipment and get this treasure back into the water so that it doesn't begin to deteriorate, grab a beer, and then relax."

"Well…" the little pain-in-the-backside laughed. "It looks like the good-luck omen you found yesterday worked, treasure hunters. You found more junk today!" The guardsman rummaged through the boat and equipment half an hour before reporting to their superior that they had found nothing out of the ordinary. The group all breathed a sigh of relief as the guardsmen exited the dock again with nothing to report to whomever they reported to.

The crew finished the task of cleaning equipment and climbed aboard *Next Adventure* to relax. Marley went aboard with the group for a quick beer before heading home. Ben grabbed a few beers from the galley, handed Marley a beer, threw himself down on the couch, took a big swallow of beer and said, "Okay, cowboy…where'd you hide it?"

Marley walked over and stood close to where Ben was sitting. Grinning, he reached behind him and pulled the bar from his shorts, placing it in Ben's hand just as he was taking another big slug of beer. Immediately, Ben dropped the bar onto the deck and spat out the swallow of beer as the rest of the group erupted with laughter.

"Damn, Marley! *That's,* just disgusting!" Ben protested.

Marley laughed. "Well, it was a better plan than you came up with, boss. And, there are six of us, which means…we can bring back six bars everyday."

"We've *got* to get a *Plan-B* together, gang," Ben commented strongly. "I surely hope there are some bigger bars to be found that *won't* fit between the cheeks of our butts," he said, shuttering in disgust.

Marley laughed again as he exited the salon room door. "I'll see you in the morning at six o'clock, sharp."

The group sat and stared at the bar once again as it lay on the floor of *Next Adventure.* Finally*,* Troy walked over and picked the bar up with a paper towel, holding it away from his body as if it were radioactive. Then, he rinsed it off in the sink. While doing so, he laughed and said, "That damn Marley's a character, man. But, what are we gonna' do with this stuff as we bring it up? We don't dare make alterations to the compressor, just yet."

Ben said, "We've been trying to have this problem for the last four years. It'll be alright for tonight. We'll take it with us tomorrow morning, for safekeeping. I have a plan that might work. But, for now…let's get showered-up and eat a bite. We've got another big day ahead of us tomorrow."

CHAPTER 5

Ben Makes A Deal With The Little Big-Man

The next morning as the group was boarding Marley's boat, Troy asked Ben under his breath…"Did you remember to bring the gold bar along? We *damn* sure don't want the little fella's boys going aboard and finding *that*."

Ben assured Troy…"I got it under control, dude. Don't ch'u worry your pretty little head."

"Okay…where you got it stashed?" Troy asked.

Ben smiled, "Hey…where do ya' think I got it stashed? It worked for Marley, didn't it…"

Laughing, Troy shook his head and said, "Boy…for *that* bar to have been lying on the bottom of the ocean all those years all by itself, it sure has gotten around in the short time it's been recovered!"

On the way back out to the site where the gold bar was recovered, the group remained silent staring dead ahead with thoughts of finding a huge pile of gold today. Ben broke the silence. "Marley…I think we're gonna' have to make a deal with the little man if we're gonna' get anything aboard *Next Adventure*. How do you think I should approach him with a proposal, and do you think it would be wise?"

"Mon, *that* man would sale his mama out if he thought it might make him a buck. I've been giving it some thought and I think you oughta' offer him an agreed upon amount everyday that he keeps the heat off of us. He's probably thinking that it's a long shot that we'll find anything, giving the fact that we've been searching for the fourth year now. He also knows that if we *do* find something and he reports it to his superior, chances of him cashing-in on anything is slim to nothing. Make him a handsome offer, which is most likely what he's waiting on, *and*…he becomes our insurance policy to get some of this stuff outta' here, and…*he's* also assured to make a few bucks rather than just a pat on the back and some worthless promotion. As I've already told you, you're gonna' have to grease his palm a little bit. Do nothing, and he *will* continue to harass us on the chance that we may find something and the chance that when he turns it in…he *might* get a cut of it."

Ben stared intently into the water on the way out to the site going over in his head what Marley had said, devising a plan of some kind in which he could make a reasonable offer to the little man. He knew that this needed to be a group decision and needed the rest of the groups input before making any kind of an offer.

The GPS gave the alarm when the boat was over the site. Marley cut the engines and threw the anchor overboard. Once the boat was secured, Ben spoke.

"Okay gang…time for a group meeting. We need to agree on a deal to offer our little pain-in-the-butt man so he'll stop with the harassment every evening."

"I agree with Marley," Troy quickly pointed out. "We should pay him off daily."

"I agree as well," Ben replied. "But, what should we offer him at the end of each day? We'd also need to dangle a major offer over his head until the day we're scheduled to leave…a little insurance that he *will not* have us searched before we're able to leave."

"Marley…" Troy asked…"In your opinion, what's a fair amount of money to this guy and what's a large amount?"

Marley responded. "Two-hundred dollars would be a fair amount, and one thousand dollars would be a large amount."

"So...there we have it," Troy stated. "We offer him two hundred a day and a thousand on the day of our departure."

"That's easy enough," Ben commented. "I brought a good deal of cash but I'm having trouble with handing him a thousand dollars before we shove off. He could *still* have us searched anyway, even after he receives the grand."

"Mon, you all are over-thinking this," Marley responded. "Offer him the two hundred per day, and then...explain to him that you'll be back next year, if all goes well for the rest of this trip. Tell him that next year you'll give him the grand on day one when you return, and two-hundred per day after that. Mon...I'm almost certain he'll cooperate with you with a deal like that. That's more money than he makes in half a year here in Jamaica. He'd be a fool to mess that up for some flim-flam promotion that he might get by turnin' you in."

"Wow, I guess you've been thinking about this, Marley," Ben replied. "Here, I've been racking my brain the last few days on what to do and all I had to do was ask you all along."

"I told you, mon...I'm not just a pretty face," Marley said turning to settle in his seat with one foot on the helm of the boat. He put the headset over his ears and started snapping his fingers to the tune of some old country song.

With the decision finally made, there seemed to be a new found enthusiasm among the group to get back to the task at hand of finding treasure. Ben and Troy were getting the surface-supplied air-unit ready for the dive while the girls were doing their usual sun-worshiping routine. Lindsay, the only diver in the group of gals, had decided to bring her gear along on this trip in order to help recover the treasure that she was certain they were going to find.

As Ben and Troy hit the water, the girls were there on the ready to hand them the scooter and metal-detector. The guys dropped to the bottom and began the process of removing another layer of the stones. First, they used the scooter to remove the layer of sand that had settled on the site overnight and then began the removal process. A layer was removed and then the detector went back and forth the entire length of the pile, but nothing was found. The entire pile was removed and searched but nothing more was found on this site. The thorough search of the pile took most of the morning. By noon, the guys were ready for a break. They surfaced, got equipment, squared away and discussed the next plan of attack.

"Okay…" Ben announced…"we're still a ways from the pillbox-site, but according to the map we drew last season…the anchor, pill box and the gold bar are pretty much in a straight line. I think maybe we oughta' switch our strategy and start covering more ground by towing." (Towing is a method of searching for large targets such as anchors or ballast piles. When visibility permits, a diver is pulled along the surface behind the boat by a rope. When the diver observes something out of place, he simply lets loose of the rope and the boat turns around and returns to the spot where the diver is located to anchor up for inspection of that area. Captain Fizz had taught Ben this method of search when he was working with him years ago on the 1715 wrecks on the Treasure Coast of Florida.)

"I agree," Troy added. "We can always come back to this spot and start the mag-search again if we have to."

"Okay…towing it will be," Ben replied. "Marley, what I want *you* to do, is…to pull me at a very slow speed on the GPS line we created…no zig-zag pattern. The visibility is excellent today and the sun is pretty much overhead which should make visibility even better. I'll only be using fins, mask and snorkel in order to reduce the drag. When I see something that I want to check out closer, I'll let go of the rope, and...*you'd* better come back to get me. Then, mark the spot on GPS and anchor-up on the site. It should be very simple that way, and...we can cover a lot of ground. Oh yeah..." Ben added..."in the event somebody spots a fin...slowly turn the boat to starboard and I'll get the hint."

On one occasion, when Ben and Captain Fizz were diving on the Treasure Coast, he was being towed in a similar fashion, just as the crew was preparing to do today. Captain Fizz was on shark-watch at that time and hollered to Ben..."Hey dude...I don't think I see a sharks fin in the water, but I have a feelin' you may wanna' get back in the boat fairly fast!" From that day on, Ben had always related towing-a-diver to trolling-bait behind a boat to catch big-game fish.

Ben and Troy looked at one anther and almost instinctively began pounding their right fists in to their left hands. It was decided...Ben had chosen paper and Troy had chosen scissors. Ben would be towed first and Troy would stand in the small tower on the boat to keep a wary eye out for any sharks that may get interested in what's going on.

Ben suited-up and tied a forty-foot length of rope to the boat cleat that had been used to tie-off the magnetometer. "Now...when we get to the pillbox site...let out a whistle, if you would, please." Then, he jumped into the turquoise blue Caribbean water for a ride. Marley eased the boat forward until Ben had the end of the rope in his hand. After that, Marley turned the boat to line-up with the line on the GPS screen and the process was underway.

Troy climbed up into the little tower and reminded Marley to let him know when the pillbox-site had been reached. Ben was peering down at the bottom for anything obvious or anything that looked out of place. Comparatively speaking, a lot of ground can be covered in this manner, but it's still a slow process. The short distance between the gold bar-site and the pillbox-site would still take a couple of hours to cover. As Ben was being pulled behind the boat and observing the bottom, he pondered on the events that must have been taking place on the big ship at this point in their voyage… *"Had the crew given up now that the hull had been breached? Were they still trying to keep broken spars, masts and sails cleared from over the sides of the ship? When lines and masts snapped and hung over the sides of a ship, the crew of the ship must have had to take their axes and cut the lines that were still attached to the vessel. The wreckage hanging over the side of the ship could snag on the shallow coral formations and capsize the vessel. What was happening on the ship at this point that had caused the Viceroy to the king to be cast overboard with the pillbox in his pocket? At that point, was everybody simply huddled-up awaiting their fate?"* Ben knew that he'd probably never know all the answers, but the thought of the human loss of life and the high-seas-drama that played-out on this very piece of the ocean was unimaginable.

About two hours into the tow, and with nothing spotted…Ben's arms were feeling a bit like jello, not to mention the fact that at this point he wouldn't be able to swim even if he had to. So…Ben dropped the rope and the boat turned around to pick him up as instructed. As the boat stopped to let Ben climb aboard, he asked, "How close are we to the pillbox site?"

"I was just gettin' ready to give Troy the word to let out a whistle, mon," Marley related. "We're almost over the site now. Did you see somethin'?"

"No," Ben replied. "My arms feel like they're two inches longer than when we started. I need to get outta' the water and take a break." Ben climbed up the ladder and collapsed on the back of the boat, exhausted.

"Nothing?" Troy asked as he climbed down from the little tower.

"Nothin', dude!" Ben replied. "Nada."

"Well…we still have an hour or so before we need to head back in," Troy said, hoping to get back into the water. "I'll jump in and you all can tow me for an hour or so. We've gotta' be gettin' closer, guys. We need to keep movin'."

Troy was in his gear and in the water before Ben could get rested up. The process was again underway while Ben was still in the bottom of the boat trying to recuperate. Marley got the boat pointed in the right direction and on the line and then asked Lindsay to take the helm while he went on shark watch.

"Lindsay, gal…you see that little boat there on the screen?"

"Sure Marley, I see it."

Well…you just keep that little boat there on the little line on the screen…it's like child's play. I'm goin' to go watch for fins up there out of the tower," he said patting her on the back.

Taking the helm, Lindsay replied with a chuckle…"This is what we're paying *you* for, Marley."

"Hey…" Marley responded…"you're paying me for my good looks, charming personality, wit…and…the chance that you may get to dance with me one day."

91

Lindsay laughed and focused on the screen while Marley climbed the ladder to watch for fins.

Troy had been towed for approximately twenty minutes while Marley was intently watching for fins. The time was getting to be later in the afternoon when reef sharks become more active. Lindsay was concentrating on keeping the little boat on the screen lined-up with the line on the screen. By this time Ben had recovered from his two hour drag behind the boat and was sitting next to Lindsay on the starboard side of the boat watching her navigate. It was now pushing three o'clock in the afternoon and the sun had started to descend, decreasing visibility from the tower into the depths of the water. Without notice, Marley sprang from the tower onto the deck.

"Fins!" he yelled in mid-air. His feet hit the deck and he yelled again… "Fins! Damnit, girl…turn the boat to the starboard and pull back on the throttle. I gotta' get Troy into the boat!"

Ben jumped up to take the helm as Lindsay slid out of the seat. Ben turned the boat to the starboard as he pulled back on the throttle and threw the engines into neutral. Marley was dragging Troy in as fast as he could when Ben joined in to help speed up the progress. When Troy was alongside the starboard side of the boat, Ben and Marley reached down and pulled him into the boat as if he were a 30-pound grouper instead of a 180-pound man. This had all taken place in a matter of about fifteen seconds. Troy was lying on the floor of the boat and still unsure of what had just happened.

"Damn, dudes…" he said catching his breath. "If you all were done for the day, all you had to do was stop the boat and let me know."

"Ya' had sharks all over ya', mon" Marley insisted.

"Well, maybe they're guarding something for King Neptune, Marley," Troy responded. "Mark the spot and let's start here tomorrow."

As the boat made a turn back toward the mainland, Ben commented as he wrapped up the tow-line. "Well, Troy... there's another chapter in our book, someday."

As Troy was absorbing what had just taken place, he glanced out at the horizon and said, "Yeah, just as I had suspected. We're gettin' closer to the Boogeyman's Island."

The rest of the group looked at the horizon and confirmed the fact that the old mansion was coming into view. However, they didn't pay it the attention that Troy was giving it.

"Marley, let's get ourselves back to the dock. I have a sneaking suspicion that the little man will be there to greet us, and...I have an offer for him," Ben concluded.

"Yah, mon," Marley replied as he took over the helm. Marley fired the engines back up and away they went. The ride back to the dock was getting shorter everyday as the group closed-in on their target. Ben was pretty quiet during the ride back as he rehearsed in his head the conversation that he would have to have with the little guy.

When Marley glanced over at Ben he could see that he was stressing over the pending conversation with the man. "Ben...the little shrimp puts his britches on the same way you do, mon. Don't sweat it."

Ben replied, "He's the least of my concern, dude. If this doesn't go right, we're at a point in this four year search that could end abruptly. I just hope everybody else has thought of this. If the little man doesn't take the bait...I don't see us getting much out of here, if anything."

"Ben, mon..." Marley interrupted..."this little joker's goin' ta bite...hook, line and sinker. I would bet my cowboy boots on it. Well…maybe my cowboy hat." Then, he chuckled. "Just having fun with you, dude. It's goin' to be fine. There's just one more thing I happened to think about that needs to be said when you're talking with him."

"What's that?" Ben asked. "You need to let him know that I know nothing about the arrangement. If he suspects that I know…he might think that I may blow the whistle on him for taking a bribe. So…make it clear that I don't know nothing."

"That's an easy sale, Marley," Ben laughed. "In fact… I'm pretty certain that he's already aware of your lack of knowledge on the issue."

When the boat was nearing the dock, Ben went below to secure the little gold bar before the goon-platoon was in sight. Marley eased the boat up alongside the dock and Troy jumped out with dock line in hand to tie the boat off. The group began throwing dive gear up on the dock to be rinsed off. Ben was on his way to *Next Adventure* to stash the bar when Marley shouted, "Hey, mon!" Ben turned to look at Marley who was gesturing with his head, nodding it in the direction of the end of the long dock where the little one and his minions were making their way toward the group.

Ben stated, "What the hell! Has this joker got us under surveillance or what?"

Marley replied, "Anything's possible, dude."

"Okay group," Ben coached. "Everybody act tired, worn out and defeated. I'm fixing to either get us a free pass, or…a premature trip back to the States."

The "little big-man" walked up to the crew with his crooked little smile and pointed to the boat. His underlings jumped aboard the boat as directed and started their search. Ben looked at the little man and remarked, "We're just simply tired, dude. We found absolutely nothing at all today, and we just wanna' relax."

"Understood," said the little guy. "But, we want to keep you honest."

Ben replied, "How about me and you having a talk aboard my boat while your guys do their thing out here." All the while, Ben was clenching his backside together so the bar wouldn't fall from his swim trunks.

The little one looked at Ben, cocked his head and said, "Okay, treasure hunter…what's on your mind?" The pair boarded *Next Adventure* and settled in the salon area for a conversation. Ben was feeling pretty relaxed about the situation by now. He had made peace with himself knowing this had to be done to get along with the hunt. He also knew that if Marley had misjudged this guys character…the hunt may as well be called off.

Ben began the conversation. "Can I get you a beer, or maybe some rum?"

"I never drink while on duty," the little man replied.

"Just thought I'd ask, because…I'm gonna' have me a beer," Ben remarked.

"You have yourself a beer, treasure hunter. Now, what's on your mind?"

"Actually, the name is Ben…Ben Carson…and what is your name, may I ask?"

"Not important!" barked the little man. "Now, get on with whatever you called me in here for…before I lose my patience."

"Okay," Ben said wrapping his mind around the subject at hand. "What's up with all this attention you're giving us? We're just trying to have some fun, relax, do some diving, help your local economy a bit, and maybe,…just maybe…find something of interest and value while we're out there. We get hassled and searched every evening.

Quite frankly, with all this hassle every evening, we're about ready to throw-in-the-towel anyway. It's looking more like we just may do that and look elsewhere for our pile of treasure."

The little man removed his hat and sunglasses and said with a cocked head and raised brow. "Do not play me for stupid, American. You have been hunting for something specific for four years now. I know there have been riches found in the past near our shores."

"Exactly," Ben quickly replied. "Four years now…and, nothing! Our original plan was to spend this year, and next year, hunting in this general location. If nothing is found related to what we think may be out there…we're gonna' abort this search and move on to the next one."

"Let's move on with this dance," the little man retorted. "You didn't call me in here alone to get to know me better."

"You're right," Ben stated. "Here's the deal, sir. We've been looking for four years. We're going to devote one more year to this, then…we're done and we're moving along, as I've already stated. I feel like our chances of finding anything in our search area is dwindling and I'm gettin' bored with it. If these searches every evening are meant to seize something of value from us, for you to turn over to your superior in exchange for the chance of some kind of petty promotion …that's a long shot for you, at best. And, most likely…you'll never profit in any way from all this. I'm willing to pay you daily to leave us the hell alone and let us enjoy what we're doing. With this deal, you're guaranteed to make some cash."

The little man's ears perked-up during Ben's delivery of his thoughts. The little man stroked his chin whiskers with his right hand as he stared out the door of the salon room. After what seemed like an hour to Ben, the little man asked, "Does Simon know anything about this deal you are offering me?"

"Simon? Oh, you mean, Marley. No sir…I would in no way involve Simon, nor would I let him know what this conversation is about," Ben replied emphatically.

"Well, then. Can you elaborate on this offer?" the little man asked as he continued pondering the offer.

Ben continued…"If, you will cease and desist with the every evening search, I'll pay you two-hundred dollars per day until we depart. Upon departure, I will also need your word that we will not be searched before we leave."

Again, the "little big man" stared out the window and stroked his chin whiskers while processing Ben's words. Then, he spoke. "That means, I'll already have your two hundred dollars a day in hand before you depart." After a brief pause, he continued…"What's my incentive to guarantee to you that you will not be searched before leaving?"

"Wow, you think of everything," Ben said stroking the little man's ego. "I hadn't thought of that. Uhhh…let's see…I've already told you that we *will* be back next year. How about I give you one-thousand dollars on the day we return next year in exchange for your word that we will not be searched before leaving this year. And...in the event that we do find some valuables…I'll throw a few gold coins your way, but…you will just have to trust me on *that* one, boss."

The "little big man" was now out of his seat and staring out the door as Ben was speaking. He thought for a few minutes before he began to speak, continually staring out the window. "You will need to give me the *grand* before leaving. I will guarantee that you are allowed to leave Jamaica without any hassle. You'll just have to trust me on *that* one, boss," he said sarcastically.

Ben went to the fridge and grabbed another beer. As he was walking back to the salon area of the boat, he said…"I trust you with that arrangement, sir. You win either way. Can't get much better than *that*."

The little man held his hand out. Ben grabbed it, shook it and said, "Deal?"

The little man laughed. "Okay…deal. But, I actually meant that the two-hundred dollars per day needs to start today…right?"

"Right," Ben replied quickly. *"What was I thinking?"* he thought to himself as he disappeared below, pulled the gold bar from his behind and came back up with two, one-hundred dollar bills. He handed them to his new business partner and said, "Hopefully, we both prosper from this deal… not just you my friend."

The "little man" took his two-hundred dollars, shoved it in to his pocket, exited the boat and ordered his men to end the search for today.

When the guardsmen were well out of ear shot, Marley asked…"How did it go?"

Ben said, "Just about as we all discussed it, with the exception that he wants the grand before we leave."

"Did you tell him that I know nothing?" Marley asked.

"Didn't have to, dude," Ben replied. "He *must* know you," Ben added in jest.

Marley laughed and said, "I believe he will keep his word on all that the two of you agreed on. He is your insurance policy from here on out. Keep him informed of what's going on, keep his palm greased and you got this deal by the gonads. I'm goin' home to my loving wife and family." The girls all give Marley a hug, and he was on his way.

After the group finished up with rinsing and readying equipment for the next day, they talked, laughed and made their way back to the boat. It was then that Lindsay said she needed to sit down. Ben grabbed her and helped her to the deck of the old rickety boards that made up the dock.

"What's wrong, darlin'?"

Once seated, Lindsay said, "I don't know. I just felt as if I was going to pass-out for a second. I'll be fine…just let me sit for a few seconds and I'll join you all on the boat."

The group stayed with Lindsay until she felt better and then made their way to *Next Adventure.* Ben walked alongside Lindsay to assist her up the gangplank and onto the boat where she seated herself on the couch in the salon room.

Mick brought Lindsay some water. "Do you need anything else?"

"Just some rest and a bit to eat. Then…I'll take me a cool shower," Lindsay replied. "Thanks, Mick."

Darlene went to hers and Troy's stateroom for a quick shower and then to the galley to prepare something for the group to eat.

Ben stayed seated with Lindsay asking every thirty-seconds how she was feeling. After a couple of minutes of his intense attentiveness, Lindsey said firmly, "Ben…I'll be fine…honest. This change-of-life thing sucks! Just let me sit for a bit, then…I'll go get a cool shower and be fine."

Mick and Troy were both looking at Ben as if to say, *"What's going on?"* Ben returned their look by shrugging his shoulders and slowly shaking his head from side to side.

Then, Lindsay reassured the group. "It's probably a combination of too much sun, menopause and not eating enough today…along with all the excitement. I'm feeling a little better now. I'm going for that cool shower." Ben saw to it that she got to their stateroom and into the shower, then made his way back to the salon room. When he entered the room, Mick could see that he was filled with concern about Lindsay.

"Ben, she's probably right about why she's feeling bad," she said trying to reassure him. "She'll feel better after she showers and gets a bite to eat."

"I suppose you're right, Mick. But, I worry about her… she needs to stay out of the sun tomorrow."

After Lindsay showered, she joined the rest of the group for supper. She was back to her chipper self and they could all see that she seemed to be feeling much better. The discussion lightened-up with Troy asking Ben about the conversation with the little man.

"It was pretty intense, Troy. But, I think he's in our pocket. I think we'll be fine." Troy could sense that Ben was in no mood to think about anything else but Lindsay at the moment.

Troy, Mick and Darlene went to the fly-bridge for some libations and to watch the sun go down. Ben and Lindsay sat in the salon room reflecting back on the day and discussing tomorrow's activities.

Lindsay yawned. "I'm going to turn in now. I love you, Ben…and I'll see you in the morning."

"Okay, dear...love you. I'm gonna' join the rest of the gang top-side."

Ben made sure that Lindsay made it down below fine and then joined the rest of the group on the flybridge. As Ben climbed the ladder to the flybridge, all eyes were on him as if to ask, *"How's she doing?"*

"She's turned-in for the evening. I think she's fine, guys…but, she's going to see her doctor as soon as we get back to Florida, I'm concerned about her."

CHAPTER 6

Treasure And Trouble

Ben awoke the following morning to find Lindsey already up and going, getting ready for the day's adventure.

"Come on, dude…let's get going!" she demanded.

"I think maybe you need to stay out of the sun and rest aboard *Next Adventure* today, dear," Ben told her.

"Ben…are you crazy? I'm not going to miss out on this adventure. I'm fine, now…let's get moving. Everyone else is already up and going, and Marley will be here in a bit."

"Okay," Ben replied. "But, you *have* to stay out of the sun. I was thinking more on it last night. Remember when we were in Sarasota on vacation with the boys? You got sun poisoning and very sick, as I remember."

"I remember," Lindsey replied. "But, I'm telling you, it's this change-of-life crap I'm going through. I'll stay out of the sun today and keep Marley company, okay?"

"Deal," Ben resigned. "I think I hear Marley's boat approaching, now."

When Ben and Lindsey disembarked *Next Adventure,* the rest of the group was on the dock helping Marley with the lines to tie-off his boat. After necessary equipment was placed on the deck of his boat the group loaded-up and shoved-off.

"Ben!" Troy shouted, as the rest of the group nursed their coffee and completed the waking-up process.

"Yeah, Troy," Ben replied.

"I was thinking last night…" Troy began to explain.

"Well, that's always good, Troy. What were you thinking?" Ben laughed.

"I was thinking that you should have invited the *little man* to join us today."

Ben gave Troy a puzzling look. "Why on earth would I wanna' do that?"

"Well…" Troy began…"we could have introduced him to towing. We could have given him the first turn at towing in the area where we spotted the sharks." Everybody laughed at Troy's comment.

"Hell…Sharks wouldn't eat *that* dude…he's too foul! Even sharks have standards, mon," Marley replied.

After chuckling at the exchange, Ben said…"Okay Cap'em Marley…let's go back to the area where we had to snatch Troy's backside from the sharks and get started there. You want the first tow, Troy?"

"You dang straight," Troy answered. "I got cheated yesterday. If we've got good visibility from top to bottom when we get out there, I'll be in the water chomping at the bit."

Marley navigated the boat back to the same spot where they'd left off the previous day. When they reached the spot, Marley pulled back on the throttle, threw the boat in neutral and said, "Man overboard! Let's find something today, mon!"

"Marley?" Lindsey said, speaking up.

"Yes, my love," Marley replied.

"How about I navigate the boat today, okay?"

"Why certainly, my love…whatever makes you happy."

"Well, Ben says that I have to stay out of the sun today," she explained. "So, I decided that this would be the best place to do just that."

Ben spoke up… "Yes… she *has* to stay out of the sun today. She had a little episode yesterday after you left the dock."

"A lot of women have *that* reaction when I leave their sight, Ben. No worries," Marley replied.

"Give me a break, dude," Ben said. "She got too much sun yesterday and almost passed-out on the dock."

"You feeling better now, love," Marley said with concern.

"Yup, all better now," she replied.

"Put your arm next to mine, love" Marley said looking at Lindsey. Lindsey put her arm next to his. "You don't need to get any darker anyway, girl… your nearly as dark as I am."

During all the verbal exchange, Troy was getting suited-up and ready to jump into the water. Once again today, the visibility was top to bottom…perfect for towing. Ben tied-off the length of towing rope that would pull Troy. Troy went over the side and peered down into the depths looking back up with a big smile. "Great visibility!" he shouted as he swam behind the boat to take hold of the rope. Marley fired up the boat and eased it forward so Troy could get the end of the rope and then lined the boat back up with the line on the GPS screen.

"Okay, Captain Lindsey…she's all yours. Just maintain this speed and heading and you'll do great." Marley sat in the seat next to Lindsey and put on his headset. Ben climbed up in the little tower for shark watch. Marley closed his eyes as if sleeping but opened one eye every so often to make certain Lindsey was still lined-up correctly.

One hour into the tow, Troy dropped the rope. Ben shouted that Troy had spotted something and Marley took the wheel to turn the boat around. He eased the boat back to where Troy was floating in the water, dropped the anchor and marked the spot on the GPS for future reference.

In no time flat, Ben was down from the tower and into the water. "What'd ya' see down there, dude?"

"Not certain…" replied Troy…"but something definitely looks out of place." Ben and Troy both peered down in to the depths as Troy pointed in the direction of the object. Ben studied on it for a bit and popped his head back up above water.

"Can't be certain, but it looks like a cannon. We need to suit-up and dive down for a closer look," he said with excitement. The pair was back in the boat and suited-up in record time. The girls and Marley were preparing the surface-supplied air system. Ben and Troy jumped back into the water, grabbed a regulator for air and dropped to the bottom for a closer look. The water in this area was a bit more shallow than the area they'd been searching, so Ben thought that this could perhaps be a bump-site such as Captain Fizz had taught him about.

Once the two men were on the bottom, Ben quickly identified two bronze cannons. Ben looked at Troy giving him a thumbs-up and pointed back to the surface. Reaching the surface, Ben instructed Lindsey to hand him the underwater video camera and the cloth tape measure that Ben always carried with him.

"Don't keep us in suspense, guys" Darlene demanded. "What is it?"

"Two, big, beautiful, bronze cannons!" Troy shouted. The atmosphere on the boat erupted while the guys dropped back down to video the cannons. Once back on the cannon-site, Ben and Troy videoed the cannons making certain to include any distinguishing markings that could be identified and then measured the length and bore of the cannons. Once Ben was satisfied that they'd gotten enough video and specifics, he pointed back to the surface. The pair surfaced and handed equipment to the girls so they could climb back aboard the boat. Once in the boat, the video was shared with everyone.

"I'm going to see if I can get through to Captain Fizz and tell him what we've found. Hopefully, we're close enough to the mainland that we can make contact." Ben dialed Fizz and made a tolerable connection with only a little crackle on the line.

"Dude, what's up?" Fizz said, answering in his patented fashion.

"Fizz…we just found two large bronze cannons!"

Fizz thought a quick second before replying. "Are you sure…because I remember two morons who got me all excited once before over nothing. They worked two days to uncover an object that they believed was a cannon off the coast of Southwest Florida that ended up being a piece of pipe."

"I'm certain, Fizz. We found them while towing. I have video that I'll try to send to you when we get back in to port."

"Take a video of the video, now…on your phone, and send it to me. If I get it, I'll have a look and call you back. I'm busy with this pirate shipwreck project in the Gulf at the moment, but I'll have a look first chance I get."

"Wha-da-ya' think? Should we search this area more or move on?" Ben asked.

"Mark the spot and keep moving forward. You don't have the means to raise them now, anyway…I don't imagine. If they *are* what you say they are…they're worth a lot of money, but I suspect you're getting close to a major find," Fizz summarized.

"Roger that, dude" replied Ben. "We'll try to send the video and move forward. Thanks a million…or several million, hopefully"

Using his phone, Ben videoed the video and sent it to Fizz. The girls were in the water at this point looking down and trying to see the cannons. Ben and Troy let them look a bit and then said, "Okay, gals…back aboard. We're moving on."

"We got a fix on them cannons, right Marley?" Ben asked.

"Yeah, mon," replied Marley. "*That*, could be my future down there."

"That may very well change all of our futures, Marley" Ben replied. "Let's move forward."

The time was nearing 10 a.m. and it was Ben's turn to be towed. Ben jumped into the water and grabbed the rope while Marley lined the boat back on course and then gave the helm to Lindsey. Troy would be on shark watch from the tower while Ben was in the water.

Ben had been towed for about twenty minutes when his phone rang. Lindsey picked it up. "It's Fizz," she said answering the device. "Hi there, my handsome Captain," she said in a sultry voice.

Fizz answered…"Well, hello there beautiful. I'd rather talk with you than Ben anytime."

"We're trolling with Ben as we speak. What's up?" she asked.

Fizz replied, "Keep dragging him, honey…don't stop unless he spots something. Those are definitely cannon from a very important ship. The crew of that ship would have been instructed to save them at all expense and would only have given them up if they were sinking. I feel like you're close to the main wreck-site and will most likely find more of them when you find the main pile. I wish I could be there, honey, but I have backers and a filming crew on this project and can't break away. Have Ben call me this evening. I wouldn't be at all surprised if you all find money soon."

"Stop the boat, girl…and turn it around. Ben dropped the rope!" Troy shouted.

"Gotta' go Fizz, Ben's spotted something else. Talk to you soon…love yooou!" Lindsey said signing-off. Marley took the helm and headed the boat back towards Ben's location. Once there, the anchor was dropped and the site was marked.

"Wha-da-ya' have, Ben?" Troy shouted.

Ben looked up at Troy. "You know how big the ballast pile is on the *El Infante,* just off Key Largo?"

"Of course I do," Troy replied.

Ben smiled, nodded his head "Yes" and pointed down into the water. "We're here, dude!" Ben shouted… "We're here…finally!"

Ben climbed back into the boat to gear-up for the dive while the rest of the group was going overboard to look down at the ballast pile Ben had located. The pile seemed to be the size of a football field and was situated partially in a sand-flat up over a coral ridge and then back down in to another sand-flat. Obviously, the big ship had started to take on water and was drafting deeper and deeper until it finally hit hard on this coral ridge and came to rest. The huge waves created by the hurricane would have then pummeled the ship to oblivion. The distance from the wreck-site to the nearest land explains why there were no survivors.

In his head, Ben was going over how this ship would have broken up from this point. He thought to himself, *"It's a very real possibility that the upper-deck structure may have sheared off and scattered farther to the East, but there are definitely riches to be found right beneath us, right here."* Again, Ben thought about the horrible loss of life and high-seas-drama that played out right here on this very spot. *"Unimaginable!"*

As Ben stood there on the deck of the boat immersed deep in his thoughts, his phone rang. Captain Fizz was on the other end and immediately began asking questions.

"I was on the phone with Lindsey explaining to her about the cannons when she suddenly hung up saying something about you spotting something else. So, what'd you find?"

"The main ballast pile, Fizz! We have found the main ballast pile! It was only about a twenty-minute tow from the bronze cannons."

"That, doesn't surprise me," Fizz replied. "So…why are you on the boat and not in the water, dude?"

"Fixin' to get back in directly. I was just mentally reflecting on what may have happened on that fateful day."

"I understand," Fizz replied. "You folks had a fairly long search…four years. Your perseverance is commendable. Most likely, there's gold, silver and emeralds, right there beneath you! Get back in there and keep me informed!"

"Deal…" Ben replied, ending the call with Captain Fizz.

"Troy!" Ben hollered. "Let's suit up and get down there close up and see exactly what piles of treasure actually look like. We've been looking for years, and…hell…we deserve this moment!"

Troy was back on the boat in a flash with the rest of the group close behind him. The pair of "now successful treasure hunters" suited up and made a splash overboard to inspect the ballast pile with a metal-detector. Once on the pile, the pair couldn't believe the enormity. Ben ran the metal-detector over the pile that lay in the sand-flat, up over the coral ridge, and back down into the sand-flat located further east. The detector couldn't differentiate one target from another since there were so many metal objects buried in the pile. Then, the pair of divers swam the perimeter of the ballast and identified at least seven more bronze cannon. This pile of stones was a hundred times larger than the pile that they searched through when the gold bar was found. It seemed to be a monumental task to move each of these stones in order to reveal its secrets, but it was a task that the pair was willing to take on.

Ben resurfaced to grab a scooter to help with the excavation of sand over the site and then quickly dropped back down to start the daunting task. The pair started on the westernmost portion of the pile as they believed that this was the stern portion and would have been closer to the captain's quarters where the lion's share of valuables would have been stored for safekeeping. Ben began his efforts in the middle of the pile. Ben would blow away sand and Troy would then come back over the spot with the detector to see what may lie beneath. The detector sounded off strongly as Troy waved it over the spot where Ben had cleared the sand. The two men started moving stones from the area until they had revealed something that was definitely metallic. It was iron, but the artifact could reveal the portion of the ship that the pair thought to be the stern. If indeed this was a portion of the stern section, it could shed light on just how the ship had gone down and also shed some light on just where the pair should concentrate their efforts. As the work to uncover the piece of metal continued over the next hour, Ben was more than certain that this was a portion of the rudder-shaft works. Then, Ben told Troy his conclusion…that he thought they should move more forward in the pile of stones to possibly get closer to where the treasure would have been stowed.

The pair moved forward with their efforts and settled close to the base of the coral reef on the western end of the pile. Ben blasted the sand away from the ballast pile with the scooter and revealed a portion of what they thought might be closer to the captain's quarters. Troy ran the detector over the area Ben had cleared and immediately got a strong hit. Ben started fanning the fine layer of sand away with his hand and revealed what appeared to be a box lying right there above the stones. Ben reached down and pulled hard on the object to break it loose from 300-plus years of encrustations. After much effort with both guys pulling, the item eventually broke loose and when the silt settled, Ben could see the edges of several coins that had once been stored in a wooden chest. These were silver coins, hundreds of them and looked to be all eight reales in size. These would have been stacked on the top of the pile in the hold. Gold would have been stored below the silver to possibly thwart theft of the more valuable coins. The guys knew they were on top of a pile of treasure that had been stacked in the ship's hold and would need to keep working their way down to the gold.

Ben looked at Troy and said. "We need to haul this up for everyone to see." Troy gave Ben a thumbs-up and popped to the surface for the length of rope and milk crate. Then, he dropped back down with the milk crate and Ben hefted the silver clump into the crate. Next, the pair instructed the hands-on-deck to haul the crate in as they made their way to the surface along with the treasure.

The crate surfaced about the same time the guys did. Marley held the rope that was connected to the milk crate and was hauling it over the side of the boat. When the crate hit the floor of the boat the group all stared at the black clump and were wondering what in the world it was.

"Oh my God!" Mick shouted. "*This,* looks like the clumps of crap that Ben had me X-ray before, except…this one is huge! If *this* is what I think it is…everybody on this boat can live a bit more comfortable. After Ben made his way up the ladder to the deck of the boat, Mick asked…"Is *this,* what I think it is, Ben?"

"Not sure," Ben replied. "Wha-da-you think, Mick?"

"Looks like a huge hunk of silver coins to me," she replied.

"And, I didn't think you were paying attention all these years," Ben chuckled. "You're exactly right… and if the documents are correct…there's more down there than Marley's boat will haul."

Once again the atmosphere on the boat erupted with cheers and even some tears. Marley sat back down in his seat and was brushing back a few tears himself. Ben walked over, placed his hand on Marley's shoulder and said, "The answer to that dream of yours has been laying here all along. You're goin' to the States to raise that family of yours."

Marley looked up at Ben in disbelief and asked, "Do you really think there's more of that down there?"

"I guarantee it, dude. That's, as virgin a wreck-site as I've ever had the privilege to work on. There's tonnage down there."

"Okay." Troy remarked. "Here's where the trouble with treasure comes in, guys. What are we gonna' do with it?"

"Well, we know there's gold and emeralds down there. We're limited in space on what we can take back to the States, so…I say we find a nice little spot to stash the silver and save our space in the air-compressor for the more valuable finds. We know a magnetometer won't pick up the silver, if by chance someone were to drag over our hiding spot. I feel it would be safe away from the wreck location. What-say-ye, Marley? How far is your cave from here?"

"It's a haul, mon," Marley replied.

"Okay," Ben said. "I say we find a nice coral overhang or two around here somewhere close and stash the silver."

"I'm good with that," Troy agreed. "But, I say we take nothing back this evening and test the little big man's commitment to your deal."

Ben shook his head in the affirmative and then said, "Good thinking, Troy…I agree one-hundred percent. We have a few hours before we need to head in, so let's make the best of it guys."

Marley dropped the load back down and the guys returned to the water to continue their salvage work. They'd only been down for a few minutes when Lindsey joined-in on the action. Ben looked at Lindsey and said, "Are you okay?"

Lindsey replied, "Yes, I'm fine. I wouldn't miss this moment for the world."

Work was underway with the group making their way back to where the silver had been retrieved. Troy waved the detector back over the area and yet another strong signal was given by the detector. Ben took the scooter to blow sand and debris away from the site and the two guys began moving stones. Several stones were removed from the area. Again…the sand, shells and debris were blown from the site but nothing could be seen. Troy waved the detector back over the site, shook his head "Yes" and pointed.

The process was repeated two more times with no results when Marley's voice came across from the boat and said, "We need to head back in, mon…storm clouds are building. Find a safe place for my future and let's get going."

Ben replied, "It should be fine where it's at, for now. Captain Fizz would say something like…'It's been here for over 300 years. I think it will be safe one more day.'"

When the group surfaced, the waves were noticeably rougher than when they'd submerged. Lindsey was the first to get out of her gear and get back on to the boat. In doing so, she was noticeably having trouble gripping the ladder and had to be helped back aboard.

"Lindsey…*you're* purple!" Mick said, taking notice of her condition.

Ben commented, "The water is a balmy 84 degrees, how can that be?"

"I don't care, Ben. Just look at your wife!" Mick barked. "She's freezing!"

Ben was the next to get back on the boat and immediately tended to Lindsey by covering her with dry towels. Marley offered his body heat by wrapping his arms around her.

Not having lost her sense of humor, Lindsey said with quivering lips, "Yuh…yuh need to ask…ask a girl for a dance fi…fi…first, Marley."

Marley looked up over his sunglasses at Ben. "She's stone cold, mon. Mick come help get her warm…we're headin' back in!"

Lindsey had begun shaking vehemently while Marley was hoisting the anchor. He fired-up the engines and the group was on their way back to the dock. Darlene sat down next to Lindsey to help restore her body temperature while Ben was kneeling in front of her rubbing her extremities.

"Are you feeling warmer yet, baby?"

"I'll be fine B…Ben…you worry too much," she replied.

"The water's not *that* cold, dear. What do you think's going on with you? You've been diving with me in colder water than this."

"We'll d…discuss this when we get back in, Ben… I'm…fine."

The boat pulled alongside the dock. Ben helped Lindsey off the boat, rushing her onto *Next Adventure* out of the brisk breeze. He helped her down and made her comfortable on the couch in the salon room covering her with a blanket. "I'm gonna' make you some coffee to help warm your innards," Ben said, making his way to the galley. "Why didn't you let me know that you were so cold down there, Lindsey?" Not waiting for an answer, Ben disappeared down below to start the coffee brewing and then quickly returned to check on Lindsey. She had once again begun shaking, but at least her color seemed to be returning to her normal complexion. The rest of the group was standing close by watching her condition with concern.

"Darlene, can you go down below and get a cup of coffee, please?" Ben asked. Darlene went below and came back up with a fresh brewed cup of coffee and handed it to Lindsey.

"Here, darlin'… just wrap your hands around this hot cup of coffee. If nothing else, it will at least warm your hands up." Lindsey sat up and took the coffee from Darlene while Ben adjusted the cover over her shoulders and threw another over her legs.

"Okay…I'm good now, guys. You all need to get the gear from Marley's boat before the water roughs-up anymore. My c…cowboy, here needs to get back home to his family…so, go on…I'm good" Lindsey urged, looking at Marley.

"Stay here with her, girls," Ben instructed. "Troy and I will go unload and rinse the gear." The guys walked back to Marley's boat which was now heaving pretty heavy in the waves. As they unloaded the gear they were discussing their concerns about Lindsey.

"Ben, if we need to tap out and head back to the States…we'll all understand," Troy said trying to reassure Ben of the will of the group.

"I'm not one for snap decisions, Troy…you know that. Besides, Lindsey would never agree to let me do *that*. Hey Marley, call us when you get home, please. Lindsey will worry about you if you don't. For some reason, she appears to like you," Ben said.

"I will, Ben. But this is just a little blow…don't worry, mon. The worst about *this,* is that I'll have to remove my cowboy hat so I don't lose it. Take care of our girl, there… I'll call in about half an hour." Before Marley shoved-off to head home, he added…"Hey mon, in case nobody noticed…no *little big man* this evening. I'll call you tomorrow morning after checking the weather. From the looks of things right now, tomorrow's goin' to be a bust."

"Troy, let's throw this gear up on the back of the boat. It's fixin' to rain anyway, and Mother Nature can do the rinsing. I'm going back in to check on Lindsey."

The guys carried the gear to the boat and spread it across the stern deck so the rain could do their work. Then, they joined the rest of the group inside.

When they arrived, Lindsey had gone to her and Ben's stateroom to lie down. When Ben went below to check on her, Lindsey's condition had seemed to improve somewhat. After making sure she had everything she needed, he returned to where the rest of the group was gathered and said, "I think she needs to go back to the States in order to see her Doc, guys. I'm not buying this menopause thing anymore…something's wrong."

"I agree," Mick said. "I think we need to take the boat back to the States when this weather lets up."

"No," Ben said, shaking his head. "I'm gonna' see if I can get her on the first flight to Fort Myers tomorrow. Mick, I'll need you to go back with her."

"That's fine, Ben. I wouldn't have it any other way," Mick responded.

Then, Darlene spoke up. "I'll be going back with her as well, guys. So…the three of you will be on your own".

"We'll talk more about it early in the morning," Ben said speaking to the group. "My thoughts are heading this boat back right behind the airplane, but I know Lindsey will have a say in all this."

Ben's phone rang. It was Marley letting him know that he was home safe. "Okay, Papa Bear. You can tell Mama Bear that Goldy Locks made it home safe and sound."

"Good deal, dude," Ben replied. "I'll let Lindsey know."

"She doing okay, mon?" Marley asked.

"She's in bed resting…and seems to be doing fine, but I think she needs to get back to the States to see her doctor. Are there any flights leaving Jamaica for the States tomorrow?"

"I can check with my buddy, Dontavious. He runs a ten seater flying-service between here and the States, but he only flies into Miami".

"Miami?" Ben sounded surprised. "So what kind of goods is Dontavious delivering in Miami?"

Marley laughed. "No ganja, mon… mostly Americans who come here for the lifestyle resorts, as they are called."

Ben thought for a bit before answering. "So our girls would be flying back with a bunch of people who like to run around in their birthday suits?"

Again Marley laughed. "Dontavious is probably the only guy who does this crossing most everyday and most likely our best bet to get her back to the States tomorrow. Wha-da-you want me to do, Ben?" Marley asked.

"Set it up. She needs to go home. I don't think the weather's gonna' be fit for diving tomorrow, anyway. Call me in the morning and let me know what your buddy's flight schedules are, please."

"I'll do it. Hey, Ben…give Lindsey a hug from me that lasts all night and keeps her warm."

"Umm…okay, dude. I had planned on that, but…I'm not gonna' tell her it's from you," Ben replied.

"Ten-four," Marley replied."

The rain had begun to fall and the wind whipped the water up enough that the waves were rocking *Next Adventure,* testing the lines that held her to the old dock. Ben stood staring out of the salon room door at the wind and waves, thinking back on a time when Lindsey, he, and another couple were in the Great Exumas on vacation. Letting his thoughts be known to the others, he said, "I hope those ropes hold, but more than the ropes, I'm a bit concerned about that old dock that we're tied to, as well." After a moment of silence, he continued speaking. "Once, back several years ago…before I got bit by the treasure-hunting bug, Lindsey and I went on vacation with Will and Beth O'Reilly, a couple whom we were close friends with at the time. We went to Georgetown, in the Exuma Island chain of the Bahamas, and rented a 32-foot houseboat for a week. It was a great time. We caught fish every morning for supper later that evening and simply took our time and moved around from island to island. Some of the islands were uninhabited, so the beach-combing was pretty interesting. Hmmm… I guess I was treasure-hunting even back then, just not for silver and gold at that point. Anyway…we were always in radio contact with the marina. One night…the weather looked like it was gonna' whip something up, so the marina radioed us and told us to tie-off to the first mooring buoy we could find. We took their advice and found a buoy, tying-up for the evening. Well…later on in the evening, we got into the rum pretty heavy, thinking all was well. Now, I've always turned in earlier than most, but with the rum kicking in and all, I went to bed earlier than normal. Will woke me abruptly around 11 p.m. He was concerned about our situation, almost to the extent of a panic.

"Hey man…you need to get outta' bed! Either we've pulled that mooring-buoy up off the bottom of the ocean, or *that* island is moving!"

I jumped up and sure enough, we were moving at a high rate of speed for the open Atlantic. Will and I both went to the stern of the houseboat and began hauling in the rope that had been attached to the buoy. Well…it was still attached, but…we also had about a six-foot long auger stake that once had been screwed into the ocean floor. We looked at each other and dropped the items on to the floor of the boat. I cranked the boat up in order to get us back to the Georgetown dock where we'd rented the boat. The weather was ripping pretty good, both wind and waves. We finally made to a safe harbor…but, what an adventure *that* was! I often wondered where we would have ended-up if Will hadn't been the night owl that he was. It's kind of scary to think about, looking back. Over the years, both Lindsey and I have covered a lot of ground and had our share of adventures and setbacks. And, one thing I *can* say…is that neither one of us regret a single second.

Enough storytelling," Ben said. "Okay, I'm turning-in, you guys. Troy…if that dock gets ripped-up from its pilings… wake me up, please."

Troy laughed. "I'll do it, dude. I wish me and Darlene had been on that adventure with you all. What is life if you don't live it to the fullest? The way I see it…if you die without creating hours of true stories to tell about your adventures…then you really haven't lived."

"Well said, Troy," Ben replied. "I'm gonna' crawl in next to Lindsey and keep her warm. See you all in the morning. We'll discuss this situation more after I hear from Marley…night guys."

CHAPTER 7

Do We Have An Accord?

Ben awoke the following morning to find *Next Adventure* still tossing a bit from the previous evening's storm, but not nearly as much as when he'd turned in. He listened to the squeaking of the rubber bumpers in place between the vessel and the wooden dock that prevented damage to the hull. He lay beside Lindsey for just a few minutes watching her sleep. His touch to her shoulder let him know she was toasty warm.

When Ben heard his phone ring he realized that he'd left it in the salon room on the upper deck. Trying his best not to wake Lindsey, he slipped out from under the covers and rushed to the upper deck. As he picked up the phone he recognized from the Caller-I.D. that it was Captain Fizz.

"Fizz…I have a good explanation why I didn't call you back last night, but let me tell you somethin' first. This, is a virgin wreck-site that we've found, dude!"

"What makes you say that?"

"Fizz…it's just as you said there'd be. Troy and I identified another seven of those beautiful bronze cannons just lying there on the ocean floor amongst the ballast. I think that if anyone else had already stumbled onto this site…those cannon wouldn't be there anymore."

"Definitely not! Tell me this…were they all around the perimeter of the ballast?"

"No, come to think of it." Ben pondered momentarily. "They were all to one edge of the pile."

"That means, she capsized before settling. If she'd gone down by the keel, most likely those cannons would've been dispersed all along both edges of the ballast. She capsized before settling, causing all those cannons to be ripped loose, if they'd not already done so. They would've all been tossed to the side of the ship that went down first. When the teredo worms finally ate away all the wood… those cannons would lay on one edge of the ballast pile. Seen it several times, Ben. All it means is, that your's and Troy's salvage efforts may be a bit tougher because a lot of what you're looking for will most likely be covered with ballast stones. Don't matter…you gotta' tear that whole pile apart anyway," he added.

"I'm certain you're correct about that, Fizz. But, I was saving this for last…we've already recovered one chest of silver coins."

"Holy crap, *dude*!" Fizz shouted. "It's a little too early in the day to drink rum in celebration of silver being found, but you can bet as soon as the hour approaches… I'll damn sure partake in some! Ole Jack Haskins research was right on-the-money again. He always said there was another rich galleon somewhere on the Pedro Banks…and now, you've found it for him, Ben. But, I've gotta' tell ya'. If Jack had lived a few more years, you would've found nothin' but a pile of ballast stone…and that's all that would've been left."

"I'm sure you're right about that too, Fizz," Ben chuckled. "Wish I could have met Jack. Hey, do me one more favor, if you will Fizz. When you have that celebratory glass of rum…call me up so we can celebrate together."

"Deal!" Fizz said.

"Now…" Ben continued. "…the reason I didn't call you yesterday evening with the news about our discovery was because Lindsey had another one of her spells after surfacing from a dive that scared the hell outta' me!"

"What do you mean, *another* spell?"

"She had a spell a couple days back. And then, she had one again when we returned to the dock last evening. She almost fainted. We all figured she'd gotten too much sun, but yesterday…Lindsay went down with Troy and I on the wreck until a storm chased us away. She'd been down about an hour or so with us when Marley said we needed to surface and head back into port. When Lindsey surfaced, it was clear that she was almost hypothermic. The water temp was about 84 degrees, Fizz. She was shaking violently and could hardly speak because of the shivers. We headed back to the dock before the weather and waves worsened, *and* to get Lindsey back to our boat to get her warmed up. She was still sleeping comfy and cozy when I got up to answer your call."

"Dude, I don't have to tell you that *she's* more important to you than every unfound treasure galleon out there!" Fizz said with concern.

"I know that, Fizz. I found my treasure thirty-plus years ago when Lindsey agreed to marry my sorry behind. I'm trying to make flight arrangements to get her back to the States today. I haven't had that conversation with her, yet…but I will as soon as she rolls out of bed. Mick and Darlene have already offered to fly back with her."

"Are you going back with her or do you plan to stay there and continue the salvage?"

"I'm gonna' leave *that* up to Lindsey, but I'm guessing she'll have nothing to do with me aborting this salvage. However, if she wants me to…then I'll be heading back, as well".

"Right answer. You take care of her and let me know what's going on, okay? That treasure's been lying there for over three hundred years… it'll wait a bit longer if need be."

"I was waiting to hear that, Fizz. I'll let you know what's going on as soon as I know. Talk to you later." Before Ben could hang up from talking to Fizz, Lindsey walked up with a cup of coffee and began asking questions.

"Who are you talking with and why are we not going out yet?"

"Fizz, hang on," Ben interrupted. "Lindsey's up and I'm sure she wants to talk with you."

"Yeah, well…put her on. I wanna' talk with her, too" Fizz replied.

"Hi there, *my* pirate," Lindsey said in her usual bubbly voice. "What's the privilege to be talking with you today, Captain?"

"Well, I called to follow-up from yesterday's excitement and to see if you folks were now successful treasure hunters instead of wanna' be's," he explained. "It appears that congrats are in order, honey…and I'm envious as hell. I'd love to be sittin' on top of a pile of silver and gold from a virgin wreck."

"Well, come on down, Captain…we just happen to *have* one of those." Lindsey replied.

"I can't get away from what I've got going on here, honey…or I'd sure love to come to Jamaica. I think Ben's got something else he wants to talk over with you this morning, so…I'll let you go for now. Now, honey…please listen to him because I think maybe he might be a little smarter than I've been givin' him credit for. He'll be in the Treasure Hunter's Hall of Fame, now…so I can't call him *moron* anymore…damn! I know what he needs to chat with you about and I agree with him, if that helps. Good-bye for now, my dear. We'll talk soon."

"Bye, Captain Fizz." Lindsey ended the call while looking up at Ben with question marks in her eyes. She laid the phone down and immediately asked Ben what he needed to talk to her about.

"Dear…yesterday, you scared the Hades out of me, and *that's* puttin' it mildly. I just now explained to Fizz what happened and he agrees with what I think we should do."

"Agrees to what?"

"We need to get back to the States in order for you to see your doctor," Ben explained.

"And leave behind four years of blood, sweat and tears, not to mention the amount of money we've spent? Not a chance in hell, Ben. Now get ready and let's get back out to that wreck," Lindsey said emphatically.

"*NO!*" Ben replied with authority. "Here's what's gonna' happen, Lindsey. You, Mick and Darlene are gonna' fly back to the States. Troy and I will be right behind you all, bringing *Next Adventure* home. That's what's gonna' happen, dear. Everybody, including Fizz agrees that *you* need to get medical attention. The water was extremely warm yesterday, and you were almost hypothermic when you came back aboard Marley's boat. Lindsey was looking down the whole time Ben was talking. When she looked up at him she was brushing back tears.

"Okay…if that's the decision that's been made, I'll agree to go home, but only under one condition. That being, that you and Troy stay and salvage that treasure."

Ben paced back and forth across the salon room floor for a long while before he finally stopped and turned around to look at her. "Lindsey, you know we've found a shipwreck loaded with treasure and we know its exact location. Who knows *how many* vessels have passed right over it without the knowledge that it was down there beneath them. Most likely, boats have even been anchored above it fishing. But, *we* found it. To me…*that*, was the quest…not so much to get rich."

"There are others involved in this, Ben…others with expectations and dreams to fulfill for themselves," she explained. "How about this…I'll go home and schedule an appointment with my doctor. Meanwhile, *you,* are seeing this adventure through. Only under those terms will I fly home, and *only* under those terms will we have an accord …as pirates say. Do we have an accord, Ben?"

Again, Ben paced as he listened to Lindsey. Finally, he stopped and looked at her. "We have an accord, *if* …you promise to go see your doctor the second you get back to Fort Myers."

"Then, we have an accord, Ben," Lindsey said smiling.

"Thank God. Okay, here's the deal. Marley has a buddy who flies a ten-seater between Jamaica and the States almost daily. When I last talked with Marley yesterday evening, he was going to check on flight schedules for me. Marley's gonna' call me after he talks with his buddy this morning."

By now, the rest of the group was coming top-side to join in the discussion of the preconceived decision and the plan to see it through.

"Okay, guys," Ben began. "Here's the deal. The plan is just as we discussed last night. The girls will hopefully get on a flight with Marley's buddy, Dontavious, in order to fly to Miami. The only caveat to the plan is…Troy and I will stay here and salvage the treasure."

"Are you sure, Ben?" Troy asked.

"As sure as I've ever been, my friend," Ben replied.

"And Troy, you *know* that I don't feel certainty that often…but, it's been decided…we're staying to salvage the treasure, dude. Lindsey wouldn't have it any other way."

Ben's phone rang…it was Marley. "Hey mon, how's my favorite dark white person doing this morning?"

"I'm good, Marley…thanks for asking," replied Ben.

"No, mon," Marley laughed. "You *know* who I'm asking about…my first-mate. How's Lindsey feeling today?"

"She's feeling much better this morning, but the decision has been made to send the girls back to the States so Lindsey can have her health checked out. Troy and I will stay here to continue with the salvage efforts."

"I agree…that's the best thing for Lindsey's sake," Marley added. But, we're goin' to get bored as hell out there without them, mon."

"Wha-da-you mean, bored, Marley?" Ben asked.

"We're goin' from tanned girls in bikinis, to the two of you pasty jokers in your knee-knocker swim trunks… boring, and kind of disgusting!"

"Oh yeah, *that*. I see what 'cha mean, Marley. How about Troy and I wear Speedos from here on out? Will that help keep your interest peaked?" Ben suggested.

"It's all good, mon…but, no Speedos, please!" Marley pleaded.

Ben inquired…"Have you heard from your buddy, Dontavious, about a flight?"

"Yes…that's actually the reason for my call, but you got me sidetracked talking about tanned skin."

"Marley…I didn't say one thing about tanned skin… that was all in your own vivid imagination, so get your mind out of the gutter. Okay…so you heard from your buddy…does he have a flight leaving today?" Ben asked.

"Yes…he has four seats left. The flight leaves for Miami at four o'clock. The girls will need to get a cab to Kingston… that's, where Donte flies out of."

"Okay…call Donte and tell him we want three of those seats, please."

"No worries, mon…I'll take care of it."

With the conversation between Ben and Marley concluded and the discussions and planning behind them, the group decided to kill some time by going on to Kingston where one can always find some type of celebration or festivities taking place. The girls had minimal packing to do, so the group was underway quickly. Ben had called for a cab while the girls were packing and left instructions to pick the group up at the docks in Freetown. While the group was walking to the end of the long dock, Ben stopped.

"Let's all have a little discussion, guys." The group stopped and Ben continued. "Look, guys…I've been thinking some more."

Lindsey quickly interrupted Ben. "There's no more thinking about this, Ben. We're going back to the States and you guys are finishing up what you started here."

"I understand that, dear…just let me finish, okay? I'll be calling everyday to check on you, as I'm certain Troy will be calling to talk with you, Darlene. And Mick, I'm sure you'll be having conversations with somebody about where you've been and what you've been up to. Nothing ever needs to be said in any of those conversations about treasure, okay? I may bring up something about some junk that we've found, but nothing…or never, anything about treasure. Deal?" Ben concluded.

The group agreed that nothing would be said and then continued the walk to the end of the dock. "Oh yeah…one more thing," Ben said. "Can one or both of you girls stay with Lindsey until Troy and I return, please?" The girls kind of all laughed a bit but said nothing. "What?" Ben asked. "What's so funny, girls?"

"*That* decision's already been made amongst us gals, Ben. It's going to be one big pool party the next couple of weeks for just the girls…*woo-hoo!*" Mick whooped.

All the girls laughed and chanted…"Party…party…party!"

"Very funny, gals," remarked Troy "Don't mention that to Marley though. He'll be volunteering to be Armando the pool boy and we won't have a Captain!"

Ben laughed at the remarks. "Have fun, girls…but Lindsey goes to the Doc first thing, don't forget!"

"I know that, Ben…we *do* have an accord don't forget. And, according to pirate law, if I'm not mistaken…an accord can't be broken," Lindsey said sternly. "My doctor will hook me up with the best of care as soon as I get back to Fort Myers…not that there's anything wrong…but they'll hook me up anyway. With it being *Snowbird Season* back home, I would be weeks getting in to see somebody, but I have connections with the best doctors in Naples. Don't 'chu fret your pretty little head about it, dude."

"Hadn't thought about that," Ben agreed. "But, you're right… good to have connections. Mick… you need to go to the appointment with Lindsey so the Doctor will get the real story, okay. Lindsey will try to brush-it-off as the change of life."

"No worries, Ben" Mick assured. "I'll go with her and make sure the doctor gets the full story."

As the group was nearing the end of the long dock, Troy glanced up ahead. "Uh ohhh…looks like we have company, Ben."

Ben sighed, "Yeah, I figured we'd be running in to him soon. I've got his payment. Actually, I'm kind of curious to see how this is gonna' go anyway…so…no time like the present."

As the group stepped from the wooden dock onto the lime rock parking area, the "little big man" sneered a bit and asked, "No treasure hunting today, folks?"

"Kinda' rough out there today, boss. And, I need to get these girls to the Kingston airport. My wife, Lindsey, here isn't feeling well and I want to get her back to the States to see her doctor. Troy and I will be returning to continue our search."

"Oh, I'm sorry to hear that," the man replied. "Have you got a ride to Kingston?" he asked.

"Yes…there should be a cab coming any time now."

The little man stuck his hand out. "My treat, folks. When the cab gets here, I'll instruct him to take you to Kingston, on me."

When the little man stuck his hand out, Ben placed four-hundred dollars in it…payment for yesterday and today. He'd passed it to the little man via a hand shake. After looking at the cash and placing it in his trouser pocket, the little man looked at Ben and said, "Pleasure doing business with you."

Minutes later the cab pulled up next to the dock where the cast of characters were standing. The "little big man" spoke to the cabby.

"Good-day, Henry…you take my friends to Kingston, on me. These ladies need to catch their flight back to the States. Be certain that the two gentlemen get a ride back to Freetown, if you will be so kind."

"Will do, Captain Stan," the cabby replied. The group loaded up in the old van and the driver set course for Kingston.

Ben looked at Troy with confusion on his face. Troy said, "Like we were just saying…it's good to have connections."

"I suppose. Hey Henry, anything going on in Kingston today?" Ben asked.

"Always celebrations going on in Kingston, mon," Henry replied. "We Jamaicans just love to celebrate…for any reason. What time is the flight back to the States?"

"Four o'clock," Ben answered. "Their flying with Dontaviuos…Simon Role's buddy."

"Ahh yah, mon…I know Donte…damn good pilot. He's only lost two airplanes in his four years of flying… one every other year...good odds for Jamaican pilots wouldn't you say?"

You could have heard a pin drop as the group looked at one another with concern on their faces. Henry looked in to his rear view mirror at his now very concerned passengers and added…"No worries, mon…Donte lost his second airplane last year, so he's good for this year if his record holds."

"Uhh…Henry…we may want to re-think this plan," Ben said with grave concern in his voice.

Henry let out a laugh that could have woken the dead. "You Americans are way too up-tight, mon, I've had the most fun with that story over the years. Donte been flying for years, mon…never lost a client…you're in good hands."

The rest of the ride to Kingston can only be explained as a white-knuckle ride as Henry swerved, darted in-and-out of traffic, passing in blind corners with the pedal-to-the-metal, while talking faster than the cab was moving. As he talked and drove, his eyes were focused into the rear view mirror more than they were on the road. The group breathed a sigh of relief when Henry announced that they had arrived in Kingston.

"Okay, guys…I'm yours for the day" Henry announced. "We have a few hours to kill before I need to get your gals to Donte…what would you like to do?"

"Take us to a watering-hole," Troy pleaded. "I'm not sure about the rest of the gang, but I need a drink after that roller-coaster ride."

"Agreed," was the rest of the groups reply. Henry pulled up and parked next to what looked like a shack, but evidently, the establishment was a favorite spot for Americans while in Kingston. The building was painted in a multitude of vibrant colors that looked as if the owners had bought any and all discontinued colors of paint in order to create an island ambiance. Once they exited the cab, both Troy and Ben kissed the ground, much as they had done after *Next Adventure* had completed the forty hour trek from Fort Myers to Freetown.

"I'll be waiting for you guys right here," Henry announced. "Don't forget, we need to get to the airport in a couple of hours so drink up and have fun."

The group walked into the shack where dollars bills, mostly signed by American tourists, had been stapled to the walls. Alongside them were signs with funny sayings written on them, as well as business cards. The dollar bills, signs and business cards covered every square inch of the interior walls. The atmosphere there was much like Ben and Lindsey had experienced in the Bahamas on Stocking Island in the Exumas. The cast of characters were friendly islanders, eager to entertain the Americans who were spending their dollars, contributing to the island's economy.

Two hours had passed like ten minutes when Henry walked into the bar and up to where they were seated. "We need to go, mon." The group paid the tab, along with a generous tip for their beautiful bartender, and then filed outside piling back into Henry's cab.

It was a short ride to the Kingston airport where the girls parted ways with Ben and Troy. Just before the girls disappeared into the security line, Ben and Troy said in unison, "Call us when you're on the ground, girls," The guys stood and watched until the girls had made their way through security.

"Well, we're on our own, dude" Ben said.

"Yeah," Troy replied. "Ya' know, I think the girls have a better chance landing safely in Miami than we have getting back to Freetown."

Ben grinned…"We'll be fine, dude… let's go."

The ride back to Freetown was just as harrowing as the first ride with Henry, but he delivered the pair back to the docks in Freetown safe and sound.

"Hmmm," Ben said as they pulled up to the dock. "I was almost expecting a welcome back from *Stan the little big man*."

Troy laughed. "I wondered whether or not I was the only one in the group who caught that…*Captain Stan the little man*," Troy said, laughing.

"Let's go grab a cold one and wait for the girls to call us when they're wheels down," Ben said. The pair walked down the creaking dock by themselves, this time without the fun loving antic of the girls. "Damn, Troy…Marley was right."

"Wha-da-ya' mean, Ben?" Troy asked.

"It's gonna' be boring without them gals…I miss them already."

"Me too, dude…me too," Troy concurred.

The guys made it to the boat, grabbed a couple beers each and climbed the stairs to the fly bridge and had a seat.

"Ya' know, Troy," Ben thought aloud. "I've been waiting for this day for a number of years…and somehow, I thought it would be more of a testosterone-charged occasion than it turned out to be. I guess the hunt was what kept me going all these years."

"Yeah, well…we're not just gonna' leave and go back home and tell everybody that we found a wreck full of treasure and then decided to leave it for the next guys dream to be fulfilled," Troy announced.

"Of course we're not…of course we're not, Troy." Ben stared out onto the beautiful Caribbean. "I guess I'm just a bit bummed out knowing that the hunt is over and worrying about Lindsey…that's all."

"She'll be fine, Ben…you made the right decision to get her back so she can be checked out," Troy said trying to reinforce Ben's decision.

"Hey Troy, have I ever told you how Lindsey and I met?"

"No… you've never offered that information, and I don't pry into people's pasts unless they're willing to contribute it."

"We were thirteen years old. I was just a dumb clod-hopper from the Midwest who trapped in the winter and put up hey in the summer for all the nearby farmers."

"Trapped?" Troy asked.

"Yeah…trapped poor little animals for their fur. It was good money back in the seventies. I wouldn't have the heart to do it nowadays, though…and even…still to this day, I feel saddened that I did it then. But anyway…I grew up in a very rural area of Indiana that had about eight miles of really bad road between our home and the nearest stoplight or resemblance of a town. Hell, I wasn't even interested in girls at the time, and believe me…now that I know what I know…I could have had few of the proverbial *farmer's daughters.* But, at the time…I was too dumb to even know that I was being come-on-to, or to even know what to do with one, for that matter. Then, somewhere around nineteen seventy-three…along comes a family from the city with four daughters and one son. The father had inherited a farm from his uncle that was located about two miles south on the same road we lived on. The daughters were all blond-haired blue-eyed beauties, but the youngest one named, Lindsey, was drop-dead gorgeous. Of course, all the neighborhood boys, who were much more experienced than me, were all lining-up to woo the girls. When the day came that I finally got to meet the family, I'll never forget it. I was so dumb-stricken when I was introduced to Lindsey, that I couldn't even talk. What a dumb hick she must have thought I was! Anyway, as the years went on, I never lost my interest in her, even when she started seeing one of the other neighborhood boys. Of course, I was jealous…but I never let it be known." Ben laughed as he continued. "She even dated my older brother for a bit…but I still never let my feelings be known. We all grew up and went our separate ways, as always happens. Lindsey married, but not very happily. Everyone questioned the relationship, but life went on. Back in those days, it seemed like the main goal for kids was to simply get out on their own and jump at the first opportunity they thought might work for them. Now-a-days, parents can't get the kids out of the basement. I married, apparently not very successfully, as I would later find out.

Lindsey and her husband had a son, as did my wife and I. I think Lindsey's marriage lasted seven years while mine only lasted four. I guess Lindsey and I were a couple of lost souls at that point simply trying to make ends meet for the sake of our children."

"Stop right there, dude," Troy interrupted. "I'm going to grab us both another couple brews…be right back." Troy went below and then climbed back up the stairs with some cold drinks. "Okay…you were at the point where you and Lindsey were just trying to provide for your children."

"Oh yeah," Ben said, continuing his story. "Lindsey worked in a factory in a larger town nearby and I was working in a local *Mom and Pop* rock mine operating equipment. One evening after work I was sitting around thinking about Lindsey, drinking beer and feeling sorry for myself. For that matter, I never stopped thinking about her. And, as beautiful as she is…I thought surely she'd already hooked-up with someone else and was living happily ever after. To this day, I don't know how I was able to get her phone number after all those years. I guess maybe some angel left it under my pillow one night. I just don't know, but I got it somehow. It was probably another month before I got up the courage to make the call. I'd been hanging around in bars trying to find companionship, but that wasn't working for me. So, one evening, I dialed the phone. That was back before the days of cell phones. When an angelic voice answered…I was once again dumb-founded, but somehow I mustered-up the courage to say, 'Lindsey?' She answered, 'Yes, this is Lindsey.' 'Lindsey…ummm… this is Ben Carson, from the old hood,' I replied. Then, she said, 'Ben, how are you doing?' I answered, in a cracked voice… 'W…well, I'm doing fine…how 'bout you, Lindsey?' She answered me with something like, 'I'm good…long time no see, Ben.' Then, I said, 'I know… yeah, it's been a long time hasn't it?' Well, during the course of the conversation, I found out that she'd quit her job at the factory and was working at one her father's business back in the city. She was concentrating on raising her son and from what I could gather and to my surprise…she was still single. I'd become somewhat more emboldened over the years and decided to ask the question… 'Hey Lindsey, how about we go grab a bite to eat one evening and talk about old times.' She laughed and reminded me, 'I'm not sure what *old times* you and I had together, Ben…but yes…I'd love to do that!' Well, Troy…about six months later into the romance, I popped *the question* during a telephone conversation. Much to my surprise, she accepted my proposal. I eventually adopted her son because the boy's father had no interest in him. I raised him as my own. We lost our son, Josh, too early, which she's never gotten over, and understandably never will. My son works in Pennsylvania in pipeline survey so we haven't seen him for years. He works all over the States for months at a time. As parents, if we did our jobs right, our kids go their own way and make their own lives, right? And now, here we are thirty-four years later in the middle of yet another adventure. That's, the story, Troy… this beer's starting to kick-in now and I need to quit before I start cryin'."

Ben's phone rang. It was Lindsey…

"Hi, dear. Did you have a good flight?"

"Yup, pretty uneventful. Donte was a freakin' hoot, though."

"Did you connect with Sonny, as planned?"

"Yes, dear. Sonny has all three of us right now heading toward Fort Myers," she replied.

"Okay, dear…Troy and I are just swapping tall tales and missing our gals."

"You'll be fine, guys. Let us know if you find the other piece of that iron thing-a-ma-jig like we found yesterday, okay?" Lindsey asked.

"You know I will, my dear. We're fixin' to turn-in now that we know you're in good hands. Night, dear…I love you," Ben said as he hung up the phone. Then he turned to Troy. "Dude…I'm turning-in after I call Marley to confirm tomorrow's adventure."

"Not far behind you," Troy replied. "And by the way… not too many couples have the kind of history and bond that you and Lindsey have together."

"I know, dude…I'm very fortunate."

CHAPTER 8

Black Hand At Last

The following morning Ben and Troy woke earlier than normal, eager to get back to the wreck-site and begin the daunting task of the salvage of what they knew would be millions of dollars of Spanish silver, gold and emeralds, and possibly the rumored golden altar. Marley's boat pulled up alongside the dock at 6 a.m. sharp. The necessary equipment was loaded onto Marley's boat and the now smaller group was underway to the site of the final resting place of, *Our Lady With The Fiery Eyes.*

"Did the beautiful ones make it back to the States okay?" Marley asked.

"Yeah, they're back. Your buddy, Donte, delivered them back without a hitch." Troy replied. "They said they had a lot of fun with him."

"Yeah…Donte's quite the ladies man and jokester. Did everybody keep their clothes on during the flight?" Marley asked, raising his eyebrows.

"You're a sick cowpoke, Marley" Ben said.

"Just joking, mon…but…them people all like to get naa…"

"Okay…okay," Ben stopped Marley in mid-stream. "Now, let's not digress too much simply because the girls aren't on the boat. We've got work to do…okay?"

The group was on site and anchored up early as work got underway. Ben spoke while suiting up. "I think I'll take Fizz's advice and video as much of this salvage as possible just in case we wanna' write a book or make a documentary someday."

"Not a bad idea," Troy remarked. "If we don't take pictures now…someday, we'll wish we hadda'."

"I think, Troy"…Ben thought for a moment before resuming…"I think I'm gonna' find us a nice little hiding spot close by for the silver stuff. Shouldn't take long because all these coral formations have nice overhangs. We may have to chase out a nurse shark or two, but they'll find somewhere else to hide."

"Roger that," Troy replied "I'll relocate the milk crate and clump of silver and get back after it."

"Oh…one more thought," Ben added. "I don't think we should use the underwater communication system anymore. I worry that somehow, somebody might pick up on our transmissions. Maybe not, but…it does concern me."

"Good with me, dude…let's get after it now," Troy replied. Ben strapped the video camera to the top of his head and fell backwards into the water with the scooter. Troy splashed in right behind with the metal-detector. When Ben touched down on the bottom he immediately pulled the trigger on the scooter The machine propelled him through the water in search of a place to store their cache. He searched all around the wreck-site as far as the surface supplied air line would allow him but found nothing in the restricted area. He made his way back to where Troy was busy removing ballast rock from the same area in which they'd found the chest full of pieces of eight. He signaled for Troy to surface. When the pair reached the surface, Ben explained that he couldn't find a spot that he felt comfortable with that was far enough away from the main site within the confines of the airline.

"I should've thought about this beforehand, but I must've had my head up my backside, I suppose."

"*We,* should have thought about it, Ben…with the emphasis on, *we,*" Troy said. "Don't worry about it, we'll bring tanks tomorrow…it's not like we don't have a dozen or so on your boat. For now…let's *find*, today…and *hide*, tomorrow." With that said, Troy dropped back down and went to work. Ben was right behind him.

The arrangement actually worked very well. The guys would salvage one day and spend the next day moving their finds to a safe place well away from the main pile. It proved to be a daunting task, as some of the silver bars they were recovering weighed in excess of eighty pounds, and according to the ship's manifest…there were lots of them…three hundred to be exact. At this point on the wreck, the guys were able to uncover two more boxes of eight reales coins and four of the heavy silver bars, but no gold yet. Heretofore, they had excavated a fairly large hole in to the ballast pile and were still getting hits from the detector every time they waved it over the spot. As they worked deeper into the ballast pile, the job proved to be more ballast-stone removing than treasure salvaging.

When the guys finally surfaced to take a break, it was just past noon.

"Holy crap!" Troy remarked. "We were down their for a bit, aye?"

"Yeah, mon," Marley said. "And, don't keep me in suspense here."

"Four silver bars and two more chests of silver coins, Marley," was Troy's reply. "And the bars probably will go eighty pounds apiece."

"You know…that's just crazy as hell," Marley replied. "I've lived here all my life…" he continued…"and believe me…I have struggled to make ends meet. I've watched Tanya and the boys do without, more than with, and this treasure was right here all along."

"That's all changed now, dude," Troy responded. "We're all richer than three-foot-up-a-bull's-behind, as my father always said back in Georgia. I never knew the exact meaning of that saying, but he always said it when he was talking about our well-to-do neighbors down the road. I grew up dirt poor too, Marley…so I know how you're feelin'."

"So, how much is one of those bars worth?" Marley asked.

Ben spoke up. "Well…if we use spot-price for silver right now…they're worth about twenty-five thousand a piece. Let's get after it Troy…time's a wastin' and we got beautiful conditions."

"Fuel that compressor up please, Marley," Ben suggested. "We're goin' back down."

The guys dropped back down beneath the surface and continued their job. They uncovered more silver bars and began to move the rocks away from them in order to expose a pile of silver bars that were a jumbled mess. *"At one point when the galleon left Portobelo…the bars were probably neatly stacked like firewood in the hold,"* Ben thought to himself as he worked at moving ballast stones. He tried to count the bars that were now exposed the best he could, and then looked at Troy while tapping the palm of his left hand with the index finger of his right which was the signal for…"I'm done!" Exhausted from their labor of love, the pair surfaced for the last time of the day.

Once they were back on the boat, Marley said, "This radio silence is killing me, mon. Have you found anything else?"

"Marley…we uncovered about another thirty of those big silver bars. No gold, yet…all silver."

"Well…don't sound so upset about finding a pile of silver bars, mon."

"I'm not upset, by any means. But, when that gold starts revealing itself…*that's* when the cash register really starts ringing, dude…that's all. We've got a day of stashing ahead of us tomorrow with what we've recovered so far today. When we finally get all those silver bars moved…I think that gold's gonna' start giving itself up."

The anchor was weighed for the day and the group was underway back to Freetown. While the boat was splashing through the waves and throwing a salty spray up onto the passengers, Ben happened to look at Troy's hands and then looked at his own. Their hands were stained black from handling and working around the silver all day.

"I'll be…" Ben said. "I once read in a book that back in the early days of the 1733 salvage in the Keys…you could tell who was working the wrecks by their hands…they were stained black from the oxide that coated the silver. The bartenders and waiters down there in the Keys during that period really catered to the guys with black hands 'cause they knew they were treasure finders and would probably leave a really good tip. That crap won't wash off…it's a badge of success for a while. It has to wear off. I've been waiting for years to see if that was true…I guess here's the proof."

As soon as the group was back on the dock, Ben called Lindsey. When she finally answered, Ben asked how she was feeling.

"I feel great," she answered. "I got in to see my doctor today and she's ordered a barrage of tests, but I really doubt that anything will come from them."

"Is Mick there? If she is, I'd like to talk with her, dear?" Lindsey handed the phone to Mick.

"Hey Ben… it's Mick. What's on your mind?"

"How'd it go today at the doctor's office? Lindsey won't give me the straight story…I'm sure of that."

Mick slowly wandered away toward the porch a bit as she spoke with Ben so Lindsey wouldn't overhear the conversation. She said in a very low voice…"If you tell her what I'm fixing to tell you, I'll never speak to you again, Ben."

"Mick…I wanna' know what was discussed," Ben replied with a stern tone of voice.

"They've ordered all kinds of tests which will take a bit of time to get the results back," she explained. "Every kind of blood test known to man, including tests that I haven't even heard of. But, Lindsey did spill the beans, Ben. She was honest with the doctor and told her that she's had more than one of these spells of feeling faint and fatigued. It turns out that it's been going on for quite a while. We've got another appointment with a cardiologist tomorrow."

"Cardiologist?" Ben asked. "Why a cardiologist?"

"I'm sure it's just to eliminate the possibility of anything going on with her heart," Mick replied. There was a long pause after Mick's assumption. Then, Ben expressed his thoughts.

"Lindsey's family has a history of heart problems. Her grandmother passed from heart failure, as did her father. I think I need to come home right now."

"I had a long talk with Lindsey last night, Ben, and trust me… you need to keep your behind right there. She feels fine right now. We've been working in the yard and hanging around the pool. She's fine. Just stay there and finish up with your dream…*that's*, what she wants."

"Well…I guess I'll stay here for now," Ben replied after some thought. "But, I want you to promise me, Mick…if you feel that I need to come home…you need to tell me… promise?"

"Promise," Mick replied.

Ben walked down the dock to help with the off loading of equipment when Troy asked, "Everything okay, dude?"

"Everything's good for now. She's doing fine."

Day three on the wreck was a grueling day of moving the heavy silver bars from the wreck-site to a nice little coral cave that the guys found earlier that morning. The bars had to be moved underwater by hand. The decision had been made not to bring anything to the surface to load onto the boat until absolutely necessary for fear of being sighted and searched. Everything that had been recovered on day two was now removed from the site and hidden for safekeeping. The time was just after 2:00 p.m when the task was completed. The pair worked later than usual on day three and began to blow the sediments away from the excavation site with the scooter. More silver bars were exposed. The guys moved another layer of silver bars from their excavated hole and then more ballast from around the edges of the hole that had been created making the excavated site much larger. Once again, Ben took the scooter and blasted the debris from the hole. Troy was watching intently as the wash from the scooter removed shells and sand from the hole, when suddenly…he made a motion for Ben to stop the scooter. Troy began hand-fanning the sand slowly when a flash of yellow suddenly appeared. What next appeared before their eyes was, gold! It glimmered just as it had as the day the galleon had gone down. Troy reached into the hole and began removing gold bars and coins from a seemingly never-ending source. It almost appeared as if a light was beaming out of the hole as the gold gleamed brightly in the crystal clear Caribbean water. The guys continued digging and digging, finding no bottom to the precious yellow metal.

Troy was no longer able to curb his enthusiasm. Ignoring the decision not to bring anything to the surface, he grabbed a handful of coins and shot to the surface, throwing the coins onto the deck of Marley's boat where he was listening to some old country tunes. Instantly, Marley sprang to his feet, picked up one of the coins and shouted.

"No way, mon! There are more of these down there?"

Troy answered, "Thousands, dude…thousands!" Then, he sank back down to join in on the fun again. By now, Ben was meticulously pulling escudos and gold bars from the hole. It seemed as if it was a well of gold that kept on giving. The guys reached into the deepest part of the hole and continued pulling up gold by the hands full, placing it in one pile just off the ballast pile. More silver bars were removed revealing yet more gold. By the end of the day… more gold bars and coins had been removed than would ever fit inside the air-compressor tank.

The two men continued their efforts for the next several days…salvaging, stashing, and returning to the dock in the evening with nothing to show for their efforts but their blackened hands. Ben would meet up with Sergeant Stan here and there to grease his greedy little palm so that he'd continue to leave them alone as he'd promised. Up to this point, the agreement was working flawlessly. Stan and his men hadn't paid the guys a visit since the deal had been struck. The time was now quickly approaching when they'd have to make the decision on what to bring back to *Next Adventure* for concealment inside the air-compressor tank.

As they were lounging around *Next Adventure* one evening, Troy grabbed a couple of cold beers and made the statement that if they stayed much longer, they were going to have to score some Red Stripe beer because they'd just about drank all the domestic beer they'd brought over from the States.

"Dude…don't think I wanna' go there," Ben replied. "We only have a few more days before we have to head back, so…we need to discuss our exit strategy. I'd like to say, let's stay and finish, but our paperwork says we'll be shoving off soon. If we ask to stay past that date…I'm afraid we'd be showing them our cards."

"Damn…didn't think about that," Troy realized. "And, I was just ready to retire from the flooring business."

"I was thinking the same thing the day we started pulling all that gold out of the belly of our lady. Probably not the prudent thing to do just yet. If this all goes well…we'll come back and make another withdrawal next year, or maybe sooner."

"Have you talked with your buddy, Fizz, since we hit the mother-load?" Troy asked.

"No…I've been trying to maintain radio silence, so to speak. He's busy with his projects, but I'm sure he's chomping-at-the-bit to hear from us."

"You think he can help us figure out how to do this all legal like?"

"Possibly," Ben replied. I plan on having *that* conversation with him when we get back. I think we should bring back some of our booty tomorrow and begin stowing it away. We can talk about it tomorrow on our way out. When we get that compressor tank full of gold, we can all live like royalty for the remainder of our days. I'm gonna' give a call home, dude…and then…I'm gonna' check in, take a shower and collapse."

"Sounds like a plan…I'm gonna' do the same."

Ben called Lindsey's phone and Mick answered.

"Hey Mick. How's Lindsey doin'?"

"Ummm…sleeping quite a bit, Ben. You want me to wake her up for you?" she asked.

"No, let her rest, Just let her know I called. Have either of you heard anything about results from the tests that have been done so far?"

"Nothing yet. She goes in for a stress-test tomorrow." Ben was silent for what seemed to Mick to be several minutes. Finally, she broke the silence. "You still there, Ben?"

"Yeah…yeah I'm still here. It seems like most of the tests they're doing are to check her heart, doesn't it, Mick."

"It appears like that's what they're looking at right now. But, they *have* to check everything," Mick explained.

"I know. I just worry, Mick…I'm very worried".

"I understand you're worried, Ben. I am too…but, they're going through the process of elimination, I guess."

"I suppose so," he replied. "In the morning when she wakes up, tell her I called and that I love her, okay Mick?"

"I will, and don't worry…everything will be fine," Mick reassured.

"Okay…I'll try not to. We'll be leaving here in a couple of days to start the trip back home…see you all then."

"See you guys in a few…be safe," Mick replied ending the call.

Ben walked up and sat for awhile on the fly-bridge staring out at the millions of stars. The light from the Boogeyman's Island caught his eye and he wondered about the stories Marley told a few years back, and…if there was any truth in them. He was in deep thought when all of a sudden his meditation was disrupted.

"Hey…if you're gonna' sit up there awhile…I'll join ya' and bring a couple cold ones with me," Troy shouted.

"Sounds good, dude," Ben replied. In less than a minute, Troy carried two cold beers up to the fly-bridge and handed Ben one.

"Everything okay back home?"

"Yeah, everything's good. They're running more tests to be certain, though. Maybe *it is* the mid-life thing after all. Right now, I'd be happy to hear *that's all* that's goin' on." Troy was listening to Ben's every word intently. He'd gotten his own update from Darlene, and according to her, it appeared to be something more than menopause. Troy thought to himself for a bit and realized that it wasn't his place to say anything at this point. He merely tried to reassure Ben.

"Could be, Ben…none of the gangs gettin' any younger…that's for certain." As Ben was listening to Troy, he was in deep thought and still staring at the light from the Boogeyman's island.

"You think the stories are true, Troy?"

"What stories?"

"You know…the Boogeyman stories, dude."

"I don't care what Marley says…" Troy explains…"he musta' smoked a quite a bit of ganja in his days to come up with a whopper like that. Probably ain't nothin' going on out there but some old recluse who just wants to be left alone and away from people. I feel the same way sometimes when dealing with clients."

"Probably right, Troy. Okay…I'm gonna' go get that shower now. See you in the morning bright and early. We'll discuss bringing treasure back tomorrow."

Ben took a long hot shower in order to try to get relaxed. He knew it was going to be a long night of tossing, turning and worrying. Worrying about Lindsey, first and foremost, and then…there was the reality of having to bring the treasure back to *Next Adventure* and concealing it inside the air-compressor tank. The last thing Ben remembered was looking at the alarm clock. The time was 2 a.m.

When his alarm went off the next morning, he wasn't ready for it. The sound made him jump up from beneath the warm covers at 6:00 a.m. sharp. He stumbled topside to brew some coffee and get the day started. After the coffee was brewing, he opened the sliding glass door from the salon room to smell the fresh ocean air. He was enjoying the solitude of the morning when he thought he heard lyrics from Glenn Campbell's, *Rhinestone Cowboy*. He thought he must be hearing things when suddenly, he realized it was Marley approaching.

Troy came up from below deck. "Thanks for getting the coffee brewed, dude."

"No worries, *Troy boy*," Ben replied.

Troy walked around Ben with a cooler in tow, looked back at him and remarked, "You just gonna' stand there, or are you going to work today?"

"Just enjoying the moment for a change, Troy. It seems like all my life has been a race to make millions for some faceless human being, and I've done a damn good job of it. I always told Lindsey that if I didn't have to work for a living…I'd be a rich man already. Turns out, that's been a true statement all along … although I was just having fun with her at the time. If I hadn't wasted my time climbing the corporate ladder and being enticed by a healthy salary all these years, and followed my dreams instead…I'd have found this wreck years ago and done moved on to another one. I'm just not in hurry this morning, Troy…the wreck's been found…the rat race is over."

"Understand," Troy said. "But, we've still got work to do Ben…let's go."

"I'll be right there, Troy," Ben replied.

Troy turned and began loading equipment onto Marley's boat. Ben got himself and his thoughts together and helped with the task. Marley's boat pulled away from the dock and got underway a little later than usual.

"Troy," Ben said while underway. "We have enough gold recovered already to fill that compressor tank probably three times over. I've been thinking about it and if you agree…I think we oughta' spend the day moving ballast-stones back into the hole where the treasure was recovered and bring back what we've already recovered back to *Next Adventure*."

"I'm good with that, Ben."

Once they were on the wreck-site, the guys worked most of the day moving ballast-stones back on top of the mother-load, hopefully for safekeeping. Then, the guys turned their attention to the task of loading the gold into the milk crate for transportation back to *Next Adventure*. They made the decision to only carry back gold bars on the first trip, as the bars were denser, containing more of the precious metal that could be transported back home, as opposed to a bunch of loose coinage. In all…seventy gold bars of around eight pounds each were hauled up and stacked on to the deck of Marley's boat. Once the task was complete, the guys sat staring at the shiny metal. They were staring at what was supposed to be delivered to the King of Spain in 1670 to help with the war efforts.

Troy finally asked, "What's this first haul worth, Ben?" Ben had to pull his phone out to use the calculator app as the numbers were more than he could comprehend in his head.

"Well…" Ben began…"seventy bars at about eight pounds each is five hundred and sixty pounds of solid gold, or eight thousand and twenty-five Troy ounces at say, twelve hundred dollars per ounce. That little pile of shiny yellow metal is worth almost eleven million dollars… possibly more, considering the artifact value. I don't know…that'll be a Captain Fizz question. Anyway we market it, guys…we're rich…and that's only about half the gold bars that we recovered. I'm doubtful we can even get these in to the compressor tank.

Marley could hardly believe what he was hearing as Ben was going through the calculations of the value of the bars. "You know, mon…I have spent who knows how many hours fishing and diving for lobster out here to make ends meet for my family. I may have looked at that same pile of rocks at one time or another and didn't know what I was looking at. I hear the ocean only gives up its treasure to those who persevere. I thought all along the treasure they were referring to *was* the oceans creatures. How wrong have I been all these years?"

Ben finally snapped back into reality. "Marley, let's weigh anchor and get this stuff back to the dock and loaded onto *Next Adventure.* Hopefully, we won't have any company. If we do, I guess we'll have to throw our fortune overboard and pick it back up later. If all goes well, though…Troy and I've got work to do this evening.

Marley weighed anchor and turned the boat toward the docks. Once in sight of the dock, Troy scanned the area with a set of binoculars to make certain they had no visitors. "Looks to me like the coast is clear, guys."

"Let's do this…" Ben said as he began putting some of the bars into dive bags and anywhere else he could in order to conceal them from prying eyes that might be around the dock. Once they were at the dock and Marley's boat was tied up, the group was happy to see that they were the only folks at the dock. The other couple of fishing boats that use the old dilapidated dock were still out for the day.

Moving five-hundred and sixty pounds of gold bars covertly from one boat to another proved to be no small chore. When the dive bags in which Ben had concealed some of the gold bars hit the deck of *Next Adventure,* they made a distinct clanking noise that was music to Ben's ears. The unloading process was completed with no mishaps or detection from locals. The gold was now safe on *Next Adventure* and ready for the next leg of the plan that would hopefully keep their future concealed a bit longer.

"Come on aboard with us, Marley," Ben said, putting his hand on the man's shoulder. "We have a few cold beers left and we need to discuss a few things." The guys had piled the gold bars up in the engine room where they'd be out of site should anybody pay them a visit, and in place for the next step…concealing them inside the air-compressor tank.

"Marley, we have to head back to the States day after tomorrow," Ben explained. "I don't think we'll have anymore room to conceal more treasure, so I don't see the need in going out tomorrow." Ben went below and got the cash to pay Marley for his services, plus a nice size tip. "Marley…this will have to do for now…but when we find an outlet to move this stuff…you'll be coming back with us to the States next time. Our pile of treasure out there needs to remain our secret to make that work, though…okay?"

"I have already told you…" Marley replied…"I have no reason to tell anybody about the wreck or its cargo, mon. If I did, there would be nothing in it for me."

"Good deal, Marley…I can promise you that you'll be living comfortable in the States soon. Take that extra cash I gave you and buy Tanya a nice dress and maybe some new tennis shoes for the boys, okay?" Ben added. "I've got us leaving at 6 a.m. day after tomorrow. Troy and I will be checking systems tomorrow and getting ready for the crossing. If you get a chance…how about you and Tanya stopping by tomorrow afternoon around four or five and we'll grill some steaks. We brought five big ribeyes and didn't get a chance to grill them before the girls had to leave."

"We would love to do that, Ben. Count us in!" Marley replied rubbing his hands together.

The guys went down into the engine room after Marley left and began the next phase of the plan.

"Troy… how 'bout you sitting in the fly-bridge and keeping an eye out for visitors…I can handle this down here." Ben stated.

"Suits me, dude. I'm not a welder or a cutter anyways." Troy took a seat in the flybridge to keep watch while Ben began to carry out the plan.

First, Ben switched on the engine room exhaust fans to remove the smoke that would be created from the cutting and welding process. Then, he took the plasma cutter and removed one end of the tank by carefully cutting the original manufacturers welds. The bars, including the bar found early in this year's hunt, were then stacked inside the tank and the end was welded back onto the tank just as planned. The whole process took about two hours and only lacked re-painting once the weld had cooled.

Once completed, Ben took a seat in the flybridge alongside Troy.

"Well…how did *that* go?" asked Troy.

"Flawlessly. I'm not just another pretty face, you know," Ben gloated.

"You sound as bad as Marley, dude. Did they all fit?"

"Had room for a few more, actually. When it cools down, you can paint it. Remember to turn on the exhaust fans so you don't get overspray all over everything though, …okay?" Ben added.

"Roger that," Troy replied.

"Well…are we officially out of beer?" Ben asked.

"No. I have my reserve," Troy answered.

"And how much is that?"

"A six pack," Troy replied."

"Hummm…" Ben thought aloud…"I've got Henry the cabby's card. I'm gonna' call him to see if he can make a delivery." Ben called Henry and explained the situation. Henry was more than happy to make a beer-run for the guys.

When Henry finally made his way to the dock with his delivery…Ben and Troy had already finished up the six pack and had started in on some tequila that the girls had brought aboard. Henry made his way down the dock with two twelve packs of American beer to the only boat docked there.

"Henry…you're a site for sore eyes!" Ben yelled from the flybridge.

"Permission to come aboard, mon," Henry asked.

"Permission granted," Ben responded. Henry carried the two twelve packs up the gangplank as Ben and Troy made their way down to pay Henry for the delivery. Ben paid Henry for the beer plus a nice tip for his trouble. "No tip, mon," Henry replied. "I'm officially off duty and would be more than happy to drink a few beers with you guys, in lieu of a tip."

The guys both laughed and said, "Well, come on up, Henry. It'd be a pleasure to have your company this evening." They all made their way back to the fly-bridge where they visited for a couple of hours while working on the two twelve packs of beer.

Ben and Troy had made another good friend in Jamaica. Before leaving Henry made the comment, "Anything you need guys, just call Henry, okay? Anything…ganja, booze, my sister will even…"

"No…no," Ben interrupted. "We're all good in that department, Henry." The guys reassured him that they'd do just that, if they needed something. This time, Henry walked back down the dock to his van with a bit of a wobble.

"I'm gonna' go do some painting," Troy said to Ben with a bit of a slur in his voice.

"How about you wait until tomorrow morning, now, Troy," Ben offered. "I don't want everything down there painted the same color as the compressor."

"You got a point there, dude" Troy agreed. With that said, Troy turned, made his way down below and fell across the bed.

Ben sat alone and drank one more beer alone while again staring out across the bay at the lights from the Boogeyman's island…wondering.

CHAPTER 9

Rough Seas Ahead And More Trouble

The guys slept-in the following morning due to the previous evening's activities along with the fact that they weren't going to the wreck-site today. Ben rolled out of bed around seven o'clock and woke Troy.

"Roll out, dude...we need to get systems checked and procure some fuel somewhere. And, you've got some painting to do too, don't forget," Ben barked.

"Okay...okay," came Troy's muffled reply from somewhere beneath the covers.

Ben went topside to start the morning's coffee brewing knowing Troy would be in bad need of it after his feet hit the floor. Then, he went up to the fly-bridge to program the GPS with the autopilot for aid in navigation on the return trip to the States. As Ben was finishing putting in numbers and coordinates, Troy walked out on to the deck below the flybridge with his first cup of coffee. Ben watched him look out over the bay wrapped with a blanket around his shoulders. He was oblivious to Ben's vantage point as he took the first few sips of the healing concoction. Ben couldn't stand it anymore and broke the morning silence.

"Hey, dude...feeling a little rough this morning are we?"

"Oh, damn...*that's* the understatement of the year! Why did you let me drink that tequila...I thought we were friends?"

"As I recall, Troy...when the six pack of beer was gone, it was you who went down and got the bottle of tequila...not me."

"You're right," Troy agreed. "I remember that, but…"

No buts," Ben interrupted. "There's a bit of the hair of the dog left if you want"

"Don't make me vomit, Ben" Troy began to laugh a bit about his over consumption. Ben laughed right along with him as Troy was going through the healing process.

"Hey…paint, dude…paint, Ben hollered. "I gave you a pass last night, but it's gotta' be done first thing this morning!"

Troy disappeared below deck to get a shower, hoping it would help get rid of the cobwebs from last night's revelry. Meanwhile, Ben went to the galley to fry some bacon and eggs that he knew would help Troy over his hangover and get on with the day's tasks. Shortly, Troy reappeared from below deck looking one notch better but still a bit fuzzy.

"Dude…" Ben began…"sit down here and eat some breakfast…get some grease on your stomach. It always helps."

Troy sat down and ate breakfast as Ben had suggested. He drank another cup of coffee and the transformation process was nearly complete.

"Okay, Ben…I'm gonna' go get that painting done now, okay?"

"Sounds like a good plan. Don't forget to turn the exhaust fans on."

"Yeah…yeah…yeah the exhaust fans!" shouted Troy. "Yaaargh, the exhaust fans matey…I got it Ben…I got it." Troy disappeared below to the engine room in order to paint the air-compressor tank while Ben went back to the flybridge to double check his GPS inputs and to also check out the rest of the electronic systems to be certain that everything was functioning correctly for the long journey back home to Fort Myers, Florida.

The guys spent the rest of the day checking fluid levels making certain that all systems were a go for the trip home. Finally, Ben said, "I'm satisfied we're good to go with *Next Adventure,* but we need to figure out the fuel situation. I'm gonna' call our new buddy, Henry…anything we need remember, Troy?"

"Uhhhm…no, can't say I remember that, Ben…sorry." Troy said shamefully.

"Dude…" Ben replied…"before Henry left last night, he said anything we need we could count on him to find it"

"Well…I missed that one, Ben."

"Well, okay…I guess I'll forgive you," Ben ribbed. "I'm gonna' give Henry a call and see if he can hook us up with some fuel. It's about three o'clock now. We should probably get the steaks ready for grilling. I expect Marley and his crew to be here shortly."

Ben called Henry's number and explained to him that he and Troy needed to leave for the States tomorrow and needed to fill the boat with fuel. He explained that he'd prefer not to have to go to a marina. He'd rather be filled up via truck right here at the dock.

"No worries, mon," Henry replied. "My buddy, Earth, runs a service that fuels the big yachts that come in to Kingston."

"Earth! Earth is really his name?" Ben asked.

"Yeah, mon," Henry said laughing. "He says his mama named him Earth because she thinks the world of him."

"That's funny as hell, Henry," Ben laughed. "Give your buddy Earth a call and tell him I need to be topped off before headin' home. I'm guessing about a thousand gallons oughta' do it. I'm shoving off from the dock early in the morning, so If he can get me topped off this afternoon, that, would be great."

"No worries, mon…Earth will be there within the hour to take care of you." Henry assured.

By now, Ben and Troy had started making preparations for the meal with Marley and his family for the afternoon. Steaks were being seasoned and marinated and the grill was set up on the aft deck of *Next Adventure*. The guys were busy working on side items to go with the steaks when they heard a loud voice and a knocking on the side of the boat.

"Hey, Mr. Carson! It's Earth…I'm here to fuel your boat." Ben walked to the dock side of the boat and looked down to see a row of white teeth and a smile a mile wide. "You need fuel, sir?" the man asked.

"Yes we do, Earth," Ben replied.

"Okay…okay, mon. I think I have enough hose to reach you out here. I'll be right back, bossman." Earth walked back to his fuel delivery truck and pulled the red hose from the truck to the *Next Adventure*. "Can you put this nozzle in your fuel bunk?" Earth asked Ben. "I'll go engage the pump and send the diesel fuel this way."

"I got it," Ben replied. "Let 'er rip, Earth!" Earth engaged the PTO on the fuel truck and began sending fuel through the hose to *Next Adventure*. The fuel delivery seemed to last for a good hour when suddenly the nozzle clicked off and the tank was full. Ben was very close in his estimate of one thousand gallons. It had taken eleven hundred gallons to fill the tank of *Next Adventure*.

"Will that be cash or credit?" Earth asked.

"Credit, if you don't mind, Earth," Ben responded. "I'm about tapped-out of cash."

Earth was rolling up his fuel hose about the time Marley and his family were arriving by boat and tying to the dock.

"Earth…" Marley yelled… "I hope you didn't rip these fine folks off, mon! Ben…you gotta watch this guy, the meter on his pump clicks in his favor!"

"You're ridiculous, Simon Role!" Earth fired back as both men laughed.

"Just joking, mon. This joker not smart enough to run a shady business and get away with it," Marley added. "How did you get hooked with this guy anyway?"

"Henry, the cabby," Ben answered as he was still not sure if the pair was serious.

"Henry…he just as crooked as Earth. How much is Henry making from this deal, Earth?"

"Simon Role…" Earth replied…"I hope you don't kiss your mama with that mouth…because you're so full of bull dung it be spilling out your mouth."

"Just having fun with you, brother," Marley said.

"Ben…this guy is the most honest guy I know on the island…I'd trust him with my wife. Well, on second thought…maybe not tonight. She's looking mighty fine in that new dress I bought her."

When Tanya stepped up on to the dock in her new dress, Earth grabbed his heart and yelled. "Oh my goodness, Mama Role…Earth had better go!" With that said, Earth fired up his fuel truck and left the dock. Their two boys followed Tanya out onto the dock. When Ben saw brand new tennis shoes on their feet, he had to swallow hard and struggle a bit to keep from shedding a few tears.

"You're looking mighty pretty tonight, Tanya," Troy remarked.

"I concur, Tanya," agreed Ben.

"Thank you, boys…" Tanya said…"But, you boys should have let me and the girls spend a little time together before they went back home."

"I know," Ben acknowledged. "And I hate that you all didn't have the opportunity. Lindsey wasn't feeling well, so we had to make some pretty quick decisions to get her back home, Tanya."

"I understand, Ben. Marley told me she was having some kind of problems. Is she doing okay now?"

"Getting lots of tests run right now, but nothing has been determined, yet. Probably nothing, but better safe than sorry," Ben added.

"Okay, gang," Troy yelled. "We got steak and your choice of sides. We have two choices…mac and cheese, or mac and cheese. What'll it be?"

"Both," Marley replied. "These two young'uns will eat their weight in mac and cheese...no worries, mon."

"Okay… mac and cheese it is then," Troy replied. "Ben if you wanna' start the steaks, I'll nuke the mac and cheese."

"Boys…" Marley yelled. "Go get our presents out of the boat for Mr. Ben and Mr. Troy, please." The boys ran to the boat and carried back one twelve pack of Red Stripe beer apiece and presented them to Ben and Troy.

"Oh…thanks boys!" Ben said as he looked at Troy and winked. "Our favorite kind."

The group conversed, laughed, and had a boaters' feast fit for a king. After the meal, they sat around on the flybridge watching the boys pretend they were pirates on the high seas in a luxury yacht.

"Ben…I gotta' ask." Marley said "Did you get things stowed away?"

"Safe and sound, I hope, dude," Ben replied.

"Have either you or Troy seen the little butt-head yet?"

"Not yet," Ben said. "But, I'm certain he'll make an appearance before we shove off in the morning."

"You can count on it, mon," Marley explained "He's not goin' to miss out on his big payday…you can count on *that* visit."

"Boys!" Marley yelled once again. "Load up. We need to get back to the house before dark. Have a safe trip back guys, and I hope Lindsey is feeling better soon. Tell her we love her and that she'll be in our prayers…okay, Ben?"

"I'll do that. Thanks, Marley," Ben replied reaching out to shake Marley's hand and giving him a man hug. In doing so, he passed a gold eight escudo coin into his hand. Marley looked at the coin and looked back up at Ben with a confused look on his face. "That's the only gold coin we brought back, Marley," Ben explained. "*That* coin will probably fetch three, maybe four thousand dollars. There are hundreds of them out there. Put it away for safekeeping. It will be a start for the down payment on your home in the States." Marley didn't know what to say and Ben could see that he was lost for words. "No need to say anything, dude…this *is* going to happen." Marley mouthed the words thank you and exited *Next Adventure* with his family.

"Well," Ben said. "I was really expecting to see our little black mailer this evening, Troy. I hope he's not planning on pulling a fast one on us."

"I wouldn't think so, Ben. We've already given him several hundred dollars of hush money. If he sells us out now…we could spill the beans on *him*…pretty sure he's already thought that through."

"Probably right, dude," Ben agreed. "Let's clean our mess up and chill for a bit before hittin' the hay…we gotta' get going in the morning. He'll probably be here first light the way I figure it."

The guys picked up and stowed the grill away before going inside for the evening while they were discussing the crossing and how best to take shifts and get rest while making the forty hour return trip back to the States. Ben yawned big and said, "Okay, I'm done…I'm gonna' get in the shower and then to bed. Probably be the last shower and good night's sleep I have for a few days." He'd no more than gotten the words out of his mouth when he heard a tap…tap…tap on the side of the boat.

"Oh…Stanley, I presume," Troy said. Ben opened the sliding glass doors from the Salon room and sure enough, there, stood "the little big man" in a flowered shirt, old corduroy jeans and penny loafers. He was looking as if he'd just gone shopping at a vintage clothing store, or had dug deep into his closet to the 1970's department.

"Wow…look at you!" Ben said, holding back a snicker. "You goin' to a disco joint tonight, Sergeant Stan?"

"Going to Kingston tonight," Stan sneered. "Might just get lucky!"

"Wouldn't surprise me a bit, Stan…you're looking mighty dapper tonight" Ben told him.

"Enough of the small talk…we have some unfinished business, American." Stan replied.

"You're right," Ben said while looking up and down the dock for any other visitors. "Would you like to step inside, Sergeant?' Ben asked.

"No," Stan replied. "We have the cover of darkness… no one knows I'm here. We can finish our business right here on the dock."

"Suit yourself," Ben replied. "Give me a few minutes while I go below." Ben went below to get some of the last of the cash and headed back up to pay Stan as agreed. "Okay," Ben said returning topside. "As I got it figured…I owe you two days and the *grand* before departure as we agreed. Is that what you remember, Sergeant?"

Stan answered, "I remember *three days* and the grand." Ben could have eaten barbed wire and spit ten penny nails because he knew that he was being taken advantage of. However, it wasn't worth arguing over. Ben counted out sixteen-hundred dollars and placed it in the greedy little hand. "So…" Stan asked…"I guess it would be safe to assume that you found no treasure?"

"Nothing this year, but we narrowed the search area a great deal and stand a better chance next year. Can we assume we have the same agreement next year?" Ben asked.

The little big man thought for just a bit before answering. "Well…if you stand a better chance of getting rich next year, I think the daily rate will be three hundred dollars. You know…inflation and all"

Again, Ben had to bite his tongue and agree to his demands. "Okay…okay," Ben agreed. "We're shoving off at six a.m. sharp tomorrow morning. I don't expect we'll have any issues…right?"

"You will have no issues, American. I have told my superiors that you're just a couple of dumb Americans ridding our water of junk. They all laughed when I told them that," Stan replied. "I promise, see you next year, treasure hunters…have a wonderful trip." Stan turned and walked away with the cash stuffed inside his corduroy, turn-of-the-century britches.

"That little a-hole," Ben said as he walked back in to *Next Adventure*.

"I heard *that*, treasure hunter…" Stan said as he was making his way down the dock laughing.

"Well…" Ben said. "I have two-hundred in cash left of what we brought. Good thing Earth took credit or we'd have had to have money wired, thanks to our little extortionist."

"Take a chill pill, dude," replied Troy. "We have eleven million squirreled away down below. I think we more than have it covered."

"Yeah, well…it's not in the bank yet, Troy," Ben reminded.

"Just a bit more of that trouble," Troy replied.

"I'm goin' for that shower now and gonna' try and get some sleep, dude," Ben said patting Troy on the back.

"Roger that, Ben. I'm not far behind you."

The guys woke the following morning, checked systems once again, as well as the latest weather and wind forecasts. It looked as if they would have fairly good weather on the return trip…but not quite as good as the trip down. The forecast was calling for four to five foot seas, which are typical of the fall months. It would add hours to their return trip, but nothing the sixty foot vessel couldn't handle. The decision was made to leave on schedule and get underway back to the States. Troy untied *Next Adventure* from the rickety old dock, pulled the bow-lines and fenders inside the vessel and shouted, "You're adrift Captain…let's go!" Ben blasted the side thrusters on the vessel to get her clear of the dock and set course for home.

The first four hours into the journey was fairly flat and they were making good time but Ben knew once they rounded the western end of Cuba and were out from behind the protection of the island…things would begin getting a little dicey.

"Well, I guess the little big man kept his end of the bargain aside from the fact that he screwed us a bit," Ben remarked.

"It's fine dude…let it go," Troy replied. "Where do you wanna deep six this welding equipment…it's not exactly the kind of equipment that you would typically see on a luxury yacht ya' know. I believe our Coast Guard might question it."

"Oh yeah," Ben said. "I almost forgot *that* part of the plan. Thanks for reminding me. This is as good a place as any, before it starts to rough-up." Ben pulled back on the throttles and they went below to bring up the equipment. The equipment was thrown to Davy Jones' locker and the journey was continued.

Just as expected, when *Next Adventure* cleared the western end of Cuba, the waves slowly began to build. Eventually, the seas looked like a washing machine with waves white capping and breaking over the bow of vessel. There was a chill in the air to make matters worse. Water ran around the superstructure of the vessel, running out the scuppers of the stern.

"Holy Shit!" Troy exclaimed.

Ben returned Troy's remark. "No turning back now, dude…we're committed!"

It was now pitch dark to make matters worse. Ben pulled back on the speed a bit to keep the bow from dipping below the waves, but kept the forward speed adequate enough to keep the vessel on course. He knew that if he pulled back the speed too much…the vessel would be at the mercy of the ocean. Turning broadside in these kinds of waves would be disastrous.

"This is a hell-of-a-lot rougher than the forecast projected," Ben shouted. "Looks more like tens and twelve's than fives or sixes to me!" He struggled to keep *Next Adventure* on course in the high seas as he switched off the autopilot and steered her the old fashioned way.

The struggle went on for hours it seemed as Ben became somewhat concerned. "Troy!" Ben yelled over the roar of the ocean and winds. "How about grabbing a few life jackets from under your seat just in case we hit a rogue wave out here!" Ben looked at Troy and saw a shade of green that he'd never seen before. He'd seen a lot of people who were sea sick but never as bad as Troy looked right now. Troy stood up and made an attempt to get the life jackets as Ben had instructed, but instead…he grabbed the railing and started barfing over the side. Once Troy had barfed a few times, Ben said, "PFD's dude…I can't let go of the helm to get them. I need you to get 'em!" Troy sat down on the floor, lifted the seat and grabbed two life jackets. He tossed one to Ben and made an attempt to put one on himself.

The cauldron went on for hours. The guys got no rest and were nearly exhausted before a noticeable improvement in the conditions came about. Finally, just about sunrise…the ocean began to lie down. Ben thought to himself… *"It seems as if Mother Ocean is angry that our vessel is carrying what once belonged to her, and now…she's trying her best to reclaim her property."*

Troy was still setting in the floor of the fly-bridge with one arm through the life jacket…it was the best he could do under the circumstances.

"You okay, dude," Ben asked.

"Don't talk to me right now, okay…I'll hurl again if I have to concentrate on anything but not hurling."

"We need to get things checked out down below, dude. It appears that we're through the worst of it." Troy finally made his way back up in to the seat and sat a bit longer with his elbows on his knees and his head in his hands.

The sun was now peaking over the eastern horizon. Ben felt a since of relief knowing that it would soon be daylight. The seas were still tossing but nothing like last night.

"I just wanted to die," Troy muttered. "Wha-ja-say, dude?" Ben asked.

"I was praying to just go ahead and just die last night," Troy repeated. "Worse than any drunk I've ever been on."

"Can you at least come sit down here and keep us on course so I can go check things out down below?" Ben asked. "It's calmed down quite a bit and not too tough to keep her on the heading."

Troy grabbed onto everything he could in order to make his way in to the captain's seat without falling. Then, he took the helm. Ben made his way below to check on things. Once inside the salon room, Ben noticed that some of the furniture had been tossed around by the angry seas. Cabinets had popped open and the contents of them were now strewn all over the floor of the galley. Everything seemed fine in the staterooms so Ben made his way on to the engine room. He grabbed the earmuffs hanging outside the engine room door to protect himself from the roar of the loud engines and opened the door. Ben breathed a sigh of relief as all appeared good. He'd been concerned all night long that the now top-heavy bench where the air compressor was mounted may have ripped loose and crashed to the floor…but all was fine. Then, he made his way up to the fly-bridge where Troy was beginning to get his color back and once again took over the helm.

"Well?" asked Troy. "Is everything okay?"

"A bit of a jumbled up mess, but nothing serious," Ben answered.

It was now a few hours past sunrise and the seas were beginning to calm once again. Ben increased the forward speed to full throttle and switched the autopilot back on.

"One of us had better get a couple hours of rest, Troy. We lost a lot of time last night…I'm guessing three maybe four hours. Why don't you go below and get some rest. I'll be fine for a bit longer." Troy didn't argue with Ben and made his way below to get some much needed rest.

Next Adventure was now back up on plane and going full-steam-ahead. Ben sat in the big captain's seat and caught himself nodding-off here and there. He was exhausted from struggling against the churning seas and warding off the chill all night long.

After Troy got some rest, the guys took turns at the helm…two hours on, and two hours off. This rotation went on well in to the next night.

The guys were now back in U.S. waters and making their way up the western coast of Florida when Ben came back up to the flybridge after one of his two hour rests carrying the 9-millimeter handgun.

Wha'cha doin' with that, Ben?" Troy watched Ben as he tossed the weapon overboard. "Well…okay," Troy remarked. But…it's gone undetected all this time…why would you throw it overboard now?" he asked.

"I'm sure we'll get a visit from the Coast Guard, Troy. They watch vessels coming out of Cuba on radar and stop most, if not all of them. I'm not taking any chances of them finding us with a weapon and giving them a reason to dig deeper…I can always buy another gun," he explained.

The sun was now coming up on morning two of the journey and the guys were overjoyed to see the coastline of Florida.

"Troy…call the girls and let 'em know we'll back to Mullet Creek soon, please."

When Troy called Darlene, she asked, "Where the hell you guys been? You should have been here hours ago!"

"We hit rough seas, ya' know…I'll tell you all about it when I've got a beer in my hand. Let Lindsey know we're almost back…okay, Darlene?"

"She's standing right here listening," Darlene replied.

Ben could now see the point of Matanzas Pass on the GPS screen. They were almost home. Ben felt the greatest feeling of accomplishment he'd ever felt in his entire life. The treasure had been found, they'd survived rough seas and ended up back at their destination…quite an accomplishment!

As the pass was coming into view, Ben pulled back on the throttles a bit and *Next Adventure* settled down into the water for the idle back into Mullet Creek. Just as Ben had expected, before rounding the pass…a Coast Guard vessel came out to welcome the guys back to the States.

"Well…here we go…" Ben said. "I figured this was gonna' happen." Ben continued on as if unaware that the vessel was coming out to meet them until the vessel turned on its lights and made it clear that they wanted to come alongside. Ben pulled the throttles completely back and put the engines in neutral.

"United States Coast Guard!" a voice barked over the loud speaker.

"I never would have guessed *that*…how about you, Troy?" Ben said sarcastically.

"We're coming alongside, Captain…please give us a hand with the lines!" the voice rang out again. The Coast Guard vessel pulled alongside *Next Adventure* as lines were thrown to Ben and Troy. After securing the lines, the voice returned. "Permission to come aboard…" the boarding-officer asked.

"Permission granted," Ben replied. The boarding-officer climbed aboard *Next Adventure* while two other guardsmen watched from the Coast Guard vessel. The officer asked for boat registration information and photo identifications. Ben and Troy both provided the officers with the identification cards and Ben asked the officer for permission to go to helm dry box to retrieve the boat information. The officer handed the identification cards to one of the guardsman on the Coast Guard vessel and motioned for another one of the guardsmen to board and accompany Ben to the helm. Ben retrieved the information requested and returned it to the boarding-officer.

"We watched your vessel come around the western tip of Cuba during some pretty rough weather," the officer commented.

"Yes, and we're beat up from the feet up. We're tired and just wanna' get home, sir," Ben answered.

"Understand, Captain," the officer replied. "What business did you have in Cuba?" he asked.

"We were never in Cuba, sir," Ben explained. "We've spent the last three weeks in Jamaica. We go there every year on vacation.

"Jamaica…okay," the officer said. "I'll need to see your passports as well then, please." Again the guys were escorted to retrieve passports and then returned back topside to present them to the boarding-officer. The officer looked at each passport which confirmed that they'd been stamped in Jamaica. The officer handed the passports back and asked, "You vacation there every year? What do you do in Jamaica, may I ask?"

"Well…you know…the Lifestyle Resorts, sir. We like going to the Lifestyle Resorts," Ben told him. The officer glanced at both men with their three day growth of beard going on and looking pretty rough.

"Okay on this end!" the guardsman who had remained on the Coast Guard vessel reported to the boarding-officer. "Their background checks are clean and nothing showed up…the guys are clean!" he shouted. Next, the boarding-officer ordered a walk-through of *Next Adventure*. The guardsman returned topside after several minutes and reported that all seemed in order. "Okay, guys," the boarding-officer said. "You can be on your way, now. And, thank you for your cooperation." He returned the guys their identification cards and exited *Next Adventure.* Once the Guard vessel was clear, Ben throttled back up and got underway again.

"A Lifestyle Resort… is that *all* you could come up with, dude? You know what he's thinking right now don't 'cha?" Troy asked.

"I don't really care what he's thinking right now, Troy…we got away with this. Next time, maybe we'll wear our Speedos when we return to the States."

"Lifestyle Resort," Troy said shaking his head and laughing.

The guys were rounding the north end of Fort Myers Beach and passed under Matanzas Pass Bridge when Troy's phone rang.

"Yes, dear."

"We thought ya'll'd be back by now," Darlene said.

"We would have, dear…but we were stopped and searched by the Coast Guard," Troy explained.

"Oh hell!" Darlene said. "Everything okay?"

"Yeah, it went well, dear…but we've got a few more chapters for our book, someday…we'll be there soon."

As the guys were making the long idle behind Fort Myers Beach and into Estero Bay where they'd connect with Mullet creek, Ben remarked, "Well, Troy…we didn't find the golden altar, emeralds, or any worked gold and silver. I wonder if it's there?"

"We've barely touched that wreck, Ben" Troy replied. "Next time, dude…next time. There's another adventure out there."

The guys were now in sight of Mullet Creek Marina where their journey would come to an end, at least for now. All the locals were there as best the guys could tell, along with the girls. The girls made their way to the dock where *Next Adventure* would finally shut down her engines and take a break. Ben turned the vessel with the thrusters and backed her into the dock. Troy was the first one off the boat, where he nearly fell on his face before getting his land-lubber legs back under him. Big John was there as usual to help secure the vessel to the dock. The girls were kissing and hugging on Troy while he returned their affection. Ben finally got engines and systems shut down and turned from the flybridge.

"Hey…what about me?"

"Well…get on down here, dude!" Darlene yelled. "We've got more of this left."

Ben climbed down and stepped onto the ground for the first time in 48 hours. He, too, had a bit of trouble shaking his sea legs but quickly made his way to Lindsey for a long awaited embrace.

"Damn, I missed you! I thought for a while there I may never see you again, but that's a story all by it's self. Let's all go sit down…we've got hours of stories to tell you all."

The group found a seat at the marina as Big John shook the guys hands. "It's on us, guys. What'll ya' have?"

"Anything but Red Stripe, John," Ben answered. Big John set up the first round of poison.

"Well…how'd we do this year, guys? Are you gonna' buy this joint…or not?"

"Maybe not this year, dude," Troy replied. "But you may be getting closer to retirement," he added.

Big John smiled. "It's on the market, guys...don't miss out," he said as he walked away.

"So…" Ben asked Lindsey. "What are the doctors saying, dear?"

"We'll get in to all that later, Ben… everything's fine, though. I want to hear the stories about your adventure."

"We can't get into that here, dear…but, I can't wait to get home where we can tell you girls all about it. We're beat…I wanna' get Fizz on the phone and fill you all in at the same time." Ben told her.

"Drink up, guys," Lindsey said. "We need to get home and see if we're rich."

The group finished their drinks and made their way to Ben and Lindsey's home where they settled once again on the lanai for the briefing.

Next, Ben dialed Fizz up on the phone. "It's about time dude…you back in the States yet?"

"We're back," Ben answered. "I want you to come here tomorrow, Fizz…we got stuff to show you. I'm gonna' call in rich to work tomorrow, and then…possibly work on my resignation letter tomorrow, as well."

"That, sounds encouraging, dude…now, let's talk about your finds…" Fizz demanded.

Ben looked at every face sitting around the table which were looking at him, hanging on every word. "The compressor tank is full," Ben said.

"Okay…full of what…air…like your head is most of the time?" Fizz laughed.

"Seventy gold bars weighing about eight pounds each, dude." The girls were numb with what they'd just heard. They were speechless. Ben added, "We could only fit about half the gold that we recovered inside the tank, and according to the manifest…there's more to be recovered. I lost count of the silver bars, but we recovered several dozen of those along with gold escudos and hundreds of silver eight reale coins."

Fizz was momentarily at a loss for words, which rarely happens! He finally spoke. "I'll be there tomorrow."

"Great," Ben replied. "I have to go somewhere and purchase another plasma-cutter somewhere tomorrow in order to open the tank. I want to cut it open around 10:00 a.m. tomorrow morning, okay?"

"I'll be there…see you tomorrow!" Fizz repeated.

"I have to go rest, guys" Ben said. "See you all in the morning for the unveiling.

CHAPTER 10

The Unveiling And Broken Heart

"Good morning, my pirate." Ben opened his eyes and looked up to see Lindsey standing over him. She'd prepared his favorite breakfast and was serving it to him in bed.

"What time is it?" he asked.

"Almost eight-thirty, sleepy head."

"I gotta get goin'," he replied sitting up in bed. "Fizz will be here at ten and I need to get somewhere and buy another plasma-cutter to cut the tank open."

"Eat your breakfast and relax a bit longer," Lindsey replied as she crawled back beneath the covers with him. "It's back to the real world tomorrow, with work and all, and I want to enjoy this last day off,"

"Yeah…about work. Actually, I was thinking about calling in rich tomorrow. What do you think dear?" Ben remarked with a grin on his face.

"Don't think I haven't given it some thought," Lindsey said with a chuckle. "Probably wouldn't be the smart thing to do just yet, though."

"You may see things a little differently here in a bit when I cut the end out of that tank. By the way, when do you go see the doctor again?"

"Tomorrow afternoon after work. I have to go talk with the cardiologist about the last bunch of tests that were done."

"So, they haven't determined anything yet?"

"Not really. Can we talk about this more this afternoon after all the excitement is over with?"

"I suppose," Ben answered. "But, I'm not gonna' drive to Ocala tomorrow. I'm going to the Doctor with you…I'll work from home tomorrow."

Ben finished his breakfast, showered and jumped in the big red pickup truck in order to purchase a plasma-cutter to replace the one that he'd thrown overboard on the trip back from Jamaica. He drove straight to the equipment dealer, purchased the cutter, and quickly headed back to pick Lindsey up and rendezvous at Mullet Creek Marina with Troy, Darlene and Mick. When they arrived, the other three were already there visiting with Big John and some of the local crowd. Ben unloaded the plasma-cutter and carried it to the boat, placing it on the aft deck. Then, he walked up to visit with the gang for a bit while waiting on Captain Fizz to join the excitement.

"Where's your buddy?" Troy asked.

"I expect him anytime. It's not like Fizz to be late. I sent him the address early this morning, so he should know the way." Ben had hardly gotten the words out of his mouth when Captain Fizz pulled in to the marina.

"Over here, dude!" Ben shouted as he waved his arms in the air. Fizz walked up to the crowd and gave Lindsey a big kiss and hug, and then turned to shake Ben's hand along with a man-hug. "Fizz, I want you to meet our good friends, Troy and Darlene Mann, and of course you know Mick."

"Hi, honey," Fizz said to Mick as he give her a big hug. "Very nice to meet you folks," he said speaking to Troy and Darlene. Big John was standing close by listening and cleared his throat very loudly.

"Oh yeah, Fizz…" Ben said after taking the hint. "This is Big John…he owns this fine establishment."

"Nice to meet you, John," Fizz said, shaking his hand. "I believe I've heard a bit about you…all good though," he added.

"I feel as if I know you already, Fizz," John replied. "I've read both your books and Ben talks about you all the time…all good, though."

Fizz laughed and again turned his attention to Lindsey. "How are you doin', darling…I heard you had to return from Jamaica early. What's goin' on?" Lindsey downplayed the whole issue.

"Probably nothing, Captain…I've had a bunch of tests run and I'm hopeful that we'll find out more tomorrow.

"You call me the minute you find something out, okay?" Fizz replied.

"I promise, I will," Lindsey answered.

"Let's go to the boat, Fizz," Ben suggested. "I wanna' show her off to you."

"Deal," Fizz replied. The group boarded *Next Adventure* where they could talk without their conversation being overheard. Ben picked up the box with the new plasma-cutter inside and carried it into the Salon room. Once inside behind closed doors, Ben began telling Fizz about the wreck, the cannon, and most of all about how much gold and silver they'd already recovered and hidden.

Fizz looked at Ben and asked, "No golden altar?"

"No, sir," Ben replied. "No golden altar, worked-gold or silver, *and*…no emeralds…*yet*."

Fizz thought a minute before speaking. "It's there, guys…the emeralds and worked-metal *are* there. Jack researched this and was certain that it's there…he just didn't know exactly where. It's possible that the golden altar is a made-up fable handed down over the years, but the jewels and worked-metals *are* there. I'd bet my ass on it!"

"Dude...we barely made a dent in this recovery," Ben replied. "I'm sure it's there, too. Now...let's go get the tank cut open...it's gonna' blow everybody's mind when you see this!"

Ben carried the cutter to the engine room where he placed it on the workbench next to the air tank. After some minor assembly, it was ready to plug in and get to work. "Okay...here we go..." The cutting process took about five minutes before the end of the tank was once again removed. All eyes were focused on the gold bars that had been neatly stacked inside the tank.

"Fizz..." Ben said looking at the Captain..."I'd be honored if you'd pull the first few bars from the tank while I record the moment with a few pictures. Troy and I may want to write our own book someday."

Fizz began pulling the gold bars from the tank while saying, "This is unlike anything I've ever seen, dudes." The rest of the group sat looking on in disbelief.

"What's those markings on the bars mean, Fizz?" Darlene asked. Fizz explained that they were assayer and tax stamps.

"These X's and dots represent the weight of the bar and purity of the gold," he added.

After all the bars had been removed from the tank, the group could do nothing but stare.

"Fizz, the way I got it figured..." Ben calculated..."if we just use current spot-gold-value...these bars are worth around eleven million."

"Could be five times that, dude," Fizz replied. "You have to consider the historic and artifact value. There are dozens of private collectors out there who'd pay multiple times over spot-value to own one of these. You need to let me reach out to some folks before making any decisions, okay? How are you plannin' on getting this stuff off here, anyway?"

"That's the easy part," Ben explained. "I'm gonna' back that big red truck of mine up here and start unloading the boat. We haven't unloaded anything from the trip yet, so there's plenty of bags and luggage that we can hide it in. Matter of fact, let's start unloading it now into whatever we can conceal it in and get it to the house."

The entire group chipped in with the chore of unloading the luggage and equipment, along with the gold, and throwing it in into the back of Ben's truck. In the matter of half an hour the chore was complete. Not one person at the marina turned their head to pay any attention or ask any questions during the process. Then, Ben turned to Captain Fizz.

"Come on to the house with us, Fizz. I have some of that twenty-five year old rum waiting on us there."

"Deal, dude" Fizz replied "I can't wait, and don't want to ask the rum to wait any longer either. I'm right behind you."

The group drove the short distance to Ben and Lindsey's home where they began to unload all the bags and luggage into the attached garage in order to remove the gold bars and store them for the time being. The bars were stacked up on the floor in their downstairs room just off the pool and lanai. Some years back, the couple had hired a local artist to paint two ships on one of the walls, one ship being…a pirate vessel engaged in a broadside battle on the high seas. Ben had always loved this painting and decided to stack the bars there for more photo-ops.

Ben finally broke out the bottle of rum. "Listen up guys…this bottle of rum's been waiting twenty-five years for someone to find that shipwreck. I've been waiting right along with it, but I hadn't realized it until now." He already had six shot glasses lined-up when he broke the seal and opened the bottle. He poured the shot glasses full and said, "Drink up, me pirates... the plunder is home!"

The morning turned to afternoon as the celebration was beginning to wind-down. Ben had noticed that Lindsey was not her usual self during the evening. She had always been the-life-of-the-party and kept everybody entertained with her wit and cute personality. She'd actually separated herself from the festivities and was now setting out by the pool by herself. Ben stepped away from the crowd briefly to join her.

"You okay, dear?"

"Yeah, I'm fine," she replied. "Just tired...that's all."

"Okay...well, I think Fizz is gonna' flop here tonight so that he and I can talk over what to do with our pile of gold tomorrow morning. If you wanna' go ahead and turn in, he'll still be here tomorrow morning to visit with a bit before you have to head off to work."

"Yeah...I'm gonna' say goodnight and go to bed, Ben."

"Sure thing, dear. Do you want me to come tuck you in?"

"It might be kind of exciting to be tucked-in by a real live treasure hunter, slash pirate." She grabbed Ben's shirt and pulled him toward her for a kiss. Then, the two of them climbed the two flights of stairs of their stilt home. When they reached the top of the second flight...Lindsey was breathing hard and looked a bit pale. Ben chose not to mention his observation to Lindsey just now, but he was secretly worrying about the love of his life. He struggled to keep thoughts from entering into his mind, like..."*What would I do without her...how would I ever get by?*" Ben tucked Lindsey in, kissed her goodnight and then joined the others on the Lanai.

"Is she okay, dude?" Fizz asked.

"I can't hide the fact that I'm quite concerned about her health, Fizz. I've seen a few things lately from her, like… the faint feelings, shortness of breath and being cold all the time, that all have me very concerned. We have an appointment to talk to her doctor tomorrow afternoon directly after she gets off work. Hopefully, we'll get some answers, then."

Troy, Darlene and Mick said their goodbyes, telling Fizz what a pleasure it had been to finally meet him.

"For some reason, I have a feeling we'll be seeing a great deal more of each other, Troy," Fizz replied.

"I hope you're right, sir," Troy answered. "It would be an honor to hang with you, sir."

"Oh please…cut it out with the *sir* crap, Troy. He's a pirate…a scalawag, just like the rest of us," Ben explained in his best pirate voice, laughing and slapping Fizz on the back. "Just teasin', dude. Troy…Fizz, here's without a doubt, one of the most honest folks I've ever met in this business. Most people in the treasure-bizz are pirates and scalawags, for sure. They only want to glean from you what you know, but will *never* relinquish any info to you in return. Fizz here, on the other hand… hell, he'll draw you a map to a treasure wreck if you asked him nice. Most honest pirate I've ever met!" Ben concluded.

With *that* said, Troy and Darlene walked out the door to go home. "See you all soon, guys," they said in unison.

Before they were able to get away, Ben shouted, "Troy! We need to talk tomorrow evening. I'm workin' from home tomorrow so's I can go to the doctor with Lindsey. Fizz and I are gonna' come up with a plan to turn this yellow pile, into a green one. Stop by and see me tomorrow after you close the store and I'll fill you in. Okay, dude?"

"Roger that!" Troy replied. "See you soon," he repeated as the couple left for home.

"So…how we gonna' do this, Fizz?" Ben asked.

"Can I have tonight to think about it and make some phone calls? I have some friends who've made a fairly decent find. Doesn't compare with your find, but…they may be willing to absorb your pile in with their meager finds in order to give them more notoriety. The difference being…they have legal salvage-rights where they're salvaging…whereas…you don't, and probably never will. The Jamaican Government shut Jack and Art McKee down on the *Genovese* wreck when treasure started coming up. I suspect they'll do the same to you, Ben, if you try to do it all legal like," Fizz explained.

"All right, dude…lets talk more tomorrow morning. Will you be a sentinel tonight and guard this pile of gold bars for me tonight, Fizz?"

"No worries, dude….I got it." Fizz answered.

"Good deal." The couch down here is actually pretty comfy," Ben explained. I've had to sleep a few times down here."

"Won't ask why you had to do that, dude," Fizz replied. "I'll just take your word for it."

Ben fixed Fizz up with blankets and pillows, and then said, "See you in the mornin', dude." Then, he walked upstairs to crawl in bed alongside Lindsey.

Ben finished his last beer for the evening, did his bathroom routine and crawled in to bed. Lindsey's feet were ice cold. The second Lindsey felt Ben's body heat spooned along side of her…her feet went straight to his crotch for the warming process.

"Holy crap, dear! That's cold!" Ben screeched as his manhood began to retreat. "Feels like you got blocks of ice on your feet." Ben took one for the team, however, and lay still while Lindsey warmed her feet.

The alarm clock woke Lindsey the following morning at 5:30 a.m. Ben awoke with her and asked her.

"Can I fix you something for breakfast?"

"Just coffee," she replied. "Start a pot of coffee, Ben… that's all I need." Then, Lindsey showered and began getting herself ready for the day. Ben brewed the coffee, poured and delivered a cup to Lindsey before going downstairs to where Fizz had spent the night.

Captain Fizz is a morning-person, like Ben, and doesn't require coffee to get his day started. Like all adventurers, explorers and treasure hunters…the fact that the next day could bestow the next big find is all they need to motivate them to get up and get going everyday.

"Dude," Ben said as he opened the door.

"What?" Fizz replied.

"Did you sleep okay, Fizz?"

"Like a log…good rum and good company always lends to a good night of sleep…or, possibly it was just the rum…not sure," he added. "How'd Lindsey do last night?"

"She seems her chipper-self this morning. When I got in bed last night, her feet were like ice. She stuck them between my legs and I kept them warm for her all night."

"Good man... if you needed help, all you had to do was ask…you know *that*, right? Fizz added with a grin.

"I always know I can count on you, dude," Ben laughed.

"I reached out to the folks with the legal State contract I was talking about last night," Fizz said. "They wanted some pictures of the bars. I'm not sending pictures out over the internet for everybody to see. I need to take one bar over to the East coast to show them."

"Wait…wait…wait. Let me relish in this moment for just a bit," Ben said. "Captain Fizz is asking me, the moron, for permission to take one of my seventy gold bars to show somebody. Do I have that correct?"

"You k*now*, of course, that I'll never stop calling you moron. Now, you want my help or not?" Fizz asked.

"Yes…I need your help, Fizz. You can call me anything that makes you happy…I don't care…just teasing."

By now, Lindsey had prepared for work and opened the door where the two men were conversing.

"How ya' feelin' this morning, sunshine?" Fizz asked.

"I feel wonderful, Captain. I spent the night in the same house with two successful treasure hunters and pirates. How much better *could* it get?"

"Uhhmm…not sure how much better it could get, but maybe you need to raise your sights a bit, honey," Fizz suggested.

"My sights are trained exactly on what I'm lookin' for," assured Lindsey. "I love my pirates and adventure…I'm good!"

The three visited for just a bit before Lindsey had to return to the work-a-day-world. "Okay, I gotta' run, fellas. When will we see you again, Fizz?"

"Soon…I'm sure, honey."

"Great! I never get enough *Fizz* in my life."

"Oh brother…" Ben remarked of the back and forth banter between Fizz and Lindsey. "Darlin. I'll meet you at three this afternoon to go meet with your doctor…okay?" Ben said after kissing her goodbye.

"Roger *that*, love," Lindsey said as she walked out the door.

"I'm gonna have to run pretty quick this morning, too, dude," Fizz explained. "I need to run to the East coast to get with some folks about this pile of gold you have here."

Fizz turned and focused his eyes to admire the pile once again. "We really only have three options, as I see it," he continued. "Option one, which would be my first hope and the most lucrative…would be to slip the stuff into somebody else's finds who has a legal contract…which are damn few, thanks to the States stance on treasure hunting. Option two, move it through the black-market and get it in to private collector's hands. The issue with this option is the fact that you're gonna' make less money, and the number of bars that need moved could take years. Option three, and the absolute worst, would be to make a great deal with a jeweler where he'd turn it into modern jewelry. You'd have to take something less than spot-value, not to mention the fact that it's just a sad thought that this piece of history could end up lost that way…but it happens. I *know* it does, for a fact. The laws, both U.S. and abroad, but mostly here in the States, have put so much restriction on treasure salvage that it's almost a non-profit deal if you follow the letter of the law. When treasure's recovered…it makes such a circus of attention that the group who finds it usually ends up in some kind of trouble…because I guarantee you there was some kind of law broken somewhere. It's for this reason that people keep the finds quiet and history is disappearing all the time into private collections, or as modern jewelry. It's a sad situation."

"I agree, dude," Ben said. "But, it's not only the treasure diving business where things are happening beneath the table due to the long arm of the government… it's everywhere!"

"I'm gonna' use your shower, dude…if that's okay," Fizz asked.

"No problem, help yourself. I've gotta' get this computer fired-up so my boss knows I'm back to work and paying taxes like a good subordinate should."

"Suit yourself, dude, but I left that rat race years ago and haven't once looked back."

"I know, Fizz …I know," Ben responded "I'm almost there…full-time treasure hunter, I mean. Once I see this pile turn to green…I may be writing my resignation letter."

"Okay, dude. I won't bother you when I leave out…I'll just grab one bar and be on my way. I'll call you and let you know how things go on the east coast."

"Deal," Ben said as he turned to walk upstairs to his home office where he sat down and worked for several hours catching up on e-mails, making phone calls, and all the other mundane tasks that he's done for a living for the last thirty-plus years. Ben thought to himself, "*I may actually be able to get the hell away from this corporate B. S. soon.*" His daydreaming was soon interrupted when his phone rang. He looked at the Caller-I.D. and it was Lindsey.

"Hi, dear. Why are you calling me in the middle of the day?"

"My cardiologist's office called and would like us in there at two o'clock instead of four." Lindsey explained.

"Oh, okay. I'll get ready and see you in bit, love."

Ben got himself ready and was at Lindsey's place of work around one thirty. She walked out the door from her place of toil and jumped in Ben's big red truck.

"Which way we goin', dear?" Ben asked.

"South, Ben. We have to go all the way to South Naples."

Ben headed south on Tamiami Trail to south Naples as Lindsey had advised. "Turn right at the next light. The doctor's office is in the complex on the left." Ben wheeled the big truck into the parking lot of the medical complex and took a parking spot in the back-forty as usual. They walked for what seemed a quarter mile in to the office, signed-in and sat down to wait for their turn. Lindsey was visibly breathing harder than normal from the little bit of physical exertion that it took to walk from the parking spot to the doctor's office.

"You okay, dear?"

"I'm fine, Ben...but why do you always park a mile away all the time?" she asked.

"I'm sorry. I don't like parking in the main crowd...you know that. I don't want some A-hole throwing his door in to the side of my truck." The couple waited patiently until they heard, "Mrs. Carson..." announced.

Ben and Lindsey stood and walked toward the nurse where she instructed Lindsey to step up on the scales. They were then led to a room in the facility that was definitely not a room where patients were seen on a daily basis. It appeared to be more of a small conference-room. Soon, the doctor made his appearance and sat down in front of the curious couple. He began with idle chit-chat asking Lindsey how she was feeling, has anything changed since he saw her last and so on such and such a day. Then, he turned to Ben.

"Mr. Carson, I hear you're a treasure hunter...that's pretty interesting. How does one get to call himself a treasure hunter?"

Ben replied, "I guess the same way you get to call yourself a doctor, sir. A lot of hard work and perseverance. The big difference being..." explained Ben..."that if a shipwreck was my patient, I'd only have to see one every ten, maybe twelve years in order to make ends meet and live like a king...whereas, you need to see patients all day everyday, with all due respect." The doctor laughed at Ben's analogy.

"Interesting career path...wish I could have half the excitement in my life that you must have in yours."

"Okay…let's talk about Lindsey, now," the doctor said, turning his attention to her. "I've run lots of tests over the past couple of weeks. I've waited this long to give you my prognosis because I wanted to be one hundred percent certain." The doctor stammered for a bit while Ben and Lindsey sat looking at him.

"So, doctor, what's your prognosis?" Ben finally asked.

The doctor looked directly at the couple and said, "Acute stress-induced cardiomyopathy."

Ben and Lindsey sat in shock for a bit after hearing the words. Ben asked, "So, can we get more details here, doc, because I have no clue what you just said other than it sounds like something to do with my wife's heart. She has a history of heart-related problems in her family, in case she didn't reveal that."

"This is not an inherent disease," the doctor replied. "This disease is also referred to as the *broken-heart syndrome* and is typically brought on by a major life altering loss of some kind."

"Like the loss of a child?" Ben asked.

"Yes…we see this more in women than men. For an unknown reason, a major heartbreak of some kind will cause the left ventricle of the heart to become distorted and eventually cause circulation issues. In most cases, the issue corrects itself after several days or sometimes weeks, and in most cases, the symptoms will pretty much go unnoticed. In Lindsey's case, however, the left ventricle has continued to distort since the loss of your son"

"So…what's all that translate into," Ben asked.

"Well…" the doctor started… "I'm going to order an echocardiogram monthly and monitor Lindsey's condition."

"Monitor her condition for what?" Ben asked.

The doctor looked at Lindsey and said, "Further distortion of the left ventricle." The doctor then looked down at the floor away from the couple.

"So, if this distortion continues…" Ben continued… "what's the outcome?"

"We'll need to get Lindsey on a transplant list and find a donor heart," the doctor replied. "The other problem here is the rare blood-type…A-negative, which is only six percent of the populous."

"I'm well aware of *that*," Ben acknowledged.

Then, the doctor replied. "Well…I have to throw it all out there to you, folks…that's going to make the chance of finding a donor pretty limited.

"Let's monitor the condition monthly and decide from the data," Ben suggested.

The doctor looked at Ben with a bit of confusion on his face. "Yes…that's, the plan, Mr. Carson."

Lindsey spoke up. "How long if we can't find a donor?"

"Two…maybe three years," the doctor answered. Depends on how far along the disease is once diagnosed. Giving that you're showing most of the symptoms already…I'd guess closer to two than three years…it's just very tough to say."

"What should we expect going forward, doctor?" Lindsey asked.

"Well…again, *that's* hard to say. I would expect much more of the same, and possibly at some point, you could begin to incur severe indigestion and chest pains, which you've shown no signs of at this point. Symptoms will begin getting more frequent, for sure."

"So, how do I get in line for a heart?" Lindsey asked.

"I'll begin *that* process immediately, Lindsey…we have all the information we need," the doctor assured.

Once she'd finished with her questions Lindsey looked at Ben. He was staring at the floor with tears in his eyes.

"Ben..." Lindsey said. "Lets go...we have some more living to do!"

CHAPTER 11

Back On The Pile Of Gold

The ride home from the Doctor's office was silent until Ben had just about passed Lindsey's place of work.

"Ben!" Lindsey shouted. "Are you going to stop and let me get my truck?"

"Oh yeah…" Ben replied as he got on the brakes hard and turned into the parking lot where her truck was parked. "My head's not where it should be right now. Sorry, dear."

"Okay…let's get home and chill, Ben. And, I *really* don't want this subject to consume our every conversation from here on…okay?"

"Okay, dear…okay," he reassured her.

After Ben had dropped her off at her truck, he made sure she got the truck started and then followed her home. He had those questions going through his mind again, fighting back hard to keep from asking them to himself, but failed. *"What'll I do if I lose her?"*

Lindsey pulled in to the driveway of their home with Ben right behind her. After parking his truck, he hesitated a bit before getting out in order to try and gain his composure. Lindsey was waiting for him to join her before she entered the house. When he finally exited his truck, Lindsey could tell he'd been crying.

"Dude…I'm not going to let this destroy me, and I'll be *damned* if I spend the next couple of years watching you walk around with your tail between your legs. Get a grip and let's get on with it, okay? That's *not* the Ben Carson I married!" she added.

Ben stood and stared at whom he now knew had to be the strongest woman he had ever known. *"She's lost a child, and now…she's gonna' be faced with a fight for her own life,"* he thought to himself. *"What a self-sided sap she must think of me for only considering my own selfish concerns."*

"I promise I'll try to be strong, dear. That's, the best that I can offer," he said looking at his wife. "Let's go look at that pile of gold and dream, okay?"

"Deal…as Fizz would say," she said with emphasis.

The couple sat in front of the pile of gold bars staring at them like two wide-eyed children looking at a pile of gifts under a Christmas tree.

"Okay…enough," Ben finally said. "We need to get to work and get these catalogued." Every bar was inspected, weighed and photographed, both front and back. Each bar was unique in shape and markings. The hand-struck markings on the bars were very crude and irregular, and all placed in different positions and places on each bar.

When the chore was completed, Lindsey asked, "Are we just gonna' leave these lying here?"

"I don't suppose they're completely safe anywhere. Troy and Darlene should be here in a bit and I was thinking that maybe they should take half of them to their place. What are your thoughts?" Ben asked

"I think that's a good plan," she yawned…adding, "It's been a long day…I'm ready for bed."

"Okay, dear. Are you gonna' go to work tomorrow?"

"Why wouldn't I? I'm not gonna' sit around thinking and let this thing consume me, okay?"

"I understand, dear." Ben said.

"What are you going to do?" Lindsey asked.

"I'm gonna' call work tomorrow morning and explain the situation. I'll be back on the job Monday morning."

"I think that's the best plan," Lindsey said. She gave Ben a kiss. "I'm beat…see you in the morning. Let's don't dwell on this, okay, Ben?" she added before going off to bed.

Ben sat alone staring at the mural on the wall and the gold bars piled in front of it, thinking to himself… *"These men were fighting and dying horrible deaths over these riches. I used to think that I'd do the same thing. I've risked a lot to recover what these men were fighting to keep. I guess the battle doesn't change much over the centuries except for the realization that the treasure's not the reason for the fight…it's life…the fight is for life!"*

Ben's thoughts were interrupted by a knock at the door.

"Anybody home?" Troy hollered.

"Yeah…come on in, dude." Troy and Darlene entered the room where Ben was in deep thought.

Not seeing Lindsey in the room, Darlene immediately asked, "Where's your better half?"

"She's turned-in for the evening…she's worn out."

"At seven o'clock?" Darlene replied. "How did things go with the Doctor today?"

"Lindsey's told me not to dwell on it, guys…when she's ready, she'll tell you, okay?"

"Okay…okay, not a problem," Troy replied. "What did you and Fizz decide?"

"Well…" Ben began…"we have a few options. Fizz took a gold bar to the east coast and talked with the folks over there who have a legal permit with the State. I haven't heard how that went, yet," Ben explained. "I expect to hear from him this evening. Listen up…I want you and Darlene to take half of these bars to your place. I don't feel good with the entire pile here in one place, and I really can't think of a safe place to keep them. Here's that trouble with treasure thing again," he added.

Troy chuckled. "Yeah…amazing how *that* keeps coming up." Troy and Ben took half of the bars and loaded them into Troy and Darlene's work van.

"You need help with unloading them on your end, dude?" Ben asked.

"We got it," Troy replied. "We got it."

"Hey, dude…we need to make sure Marley's taken care of, okay?"

"Uhhm...of course we will. That's, what we told him. Why are you reminding me of that?" Troy asked.

"I just wanna' be sure that the promise is kept, that's all."

"Why wouldn't we keep our promise?" Troy thought to himself as the couple was leaving to go home.

After Darlene and Troy left, Ben was once again sitting alone pondering the next leg of life's journey while staring at the ships on the wall engaged in battle on the high seas. He was in deep thought when his phone rang.

"Dude…" he heard… "how'd your doctor visit go?" Fizz asked.

"Uhhh…not real good, Fizz. To tell ya' the truth, I'd rather explain the next time we're all together. I think Lindsey would prefer that, as well, okay?" There was a long silence on the other end.

Fizz finally asked, "So…is everything alright?"

"I'd be lying if I answered yes."

"Okay…I'll respect that," he replied.

"Tell me, Fizz…what'd you find out on the east coast today?"

"The folks on the east coast aren't willing to take on such a huge amount under their contract. I hate to agree with them but they say the State's not dumb enough to believe that all this came from the wreck under their contract…and they're probably right. I've reached out to some folks who sell to private collectors and expect to hear something soon."

"Alright…can we hook back up this weekend and talk some more?" Ben asked.

"Sounds good," Fizz replied. "See you this weekend."

As Ben sat in a trance thinking, he heard one of the screen doors open to the pool enclosure and turned to see Troy and Mick standing outside on the lanai peering through one of the sliding-glass doors.

"Come on in, guys. What you doing here?"

"We want to know what the doctor said," Mick answered.

"Sorry to be back here bothering you, Ben…" Troy added, "but, Darlene and I went down to the marina after leaving here earlier for a cold one and Mick was there. The two of us decided to come see you."

Ben stared at the floor for few moments before saying anything. He finally looked up at Troy and Mick.

"I'm gonna' tell you because it wouldn't be fair of us not to, but…you have to promise that you'll not spread this around nor let Lindsey know I've told you. Going forward, she doesn't wanna' be treated any different…okay?"

"Okay, Ben…we promise," both Troy and Mick replied. Ben told them everything he knew at that point. Afterward, Troy looked at Ben and said, "I feel like a horse just kicked me in the gut, Ben…I don't know what to say."

"I don't want you saying anything. We don't want to be treated any differently."

"I understand," Troy assured. Mick was speechless and fighting back tears.

"Mick, she'll tell you when she's ready, okay?" Ben explained. Mick shook her head, "yes", but still couldn't find any words. "Nothing changes right now…we still go to work and come home…just like always. I'm gonna' call work tomorrow and explain the situation to my boss. I'll be working from home the rest of this week and return to the Ocala area next week. Mick, I'd like for you to stay here while I'm gone, alright?"

"Sure, Ben…sure…whatever you need."

****

The weeks and months passed without a donor who matched Lindsey's blood type to be found. The doctors had given her medicine to slow down the progression of the condition but the monthly tests were showing signs of further distorting. She'd been given a special phone to keep with her at all times so that when a donor heart became available, the doctor would call her phone, whereas Lindsey would drop whatever she was doing and prepare for the procedure. She was given instructions to never be more than one hour from the hospital where the surgery would be performed.

Both Ben and Mick had noticed the fatigue and shortness of breath getting worse. She'd also had a few more of the light-headedness and fainting-spells. Ben made the decision for her to take a leave of absence from work…against Lindsey's will.

"It's best, dear," he explained "I worry about you driving."

Ben became more and more concerned for his wife as time dragged on and symptoms became more regular. He knew that finding a donor heart would take a miracle of some sorts.

Weekends were spent close to home waiting on that phone call. The boat that was usually out on the weekends hunting artifacts had been setting idle in the driveway for some months now. Fizz had been successful moving some of the bars through private collectors and money was coming in…a lot of money! More money than anyone in the group had ever seen.

Ben woke one Saturday morning and went down to his favorite room in the house where the mural of the ships had been painted. He sat and thought…and then he paced and thought. The thoughts of having to go through life without Lindsey were again flooding his head and he really wasn't sure he was strong enough to go through that. He thought of how strong Lindsey had been while dealing with the loss of their son and knew that he didn't have that same strength. He'd heard it said that after losing a child… the loss of a parent or spouse would be nothing in comparison. Ben thought about that to himself and concluded. *"I'm not sure I'm willing to test that theory."*

The time is now 9:30 a.m. Lindsey hadn't gotten out of bed yet when Ben walked upstairs to check on her. He pushed open the door.

"You awake, dear?"

"Yeah, I'm good…just lying here relaxing and listening to the mockingbirds sing."

"You want me to fix you some breakfast?" Ben asked.

"No…let's go out for breakfast."

"Okay…well then, you need to get moving or we'll be looking for lunch," he explained.

"Always in a hurry, Ben…why are you always in a hurry?" Lindsey asked.

The weekend passed and Monday morning found Ben getting ready to go earlier than usual.

"Oh…why you up so early?" Lindsey asked, yawning.

"Got an earlier than normal Monday meeting," Ben replied. He packed his usual stuff and kissed Lindsey good-bye, leaving the house and heading toward Tamiami Trail as usual. But this morning, he turned the big truck south instead of north. Ben had secretly made flight arrangements over the weekend with a commuter flight service out of Miami to take him to Jamaica.

The small aircraft landed in Kingston at noon, straight up. Ben cleared customs and stood outside the airport all alone. He pulled out his wallet where he had Henry the cabby's business card stashed, along with a large sum of cash, and dialed the man's number. Henry answered with…"It's always a beautiful day in Jamaica…how may I be of service?"

"Henry…it's, Ben Carson."

There was a bit of a silence on the other end and Henry finally asked…"Ben Carson…should I know you?"

"You got pretty wasted on my boat back in October with me and my friend Troy down in Freetown," Ben reminded him.

"Oh hell yeah, mon," Henry replied. "What can I help you with my friend?"

"Well…Henry…you told me if I needed anything, that you was the guy to talk to here on the island."

"That's right," Henry answered. "Whatever your needs are…I can help."

"I'm at the Kingston airport, and I need a ride. Once you get here, I'll explain further, okay? It's necessary for me to keep this visit a secret, though."

"No worries, mon…I'll be there in about an hour. I have another fare right now and will be there as soon as possible."

"That works for me, Henry…I'll be out front waiting." Ben sat patiently in front of the airport and waited for Henry's cab to pick him up. He spent the time thinking about Lindsey and how he needed to proceed with his plan.

When Henry's van pulled up to where Ben was awaiting, Henry stepped outside the van to load Ben's luggage.

"Traveling kind of light aren't you, boss?"

Ben shook Henry's hand. "Yes…once we get going, I'll explain." Henry tossed Ben's one small bag into the van and headed toward Freetown.

"Okay…" Henry asked…"what do you need from me other than a ride?"

"Troy and I stayed at a little dive just outside of Freetown a few years back," Ben explained. "I need a room there for a few nights. Then, I need to rent a boat with GPS along with some dive gear."

"Can do…can do, and can do." Henry picked up his phone and called the little motel Ben had described. "Angie, my love…Henry here," he said when his call was answered. "I have a friend who needs a room for a few nights with special rates…okay?" Ben could hear the other person talking but was unable to make what they were asking. Then, Henry said, "Male, Angie…my friend is male, but nothing funny, and yes…I remember telling you we'd do *that*, but business got hectic. Can we discuss this later, Angie? Now, is not the time." Henry assured the woman they'd discuss matters later before cutting off the call.

"Guess I'm not getting the special rate, huh Henry?" Ben laughed.

"Yah, mon," Henry laughed "Angie gonna' fix you up. I just forgot I had told her a few weeks back that I'd pick her up and take her to Kingston for a night out, and didn't do it. A better opportunity presented itself…ya' know, mon?"

"You don't have to explain to me, Henry. How 'bout stopping at the nearest dive shop so I can rent some gear… and, how about the boat?"

"What kind of boat you needing?"

"Something around 25-foot or so, I guess."

"My buddy, Lonnie, will be able to help with that."

"Is Lonnie's boat anywhere close to where Marley docks his?" Ben asked.

"No, mon. Why you ask?"

"Because Marley *cannot* know that I'm here under any circumstances, okay Henry?" Ben explained, emphasizing the fact. "I'm not doing anything underhanded that would hurt him. I think too much of him and his family to do that. You're just gonna' have to trust me on this...he can't know I'm here."

"Okay…okay," Henry replied. "I have no need to tell him."

"Thanks…I intend to tip pretty big while I'm here, so don't forget."

Henry procured the boat for the next morning for Ben and then stopped at the dive shop where Ben rented all the gear that he'd need. He'd brought a lot of cash with him so Lindsey wouldn't be able to see any on-line activity with their accounts which would give away the fact that he was in Jamaica.

Next, Henry drove Ben to the little motel where there was a beautiful woman setting out front. The woman was wearing a very short, tight skirt that showed every curve.

"Is that Angie?" Ben asked.

"Yeah, mon…that's her."

"Well, that better opportunity you were telling me about must have been a damn good one!" Ben told him.

When Angie saw Henry's van pull up in front of the motel, she got up from her chair and very seductively walked back toward the office, making certain that Henry was paying attention to her.

"She's doing that crap on purpose, mon…you know that, right?" Henry explained.

"I don't know, dude. But, I am sure she wants to be certain to show you what you missed out on."

"Angie, *baby*!" Henry hollered once he'd parked the van. Angie turned around, looked at Henry and then walked inside without saying a word.

"Now, there's a woman scorned, if ever I saw one," Ben commented. He instructed Henry to take the dive gear and load it on the boat at Lonnie's place for him and then passed him a couple hundred dollars.

"There must be a pretty good tip in there…" Henry suggested..

"I told you…I'm gonna' take good care of you while I'm here, but you need to take good care of me, and keep quiet about me being here to Marley."

"No worries," Henry assured.

"Pick me up tomorrow morning around eight," Ben instructed.

"I'll be here."

It was getting late in the evening and Ben was beat from the driving, the flight and the stress of the whole matter. He just wanted to get checked in and get to his room for a hot shower before lying down. He had tomorrow already planned out and knew what he needed to accomplish. He prayed that things would go as he needed. Ben sent a text to Lindsey saying, "*I love you!*", as he typically did while out of town, and then turned-in for the evening. It wasn't long before he got a text back saying, "*I love you, more!*", which was also typical. Ben felt certain after receiving the text that Lindsey didn't suspect a thing.

After a long, restful night's sleep, Ben awoke the next morning at 6 a.m. He stood in front of the mirror for a while looking at himself conjuring-up memories of his and

Lindsey's marriage…the good times they all had while the boys were little and growing up, and just how wonderful Lindsey had fulfilled his life. Tears came to his eyes while he reminisced, but none rolled down his cheek. He wiped them from his eyes and then removed the razor from his bag to cut the mustache and goatee off that he'd worn for years. He deemed it necessary just in case he ran into Marley or possibly even the little big man. They, may possibly be the only two who might recognize him and question why he has returned.

Henry arrived right on time at eight a.m., just as instructed. Ben jumped in the van. "Hey mon…you're not the guy I came to pick up," Henry joked.

Ben laughed. "Turns out Angie doesn't like facial hair, Henry."

"Get out of here! Are you serious?" he replied.

Ben laughed again. "Not serious, dude…let's go to the boat."

"Here we go," he said, pulling the van out of the motel parking lot.

In no time, Henry pulled up in front of a better than average looking home, especially for Freetown.

"I thought the boat would be at a marina…" Ben said.

"No, mon…Lonnie keeps the boat behind his home."

"*Better yet,*" Ben thought to himself.

The pair walked behind the house where the boat was tied to a dock. The dive gear had been loaded, as Ben had instructed, and Lonnie had seen to it that the boat was full of fuel.

"Two hundred dollars for the day," Henry said.

"That's fine," Ben agreed. Ben handed Henry a hundred for his services, and then two hundred for Lonnie's boat. "Do we need to talk with Lonnie first?"

"No need," Henry explained. "He's off making other deals somewhere…you're good to go."

"I'll call you when I get back in, dude…thanks for everything" Ben added before shoving off.

Once Ben had cleared the canal and was in the bay he stopped to program the GPS. He pulled the piece of paper from his wallet where he'd written down the coordinates of where he and Troy had stashed the rest of the gold they had recovered. Once the numbers were in, he hit the button that said, *navigate to,* and he was on his way. With the water so smooth this morning, Ben knew he could make good time. He pushed the throttle full-forward and the boat responded by jumping up on-plane for maximum speed. The GPS screen indicated to Ben that he'd be at his destination in thirty-four minutes. He kept the throttle full-forward and was floating over the top of a pile of gold at exactly the time that the device had given.

Ben tossed the anchor in order to hold the boat over the spot. Then, he suited-up for the dive. Once on the bottom, the coral-heads all looked the same. He knew that the shifting sand had most likely covered their pile so he fanned the sand desperately under the head where he thought the pile must lie.

He'd spent close to an hour beneath the water, practically depleting the compressed oxygen tank supply. He had to surface to retrieve another tank. He'd only rented two tanks so he knew he needed to find the pile of gold quickly on the next dive. While on the surface, he took another look at the GPS screen. "*Should be right over the top of it,*" he thought to himself. He looked through the boat for something that he could probe the sand with. He finally found a fiberglass fishing-rod that would work great. He broke the rod in half and took the smaller section down with him to probe around the coral-head where he thought the pile should have been. When probing, it's fairly easy to distinguish when the probe has passed through the finer sand layer and enters the coarser shell layer below. Once back on the bottom, he started the process by probing down until the coarser layer was struck and then moved along, knowing the pile should only be covered by finer sand.

    Ben had probed about twenty holes when he finally met resistance about twelve inches deep, piercing only the fine sand. Next, he moved the probe over about six inches and probed, once again hitting the resistance at about the same depth. Repeating the process in the area four more times and getting the same results, he began fanning the sand away. In no time, he was looking at the yellow gleam of the gold bars he and Troy had removed from the wreck-site. He realized that he'd underestimated how much sand would have shifted in covering the pile. He grabbed one bar and shot to the surface. He thought to himself, *"One bar should be enough to complete the next step of my plan."* By the time he'd surfaced with the bar and climbed back into the boat, the time was approaching noon. Ben had spent more time relocating the pile of treasure than he'd anticipated. He sat and thought about the next step in his plan and knew that it was the make-or-break part of the plan. He also thought that the more time he spent in Jamaica…the more likely the possibility that he'd be discovered there. He pulled the anchor up and moved off the site while thinking through his next move. He finally reached the decision to go back in and carry out the next step of his plan tomorrow which would give him a full day to see it through, if needed. He then removed the coordinates from the GPS and headed the boat toward Freetown.

Once he'd returned to Lonnie's place, Ben called Henry to be certain that he was free to pick him up.

"I can be there in ten minutes," was Henry's response.

"Perfect," Ben replied. "See you then." Ben was tying the boat to the dock behind the house when Henry walked back to meet him. "I need these tanks filled, Henry."

"No worries, mon," Henry replied helping Ben remove them from the boat.

"Henry…let Lonnie know that I'll need the boat again tomorrow, if you would please, and…oh yeah…let him know I owe him for a fishing pole I broke."

"You broke a pole?"

"Yeah…I hooked a big one," Ben explained.

"I'm not gonna' ask," Henry replied. The guys loaded the tanks into Henry's van and headed toward the motel as Ben had instructed.

"The day is still young, Mr. Carson. Would you like to go to a watering-hole somewhere before going back to the motel?"

"No…no thanks, Henry. But, I do need you to stop somewhere and go in to get me something to eat, and then take me back to the motel."

Henry stopped by a little "Mom and Pop" eating joint to get something for Ben to eat and then returned him to the motel.

"Same time tomorrow morning, Henry," Ben instructed as he handed Henry another hundred dollar bill. "Thanks, mon…I'll have these tanks filled and loaded for you."

Thanks, dude. See you in the morning."

Ben went straight to his motel room where he removed the gold bar from the hip pouch that he'd taken with him and threw it on the bed. The small, heavy bar sunk a bit into the bedding where he left it while he went to get a much needed shower. After showering, Ben flopped down on the bed and thought for the next hour about the next phase of his plan. *"This next move could go very badly,"* he thought to himself. *"There's no way of knowing which way it might go. It could very well be the end of everything."*

Later that evening, Ben texted, *"I love you,"* to Lindsey. In just a few seconds he got back the expected, *"Love you more!"*

CHAPTER 12

Ben Shakes Hands With The Boogeyman

The alarm on Ben's phone woke him Wednesday morning at 7 a.m. He laid still for just a bit rehearsing in his head the way he'd hoped and envisioned things would go today, not fully knowing what to expect. After getting out of bed and ready for the day, the last thing he did before exiting the motel was to strap the hip pack on and secure the gold bar inside.

Henry was right on time at 8 a.m. Ben jumped into the van for the short ride to the boat.

"Good-morning, Ben Carson! Did you sleep good last night?"

"I slept fine Henry…and, a good-morning to you, by the way."

"Angie's not coming to see you at night, is she?"

"No, I haven't seen Angie since I checked in, Henry. However, if she *had* come to see me… I suppose you know that you'd never have a chance with her ever again," Ben joked.

"Give me a break, mon," Henry laughed.

By the time the two had finished their locker room trash talk, the van pulled up in front of Lonnie's home.

"She's ready to go, boss. Tanks are filled and loaded, just as you had requested."

"Good man, Henry," Ben said, handing Henry another three-hundred dollars…one-hundred for Henry and two-hundred for Lonnie.

"Henry, I'm not quite certain what time I'll be returning today. It may be late, or it may be within a few hours…I'm just not sure."

"Just give ole Henry a call and I'll get here as quickly as possible."

"Okay Henry…thanks," Ben said as he walked around behind the house to the boat. He climbed into the boat and untied it from the dock. He wouldn't need to program the GPS today for he knew his destination. Making his way out the short canal to the bay, he jumped the boat up onto plane for a short ride south to the Boogeyman's island. Ben had decided that he'd simply pull right alongside the dock like he owned the place and let happen what may.

When he arrived at the Boogeyman's dock, he did just that. As he was tying-off to the dock he heard the sound of barking and snarling coming straight at him. Looking up the hill he saw two large Doberman Pinschers running toward him as fast as they could. They were clearly coming to rip him apart. He quickly untied the boat and shoved away from the dock, fired up the engine and moved a safe distance back away from the dock. Then, he sat for a few minutes watching the barking dogs, drooling and growling. He was wondering whether this was the end of the plan or not when he looked up the hill again and saw two very large Jamaican bruisers coming to see what had alerted the dogs. The closer the two menacing figures got to the dock…it was clear that these guys could have been defensive lineman on a professional football team. When they reached the dock, the two giant men stood staring at Ben as if he was out of his mind for not turning around and dismissing himself from the situation. The two dogs continued snapping and snarling until one of the huge men spoke.

"That's enough…that's enough…good dogs!" With that said, the dogs sat down but were clearly ready to attack if the situation deteriorated. "You're trespassing…you have no business here…you need to leave…now!" one of the brutes shouted.

"Can't you just hear me out?" Ben asked.

"You don't have anything to say to me," one of the guys said as he pulled back his vest to reveal a shoulder slung sidearm. Ben raised his hands and said wait…wait…wait! I'm not armed. You wouldn't shoot an unarmed man would you?"

"That never stopped us before," the big man replied as he and his partner laughed. "Now get yourself outta' here before I shoot your boat full of holes!"

"I've got something I think your boss may be interested in," Ben told the behemoths. "If you'll let me get a little closer…I'll toss it over for you to see. Maybe you can see it from there. It's one of many gold bars from a shipwreck," Ben told them as he held the bar up for them to see. After a few seconds passed, one of the men shouted to the dogs.

"Brutus…Maggie…up the hill and stand guard!" The dogs sprang to their feet and ran up the hill a short distance, staying in sight of the dock and the event that was unfolding there. "Come on in a little closer," one of the men shouted. Ben pulled within ten feet of the dock. By this time both men had revealed their sidearms. "Close enough. Now…toss that over here!" Ben tossed the bar up onto the dock. One of the men stooped to picked it up while the other man kept his eyes trained on Ben. The man who picked up the bar carried it to the lands end of the dock and held it under what appeared to be a surveillance camera. The man was talking to someone whom Ben could only think was the Boogeyman. Then, the man who was standing beneath the camera turned and asked Ben a question. "What is it that you want?"

"I want to talk with whomever you're talking with, I think," Ben replied.

"Why should we allow you this conversation?" the big man asked.

"Well, like I said...I know where there's a fairly nice pile of these, and...I need a favor," Ben explained.

Again, the man at the camera appeared to be talking to himself. After a few minutes the man hollered..."Brutus...Maggie, on up the hill and stand down!" The dogs turned and ran up the hill out of sight while Ben was ordered to tie-off his boat. He did as he was ordered, tying-off the boat to the dock. Once on the dock and standing closer to the two men, they appeared to be even larger. He felt like a mere speck of a man standing next to these big dudes. "Turn around and put your hands behind your back," one of the men ordered. Ben complied and one of the men tied his hands with zip ties.

"That's really not necessary," Ben said.

"If you're goin' up that hill it is," he was told.

"Okay. Okay," Ben replied. "How 'bout the dogs...are they caged?"

"No, they've been told to stand down and they wouldn't dare disobey a command," one of the men said. "Trust me though...all I have to do is shout, *Chaos,* and they'll rip you limb from limb."

"Okay...far be it from me to test their obedience," Ben said as he was nudged to proceed up the hill.

The walk up the steep hill was brutal for Ben with his hands tied behind his back. The big mansion was now coming into view along with a tall, ornate cast-iron fence covered in cactus and other indigenous plants surrounding the entire complex. The whole compound was built on a windswept rocky formation that looked like something right out of a Count Dracula movie. As the group approached...the big gates opened creating creaking and popping noises that added to the creepiness of the situation. Once inside the gate, Ben could see the dogs standing in front of a big door that was clearly the main entrance to the mansion. The big men continued to nudge Ben closer to the big door and the dogs.

"Are you sure these guys are okay with this...have they been fed today?" Ben asked.

"Don't make any stupid moves and you'll be fine," one of the men said. When Ben walked up the steps to the big door, it swung open with a long, eerie, creaking sound to reveal what could only be explained as a museum. As he was escorted through the entryway, he made mental notes of artifacts from around the world. He saw rare Egyptian pieces, African shields and crude weapons, Central and South American Inca and Mayan displays, Ming Dynasty porcelains, pre-Columbian pottery, Aztec treasures from Mexico, medieval armor and weaponry and most importantly, a lot of shipwreck artifacts. At that moment, Ben knew that what he had to offer the Boogeyman was right down the ole boy's alley.

The two big brutes lead Ben to a door just off the right side of the main entry room. As they approached the door, Ben heard a voice coming from somewhere on a speaker, "He may enter...remove the restraints."

One of the big men cut the ties from Ben's wrists, opened the door and said, "We'll be waiting right here... don't forget." And then, in a very low voice, the other big fella said, "Yeah...that's right. And whatever you do... *don't* use the word, *chaos,* in your conversation!" he told Ben, handing the gold bar back to him to present to their boss.

"I'll try to remember that," Ben said as he was nudged again to enter the room behind the door. He walked into the room and was once again taken aback by the thousands, if not hundreds of thousands of dollars worth of rare artifacts from all over the world on display inside the huge room. Ben stood still while looking around for the source of the voice that he'd heard out in the entryway.

"Over here…" Ben heard. "Come over here." Ben turned his head toward the voice and saw a small statured man sitting in a large chair. As he walked closer to the man, Ben spotted a small Yorkshire Terrier sitting in the man's lap wearing a pink ribbon in its hair. The cute little dog growled as Ben neared her master. "It's fine, Izzie," the man said reassuring the little dog as he rubbed her ears. "You'll have to excuse her…we don't get many visitors. In fact…you're the only unexpected visitor we've had in years. If you hadn't had that gold bar…most likely, your boat would have been shot full of holes," the little man added.

"Well, at least she won't rip me limb from limb," Ben said.

"Oh…Don't underestimate her," the man said. "She has the heart of a lion...she fears nothing…not even Brutus and Maggie, whom I know you've already met. This little girl lets them know who the boss is."

As Ben moved yet closer to the man, he could see that he was a very small man who looked to be in his seventies, maybe early eighties. Ben surveyed the room some more to be certain the two of them were alone. He finally asked. "So, you're the Boogeyman?"

"Boo!" the man said, laughing a bit. "Hard to believe, I know. Have a seat and let's talk about why you came here." The two men shook hands before beginning their conversation.

"I've been coming to this area for the last four years in search of a treasure-laden Spanish galleon that went down during a hurricane in 1670." Ben handed the gold bar to the man. "There's several more where this one came from."

"So, it would appear that you've found the wreck-site," the man stated.

"Not the main site…at least no yet," Ben told him, fibbing a bit. "We've found what's called a bump-site where the ship bottomed while in a trough between two waves. The bottom was ripped open enough to let some of the contents spill out. That, is where this bar and several more about the same size were found."

"So…I suppose you've come to ask me if I'm interested in purchasing some of the bars and artifacts?" the man asked.

"No," Ben replied. "In fact, sir…I really didn't even know that you were a collector until I entered your home. I must say that you have quite an impressive collection. How long does it take to amass a collection like this?"

"You haven't seen anything," the man told Ben. "I've been collecting for fifty years. I buy from other collectors and the black market. When I was younger…I was like you, I suppose. I traveled the world in search of lost riches and adventure when I wasn't doing what actually paid the bills."

"So, if you don't mind me asking, sir…what paid the bills?"

The man replied to Ben's question. "I was a surgeon… world renowned. I was all over the world performing tedious and dangerous surgeries during the time when it was said to be impossible. I performed the surgeries and then picked up artifacts from wherever I was in the world at the time," he explained. "I'm retired now and only consult when necessary."

Ben thought to himself while the man was talking. *Well, the surgeon part of the story's correct."*

The man interrupted Ben's thoughts. "So…if you're not here to sell artifacts…what brings you here?"

"Well, sir…" Ben started. "My wife, Lindsey…whom you would love, by the way…because she loves adventure and artifact collecting more than I do. Well, sir…she's very ill, and I was hoping I could get your help and compensate you with more of these gold bars."

"You know, son…" the man continued…"I'm not really interested in the value of the gold. I'm more interested in the artifacts themselves. This ship of which you're looking for…surely you have an idea of what it was carrying to have spent four years looking for it."

"Yes, sir…I do know. I have the manifest of the cargo that was loaded before the ship left Portobelo." Ben told the man the complete story as the man listened intently. Ben finished his narrative with…"And the most intriguing part of the story is, that a solid gold altar was reported to have been aboard, but not recorded on the manifest."

The man was hanging onto Ben's every word. When Ben finished telling his story, the man asked, after thinking a bit. "This gold altar of which you speak…was there an architect by the name of Montessori in your research?" Ben was amazed with the man's question and answered immediately.

"Yes! Hernando Montessori…so you've heard the story?"

"Of course I have. Whomever finds that altar will have made the King Tut tomb discovery take a back seat. I'm sure you're aware that there *are* legalities that have to be overcome in order to take ownership of a wreck. Do you have legal rights?"

"No, sir…I don't."

"Do you think the wreck is close by here, at this location?"

Again, Ben stretched the truth a bit and said, "I'm guessing the main pile should be on the Pedro Banks somewhere about fifty miles southwest of here."

The man thought for a few minutes before replying. "I own the flea-bitten jackals who run this sovereignty," he explained. "I *could* see to it that your group would be given the rights to a salvage…with strings attached, of course. Now…back to your wife. What exactly is her condition and how is it that you think I can help her."

"Well, sir," Ben began. "In layman's terms, she has the broken-heart disease from the loss of our son."

The man thought for a bit before replying. "Acute stress induced Cardiomyopathy. I'm familiar with it. How long ago was she diagnosed?"

"I guess the actual diagnosis was made about four or five months ago now, but the symptoms have been there for going on a year now. Long story short, she needs a heart transplant."

The man thought for a while and asked, "I suppose she's already on a donor list, isn't she?"

"She is. The problem is…the blood type. She's A-negative. We've been told that only about six percent of people have that blood type…making the possibility of finding a donor heart pretty slim."

"That's an accurate statement," the man said. "So… what makes you think I can help with that?" the man asked, sounding a bit agitated at this point.

"Okay…here's what I was thinking…" Ben said. Two hours passed while the men worked out the details of Ben's plan. After a few moments of silence, Ben finally asked, "Is this possible, or do I need to work from another angle?"

"The only other angle you have, is to wait on a donor heart that may never come," the man explained. "I have associates all over the world," the man continued. "I'd have to get them involved, which would require money, and a lot of it for what you're asking."

"How much money are we talking about?"

"At a minimum, you're going to have to come up with four million just to get them onboard with this," the man answered, watching Ben for his reaction.

"Deal!" Ben replied without a flinch or hesitation. "I'll have enough gold bars on your dock tomorrow afternoon to cover that."

The man shook Ben's hand and said, "I'll start contacting people tomorrow after seeing the gold."

The two men walked out of the room talking about artifacts. They walked through the entryway stopping and talking about every display they passed. The man was impressed with Ben's knowledge of history and stories that backed up his knowledge. As they walked through the big door to the outside, the man ordered one of the big fellas to bring the golf cart around. The man took Ben down the hill to the dock. Ben again shook his hand and told him that he'd be back with the gold as promised, tomorrow afternoon.

"Oh yeah…" Ben added. "Can you call off Brutus and Maggie when I get here with the delivery tomorrow."

The man laughed. "I'll see to that."

"Okay…thanks," Ben said reaching to pet Izzie the little Yorky that never left site of her master. Izzie raised a lip to reveal some tiny teeth and made a small little growl. "Okay. Okay…" Ben said. "I'll just be on my way now."

Ben jumped in the boat, untied it from the dock and made his way back to Lonnie's dock feeling as if a major load had been removed from his heart. Not only had he accomplished getting his plan in place to help Lindsey, but he'd also inadvertently found a way to salvage the remaining treasure, possibly accomplishing it legally with the Boogeyman's help, of all people. He couldn't wait to share the news with Fizz but was unsure how he'd accomplish that, without uncovering the fact that he'd been back to Jamaica. *"The plot thickens,"* he thought to himself.

Ben informed Henry that he'd need Lonnie's boat one more day and to pick him up again the same time tomorrow morning. He also informed Henry that he'd be flying back to the States Friday morning on an early flight with Dontavious and would need a ride to the airport.

Ben sat in his room that evening and did some quick math to determine how many bars he'd need to deliver to the Boogeyman in order to get him to begin contacting his associates in order to make things happen. He decided twenty-eight of the bars should get him to the four-million dollar number that the Boogeyman had requested. He'd go out tomorrow morning, raise the bars and deliver them to his new friend, the Boogeyman.

Ben also had a few other details to work on that evening in order to complete this leg of the plan. He sat at a small desk in the motel and worked on a note. The note was very difficult for him to write but he knew that it needed to be done to explain some things. Once the note had been written, he folded it up and placed it inside a small dry box that he'd brought from home with him for safe keeping. Once this task had been completed, he was both physically and mentally exhausted. Then, he showered, sent his usual text to Lindsey and collapsed on the bed for the night.

Thursday morning found Ben raring to go to get this deal moved along a little further. Henry pulled up at 8 a.m. sharp and they were on their way.

"Dude…" Ben asked. "Does that Mom and Pop diner we stopped at earlier in the week serve breakfast?"

"Yah, mon…best breakfast on the island. You need to stop there?"

"Yeah…I do! I'm hungry as hell, dude. I didn't eat all day yesterday. Angie fixed me supper night before last at her place, but she didn't call me last night for supper."

Henry let out a thunderous laugh. "I know you're full-of-it this morning! You're just pulling my leg, mon. Angie can't boil water without a recipe!"

"Well, a woman that looks that good doesn't need to cook anyway, I suppose," Ben laughed.

Okay. Okay, mon. I know I screwed-up when I stood her up…stop rubbing it in now, okay?" Henry chuckled.

Henry pulled into the little diner and Ben instructed him to go in and get him something to go. Henry walked in the colorful establishment and reappeared a few minutes later with a styrofoam box full of hot food, to go. Ben opened the box to see scrambled eggs with some kind of meat in it and fried potatoes. He dug into the food and finally asked Henry what the chewy meat was in the eggs.

"That, is conch, mon. It's the diner's specialty. Why do you ask?"

"Conch…for breakfast?" Ben replied.

"Yeah, mon…you don't like it?"

"Yeah! Yeah it's good, dude. Just a little different… that's all. These eggs…are they chicken eggs?"

"Yeah, mon," Henry replied.

"Okay. I just wanted to be sure they weren't turtle eggs or something."

Ben finished his breakfast as Henry was pulling up in front of Lonnie's house. Once again, Ben paid Henry for his services and handed him another days rent on the boat, as well. Ben jumped into the boat and got underway to make another withdrawal from the pile of gold. Once clear of the canal and in the bay, Ben stopped the boat and re-entered the coordinates into the GPS. The water was again flat and the morning was beautiful as Ben was full-throttle to the site.

Once on site, Ben suited-up and fell off the gunnel backwards into the turquoise water. When he touched down on the bottom, this time he re-located the pile with ease and began hauling gold bars up until he'd retrieved twenty-seven bars. Then, he climbed back into the boat and re-positioned the vessel over the wreck-site. He suited back up, removed the dry box with the notes from the hip pack and attached the box to a small orange float that he'd found on the boat with some fishing line. Then, he dropped back down into the water and concealed the entire package beneath some ballast stones in order to hold it in place and then re-surfaced.

Ben remembered that he'd told the Boogeyman that the wreck-site was a fifty mile run out from his island. He thought that if he made his way to the island now to deliver the gold…the Boogeyman might question him again on the location of the site. He decided to kill a couple of hours just floating around and relaxing before heading to the Boogeyman's Island to delivery the goods. He weighed anchor and simply floated with the current while in deep thought, pondering all that he'd accomplished this week. He thought about Lindsey and how life can change from adventure and jubilation to heartbreak in the blink of an eye.

A couple hours passed quickly. Ben fired-up the engine and turned the boat toward the Boogeyman's Island. As he was pulling up to the dock he kept a wary eye out for Brutus and Maggie. He tied the boat to the dock and waited, knowing that he'd be seen on the surveillance cameras. It wasn't long before Ben saw the golf cart making its way down the hill with the small elderly man and one of the behemoth bodyguards as chauffeur. The pair pulled the cart right out onto the dock alongside where the boat was tied-off.

"You have a delivery for me?" the Boogeyman asked.

Ben began unloading gold bars while the other two men looked on with amazement. When he'd finished unloading the last bar, he said, "There's twenty-seven bars…and…with the one you already have in your possession…that makes twenty-eight. That's gonna' be real close to the four million you requested at current spot value…five times that when artifact value is considered." Ben remembered what Fizz had said after unloading the bars from the compressor tank that they'd smuggled back to the States.

"How much more did you say was on the ship?" the Boogeyman asked.

"Enough gold, silver, jewelry and emeralds to fill this boat full several times. She is without a doubt one of the richest wrecks laying in these waters. There should also be several bronze cannon at the site when it's located…and hopefully the gold altar," Ben added.

"I don't have a bronze cannon. That, would be a great addition to my collection," the small man remarked.

"I'm sure it would," Ben agreed.

"Well…it looks as though you kept your end of the bargain," the Boogeyman told Ben. "I'll start making phone calls and getting things moving for my end of the deal. You will need to be patient with me…finding an associate who will complete your request could take some time."

"How long is, *some time?*" Ben asked.

"Possibly a month, maybe two. You need to understand…" the Boogeyman continued to explain… "there will be piles of documents and files to create in order to pull this off. It's not going to happen over night. Go home and you'll be hearing from either myself or one of my associates."

"Okay, sir," Ben replied. "Can I get your name, sir?" Ben asked.

"We can skip *that* information," the man said. "It's not necessary."

Ben shook the man's hand once again and untied the boat. "I'll be waiting," Ben hollered as he pulled away from the dock. When Ben was well away from the dock he stopped the boat and deleted the coordinates from the GPS. He thought hard on a lot of things as he made his way back to Lonnie's dock. He wondered if the man had just ripped him off. He thought to himself… *"What if we find a donor heart before the man gets back in touch with me. I'm pretty sure he's not gonna give me a refund."* Then, he answered his own concerns with… *"If a donor heart comes available before the man gets back in touch with me…that, would be a prayer answered. Screw the gold."* He also thought, *"The man is interested enough in this project for his own gain, that he surely would try his best to keep his end of the bargain if it comes to that."* Ben shook the negative thoughts from his head and before he knew it, he was tying the boat off to the dock behind Lonnie's house. He made the phone call to Henry to return him to the motel and Henry was there to pick him up in short order. The pair loaded the dive equipment into Henry's van and headed toward the motel.

"Can you return this stuff?" Ben asked Henry.

"Sure, mon... no worries."

As Henry was dropping Ben off at the motel, Ben said, "Don't forget my flight tomorrow, dude."

"Yah, mon...I got you covered... you okay?" Henry asked.

"I'm okay, Henry. I'm just beat and need a shower. See you in the morning," Ben said as he stepped out of the van.

When Ben reached the motel room, he looked into the mirror and thought, *"I've got some explaining to do as to why I shaved my face after all these years."* He showered and lay on the bed for what seemed to be hours simply thinking. His thoughts were always about Lindsey and how much he loved her. He couldn't help but get a little emotional as a few tears began to roll down his cheeks. He sent the nightly text to her along with an added note...
"You had my heart from the very start...see you tomorrow!"

CHAPTER 13

When Death We Don't Part

Ben awoke Friday morning with excitement knowing he'd return home to Lindsey before the day was over. Packing what little he'd brought with him, he prepared to leave and then walked to the office to check out. When he arrived at the front desk, he was surprised to see Angie standing behind the counter.

"Good morning," she said with an angelic voice.

"And a good morning to you, Angie!" Angie looked at Ben with surprise. "How is it that you know my name, sir?

"You checked me in Monday when my buddy Henry dropped me off here. He told me *all* about you."

"Henry!" She said with a hint of disdain in her voice.

"You're all he talks about…all good stuff, I might add. You must be pretty special to him?"

"Huh…*that* two-timing womanizer! I wouldn't give him the time of day."

As Angie completed Ben's check out, Henry pulled up to the motel and honked his horn to let Ben know he was waiting.

"Okay, thank you my dear…but really… you *may* want to give Henry another chance. I'm pretty sure he knows he messed up," Ben said defending Henry's character.

"You tell Henry that I'll let him dream of me…that's all he's getting!"

Ben chuckled. "I'll be sure to tell him…and again, thank you for the stay."

Ben left the motel office and walked out to Henry's van. He knew he had another hair-raising ride to the Kingston airport ahead of him.

"Good morning, Henry," Ben said as he climbed in the passenger side of the van.

"Good morning to you too, Mr. Carson."

"Guess who checked me out this morning Henry?"

"Uhhhm…let me guess. I'll bet it was Angie. Is she working the desk this morning?"

"You are correct my friend," Ben said with a slight chuckle. "She was wearing another one of those tight skirts, too…looked like a burlap bag full of bobcats. I wish I knew where she gets those skirts…my wife would look *great* in one of those!" he added with emphasis on the word, great.

"Damn!" Henry said, envisioning what Ben was explaining. "So…what was said?" Henry asked.

"Wha-da-ya' mean?" Ben asked, playing dumb.

"You know what I mean…was anything said about me?"

"Yeah…yeah, she did mention you dude. She said something about trying to hook up with you again. She had nothing but good things to say about you Henry. I think you should make another attempt to woo her, dude."

"I *might* just do that…thanks, Mr. Carson." Henry replied.

When the van pulled up in front of the airport, Henry had a few parting words for Ben. "Be sure and keep your clothes on for the duration of the flight, Mr. Carson. Dante's clientele is known to get a bit freaky on the flight back to the States."

"I'll keep that in mind Henry. And, don't forget…I was never here…okay?" Ben reminded him.

"Yah mon…I don't know anything!"

"Funny…that's what Angie said about you this morning, dude." Ben laughed and handed Henry five one-hundred dollar bills. "Like I said before…I was never here." Then, he turned to catch his flight.

Ben climbed aboard the small commuter aircraft and grabbed the first available seat. It was clear to him that the other passengers had been enjoying themselves at the resorts and obviously had already consumed a number of Bloody Marys earlier this morning. The female passengers were all comparing their lack of tan lines. The flight was very entertaining, to say the least!

As soon as the flight touched down in Miami, Ben jumped on a shuttle to take him to where he'd left his pick up truck before flying out of the country. The ride over across Alligator Alley was always a monotonous trip with nothing to see for miles but a sea of grass that makes up the Everglades. Every once in a while you might catch a glimpse of a gator lying on the bank of the ditches that run along both sides of the highway.

Ben pulled into his drive just before 2 p.m. He walked into the garage and through to the downstairs area of the house where everyone usually hangs out, but the room was empty. He walked upstairs and found Mick sitting on the upstairs deck reading a book. He opened the sliding glass door to the deck and stood in the doorway.

Mick looked up from her book. "Welcome home, Ben!" She was taken aback after seeing Ben's clean-shaven face. "Wow...*that's* a different look. What did you do *that* for?"

"Just needed a change...that's all. Where's Lindsey?"

"She's lying down…she sleeps quite a bit lately," Mick replied.

Ben walked into the bedroom where Lindsey was sleeping and laid down beside her.

"I'm home, dear," he whispered, rubbing her cheek with his chin.

Lindsey looked up into his face. "Ben, I told you years ago that I prefer you with whiskers. Why did you do that?"

"Just needed a change, that's all dear."

"Well, then…let it grow back," she insisted.

"Okay…okay, dear. I'll let it grow back," he assured her. "How've you been feeling?"

"Okay," she replied. "Just needed a little nap…I'll be out in a few minutes." Ben jumped up off the bed.

"Okay dear…how about we go to the marina this afternoon and stay on the boat this weekend?"

"That, sounds like fun! Give me another few minutes or so and I'll get ready, okay?"

"Deal!" Ben said, and then he walked back out onto the deck where Mick was reading her book. She put her book down when she heard the sliding glass door open.

"Have you heard from Fizz this week, Ben?"

"No," he replied looking at his phone as if to be checking missed calls. "Why?" he asked,

"He stopped by here during mid-week and picked up some more gold bars and left a pile of money." Mick explained. "Lindsey's worried about having all this cash lying around the house."

"Sounds like a good problem to have. I have to talk with Fizz this weekend before heading back up north next week. Troy and I'll get it figured out."

"Okay…but Lindsey doesn't need anything else to worry about, that's all I'm sayin', Ben," Mick explained.

I understand, Mick…I'll deal with it," he assured.

After Lindsey's nap, she got ready for the evening and walked out on to the deck looking as beautiful as she had the day she and Ben married.

"Wow, you look nice, dear."

"Thank you, Ben. Are you going to do a little something with yourself? You must have had a rough week. You're looking a bit dog-eared," she added.

"Thanks for the compliment, dear," Ben said sarcastically.

Ben, Lindsey and Mick climbed into his truck and made the short drive to the marina. Before leaving, Ben had called Troy to let him know that he needed to discuss a few things with him.

When Ben's red truck rolled in to the marina…Big John immediately set up rounds on the table where a sign was now hanging that read, **Treasure Hunters, Pirates and Bullshitters Only**." When Ben saw the sign, he laughed.

"I guess everyone in this establishment could be accused of one or two of those titles. Nice touch, John. I like it."

When Troy and Darlene arrived and joined the group, Ben immediately went into the conversation of the cash.

"I hear Captain Fizz stopped by this week to pick up some more bars and dropped a large amount of cash."

"How much is a large amount?" Troy asked.

"I don't know, dude. But, it's enough to make the girls worry about having it around."

"Well, what's the difference between having the bars lying around versus cash, Ben?"

"I know, dude…I feel the same way…but, the girls are worried about the cash and I suppose they're right. The amount is gonna' continue to increase, so we need to have a plan. Fizz is getting the bars sold faster than I'd imagined he would, and the pile of cash continues to grow. It's a great problem to have, but we need to make a decision, that's all," Ben explained.

"Well, let's just open a few accounts in different banks," Troy suggested.

"No…no banks, Troy. Your life becomes an open book when you deposit money into a bank. I have very little trust in the banking system. And, if you think they're not run by the government, then you need to get your head out of the sand. At some point, we'd have to answer about the number of large deposits and probably end up having to pay taxes on the money…no banks!" Ben reiterated.

"Okay…well, we need to give it some thought," Troy replied.

"I have to call Fizz and discuss some other matters," Ben explained. "I'm sure he's been faced with this more than once and can lend some advice."

The group enjoyed the evening but kept the weekend celebration to a medium roar. Alcohol was off limits to Lindsey…doctor's orders. So, Ben sat and drank water with Lindsey after he'd consumed the one round that Big John had set up.

After a few hours of talk and laughter…Ben boarded *Next Adventure* to be certain all was good on board for the weekend stay. He also took this time away from the crowd to call Captain Fizz.

"Dude!" Fizz answered. "How's my favorite wench?" he asked.

"She's okay for now, Fizz," Ben replied

"Okay…well, give her a kiss from me, okay dude? By the way, did you see your pile of bars is getting smaller and the pile of green is getting larger?"

"I sure did. That, trouble with treasure thing keeps appearing, though."

"Wha-da-ya' mean?" Fizz asked.

"All this green," Ben answered.

"That's the easy part that I was going to talk with you about," Fizz replied. "You simply invest it in my projects and you're all set…the government will never question a thing," he added.

Ben laughed. "I'm sure some of it will be helping push your projects along, but we still have a major investment ahead of us on this wreck in Jamaica. I need to have a face to face meeting with you real soon to inform you of some new developments down there."

"Okay," Fizz replied. "I can come down there or you can come up here, either way."

"I'm in the house up north from your location next week, so you can stop by there on your way up to Ocala if that works."

"Actually, that's perfect," Ben explained. "How about Monday morning around nine o'clock?"

"Deal, dude…meet me at the Waffle House at the exit where you get off to come to my place. I'll let you buy me breakfast with some of that green you're so worried about."

"Deal!" Ben replied. "See you Monday morning."

Ben walked back out and took his seat with the rest of the gang. He was clearly beat from the week that he'd just had, along with the air travel and stress of it all. He could see that Lindsey was over it as well and ready to chill on the boat.

"Okay guys. Lindsey and I are gonna' go chill on *Next Adventure.* Troy, I need to have one more conversation with you before you head out for the evening. Come see me before you and Darlene give it up for the evening, ok?"

"No problémo, dude…I'll be down there in a bit," Troy answered.

"I need to go too, guys," Mick added. "I haven't been to my place all week and I need to check on things there." Mick gave everybody a hug and asked Big John if he would take her to Ben and Lindsey's place where she'd left her car.

"Sure thing," John replied. "Your chariot awaits my lady." The pair jumped on John's golf cart to drive Mick the short distance to Ben and Lindsey's place.

"Thanks, John," Ben said as he and Lindsey made their way to *Next Adventure.* Once onboard, Lindsey told Ben that she was going to turn in.

"Darling…I'm kinda' tired. I'm going to lie down."

"Okay dear. I'll be there shortly. I just wanna' go up on the fly-bridge and check some things out up there."

Ben climbed the ladder up to the fly-bridge and sat at the helm pondering a few things when Troy walked up with a bottle of Ben's favorite beer.

"Thanks dude," Ben said. "But, I think I'm done with the booze for a while."

"No problem…I understand…I think," Troy replied. "Now, about this conversation…" Troy asked.

"Oh yeah…I know I've already told you that we need to be certain Marley is taken care of, as we promised. I also need to be sure that Maria…in Spain, is compensated fairly well for her part in this. Twenty-five or thirty-thousand dollars would be adequate, I think."

"Why do you keep telling me this, Ben?" Troy asked. "I'm fine with it…so don't worry" he assured.

"Also…" Ben continued…"I'm meeting with Fizz Monday morning up at his place to discuss this mounting pile of cash and a few other details. I'll call you from Ocala and fill you in on that conversation, okay?"

"Roger that! I think Darlene and I are going to call it a night too, dude," Troy replied as he got up to climb back down the ladder.

Ben sat for just a bit and stared at the beer Troy had brought him. Then, he stood, picked up the beer and dumped it into Mullet creek. He sat back down looking over the side of the vessel and watched the suds that had formed flowing out with the tide and thought how quickly life can change. He was more motivated than ever to take better care of himself.

The weekend passed quickly with Ben and Lindsey relaxing on the boat. A few visitors stopped by but for the most part the couple spent a lot of time together with just the two of them enjoying each others company. They left *Next Adventure* Sunday evening and returned home so Ben could get ready to go up north to Ocala on Monday morning and explain to his boss why he didn't show up for work last week...but most importantly, to meet with Fizz.

He woke Monday morning and threw together the usual stuff he traveled with. He shaved before leaving, being careful to leave the mustache and goatee as Lindsey had requested. He gave her a kiss reminding her that Mick would be there when she got off work to spend the nights with her.

"I'll see you soon, dear...I love you," he said as he left the house.

As he was driving, Ben thought about the conversation he needed to have with Fizz. He knew Fizz would keep his secret...he wasn't in the least bit concerned about that, but he did wonder how Fizz would respond to the real reason he'd returned to Jamaica.

Ben was at the exit where he was to meet Fizz for breakfast before he knew it. Turning off the Interstate, he parked his red truck in the parking lot of the Waffle House and walked into the restaurant.

"Good morning," came a voice from behind the counter.

"Good morning," Ben replied as he looked around to see where the greeting had come from. He took a seat in a corner booth where he felt the conversation would less likely be overheard and waited on Fizz who rolled in at nine a.m. Ben watched as the Captain made his way from the parking lot to the restaurant. As Fizz entered the restaurant, he heard a voice speak to him.

"Good morning..." He looked around to see where the greeting came from.

"Good morning," Fizz replied sitting down at the booth with Ben. After sitting down he laughed. "I've been coming here for years, but I've never been able to figure out who's greeting me."

"Same here, dude. I've eaten in every one of these joints along Interstate-75 between southwest Florida and Georgia and haven't figured it out yet."

After the two men ordered their breakfast, Fizz remarked. "Okay dude...what's on your mind?"

"To begin with, I was back in Jamaica last week by myself, but *that* needs to be kept quiet, okay?"

"Okay...your secret's safe with me. Why did you go back to Jamaica?" As Ben filled Captain Fizz in on all the details, he listened intently.

"First of all, I found a surgeon who can help Lindsey, which was the main reason I returned. But, here's the clincher, Fizz...the surgeon is a collector of ancient artifacts. He's the guy who owns the island I was telling you about, you know...the one who the locals call the Boogeyman. Anyway, the surgeon had made a comment to me that he owns the local bureaucrats and has the ability to convince them to allow our group to salvage the remaining treasure in a legal manner...with strings attached, of course. I know for sure he's gonna' want a bronze cannon out of the deal," Ben concluded.

"Wait...wait...wait! First of all..." Fizz began questioning..."you say you've found a surgeon who can help Lindsey? And now you're telling me this guy's a recluse who lives on an island in Jamaica? What the hell are you thinkin'?"

"Fizz, you're just gonna' have to trust me on that, okay?"

"Okay, dude," Fizz replied with a concerned voice. "However, I think you need to think through this one a great deal more, though." Fizz shook his head in disbelief. "Now, back to the other matter," he continued. Asking for a bronze cannon out of the deal doesn't seem to be too much of a request, especially if he can get us legal ownership of the wreck."

"There's probably one more thing he may ask for," Ben explained.

"What's that?" Fizz asked.

"The gold altar, if indeed it does exist."

"How would he know about the golden altar?" Fizz replied with surprise.

"Okay…I mentioned the gold altar during our conversation, but he was already aware of the story and even knew the architect's name who had the altar designed. He knew the story before I told him," Ben explained.

Fizz thought for just a bit before asking another question. "So, what's this guy's name, Ben?"

"I only know him as the Boogeyman at this point. I asked him his name and he told me that it wasn't necessary that I know, so I didn't press the question any further."

"Albert Von Schmidt," Fizz said. Ben raised his eyebrows.

"Excuse me?"

"Albert Von Schmidt. When Jack was researching wrecks in the Caribbean, he ran across some old newspaper articles from the nineteen-fifties that talked about a German man with an expansive collection of artifacts like you've described. He was trying to mount an expedition to search for a lost galleon that possibly carried a fabled golden altar. He was unable to attract anyone who was interested in putting an expedition together, so the story was forgotten like so many other stories over the years. I've told you that both Jack and I believe that the altar does exist. I think you may have finally found the resting place of that artifact...and, I believe ole Albert thinks you have, as well. Albert hasn't been heard from for years. I suppose he must have been chalked-up as dead by now. And now...my student, Ben Carson, has found him alive and well! I believe *that's* a treasure find in itself! Damn!" Fizz continued..."Jack was all over this situation before he passed. Like I've already said...if Jack had lived a few more years, the wreck you found would've already been salvaged. I believe he was *that* close."

"Well, I've given the man your name Fizz. He's expecting you to come visit someday and work through the details of the salvage. Marley and Troy will help you with its location," Ben explained.

"You talk as if you're not gonna' be there. What's up with *that*?" Fizz asked.

"Uhhm...yeah...of course I'm planning on being there, but with Lindsey's condition and all, you just never know."

"Lindsey's gonna' be just fine, Ben. And this galleon's been on the bottom for well over three-hundred years. It *will* wait a little longer."

Yeah...okay. The other situation I need to discuss with you is about all this money. I figure you must have been faced with this situation a few times during your career. What can we do with all this cash?"

Fizz laughed a bit before replying. "I know, it's like you're rich, but don't have two nickels to rub together...

frustrating as hell! Bury it, stuff your mattress with it, but whatever you do, don't put it in the bank. When we get legal rights to the wreck, all those problems will go away," he explained.

"I suppose you're right, Fizz. For now…I need to get on up north and see if I still have a job. I'll see ya' soon." Ben finished his breakfast, shook hands with Fizz and headed north.

Ben drove the remainder of the way to work and explained to his boss why he'd been absent from work the previous week. He really didn't care whether he'd be fired over it or not. He simply knew that he needed a paycheck to continue being deposited so that Lindsey had no reason to concern herself with the matter.

Two more weeks had passed and Ben was concerned that he had been hoodwinked by the Boogeyman. Then, one morning on his way to Ocala his phone rang with a number on the Caller-I.D. that he didn't recognize.

"Mr. Carson?" the voice asked.

"Yes...this is Ben Carson."

"My associate, whom wishes to remain silent in this matter, has reached out to me in order to assist with an issue you have. Are you familiar with what I'm speaking of?" the voice asked.

"I am," Ben replied as his heart began beating a hundred miles an hour and his hands started to sweat to the point that he had to wipe them off on his jeans to keep a grip on the steering wheel.

"I have a briefing set up at my office in Tampa tomorrow. Can you make it here to meet with me?" the voice asked.

"I'll be there," Ben replied. "Just tell me what time and send me the address.

"Perfect..." the voice said. "I'll text you the details. See you tomorrow, Mr. Carson."

A genuine feeling of relief come over him that he'd never felt before. Now, he knew that he'd not been ripped off by the Boogeyman, and most importantly...he was doing what he felt was the only thing he could do to help Lindsey. He pulled off the Interstate at the next exit to find a motel to spend the night and to also type-up a resignation letter to send his boss.

Ben pulled off the road just past Tampa in Pasco County and got a room at a motel. He typed the letter of resignation and paused a bit before pressing send. He had to be in downtown Tampa tomorrow morning at 8 a.m. He spent the night tossing and turning and thinking to himself, *"How can this diabolical plan actual be carried out?"*

Tuesday morning, Ben was at the address sent to him well before 8 a.m. The building appeared to have been a medical facility of some sort at one time but was now very outdated in appearance. The parking lot had very few cars in it and grass was growing through the cracks in the asphalt. Ben thought to himself, *"This looks like a scene from some nuclear holocaust movie."* He walked up to the front door and surprising enough, the door was unlocked. He walked into the reception area where he saw a young girl working behind the desk.

"How can I help you?" she asked.

"Uhh...yeah. My name is Ben Carson. I have an eight a.m. appointment."

"Oh yes, Mr. Carson. You're here to see Dr. Altenbach on the third floor. Just go right down this hall and the elevator will be on your right, Mr. Carson. Have a nice day," the receptionist said.

Ben made his way to the elevator and proceeded to the third floor. The elevator door opened to what appeared to be a full blown hospital. He entered at the nurses' station where he was asked whom he was there to see.

"Uhhm…Alten something…" Ben said.

"Altenbach?" the nurse replied.

"That's the name," Ben said. "Altenbach."

"And your name?" the nurse asked.

"Ben Carson, ma'am."

The nurse picked up the phone and called Dr. Altenbach who met Ben at the nurses' station. After introductions were made, the doctor said, "Follow me, Mr. Carson. I have a conference room reserved for our meeting just down the hall." The two men entered the conference room where the doctor got right to the details of the meeting.

"Mr. Carson…you must understand that this type of request is far from typical. Typically speaking, we see loved ones offering their liver, kidney, and sometimes even a lung. A heart, on the other hand, is very rare…but indeed, it has been done. You will need to take your own life on the day of the organ removal. I'll get more into the details of that, later," the doctor explained. "I have been in touch with your wife's doctor in Naples in order to let him know that we may possibly have someone here in Tampa that is currently being screened as a possible donor for your wife. I will need to verify the blood-type before informing the doctor in Naples that we have a definite match. A-negative blood-types are few and far between," the doctor explained. "Are you sure that your blood-type matches your wife's, Mr. Carson?"

"I'm certain," Ben explained. "Back several years ago, I would have died if it weren't for Lindsey. I had an accident at work that required several blood transfusions. She provided the blood that I needed to stay alive. I owe her this."

"I believe you, Mr. Carson. I just need a sample to send to your wife's doctor"

"Do what you need to do, Doc," Ben told him.

The doctor ordered the blood drawn from Ben to be sent to Naples to Lindsey's doctor for blood-type verification. Afterward, Ben reminded the doctor that he'd said he would explain in further detail how Ben would take his own life on the day of the organ removal.

"Oh yes," the doctor said. "It will be painless and fast, Mr. Carson. You will have an I.V. placed in your arm. You will administer the solution yourself by pushing a syringe that will stop your heart. Your heart will be removed and transported to Naples to your wife."

"And when do you plan on performing this procedure Doc?"

"Tomorrow, if we get confirmation back from your wife's surgeon in Naples that it's a match."

Ben nodded his head "yes" and said, "Okay…I have a little time to make some phone calls. I have some voices I want to hear before my body goes," he explained.

"I understand," the doctor said. "I would suggest making calls to those you wish to make amends with and especially to those you love."

"Yeah…I know who I need to call."

Ben traveled the short distance back to the motel where he sat and made a list of those he intended to call. He called his son in Pennsylvania and talked with him for close to an hour. Then, called his brother in Indiana and both his grandchildren. He called his mother, which was an especially tough conversation knowing that this would be the last time he'd hear her voice. And then, he called Lindsey.

"Well…I'm certainly surprised that you're calling me. I always look forward to your text, but a phone call is even better!" she said.

Ben paused as he heard her voice. He knew this was going to be the last time.

"I just wanted to tell you that I love you, dear." That, was all that he could muster-up.

"I love you too, dear…what's up with you?" she asked.

"Nothing…nothing, dear. I just wanted to hear your voice, that's all. I'll be with you soon, dear…take care," he said.

Lindsey simply replied with…"I love you, Ben."

The following morning around eleven a.m. the phone call came from the doctor's office in Tampa. I made the short trip to the office arriving around eleven-thirty. Shortly after, I was prepared for the surgery and then the syringe that would stop my heart was placed in my hand. As I lay there, I thought to myself how eerie this all seems, in slow motion and kind of hazy. In my mind, the voices I was hearing were echoed and muffled. As I prepared myself mentally for what I knew needed to be done, I heard Lindsey's voice speak in that same echoed and muffled manner, *"I love you Ben…I love you Ben…I love you Ben.* Then, I pushed the plunger of the syringe. As I lay there waiting for the drugs to take effect, I faintly heard the ringing of a phone. The time was just after 1 p.m. I thought to myself… *"I must be slipping into the spirit world…"* and then once again, I heard the sound of a phone ringing, and then…the flat line sound of the heart-monitoring device.

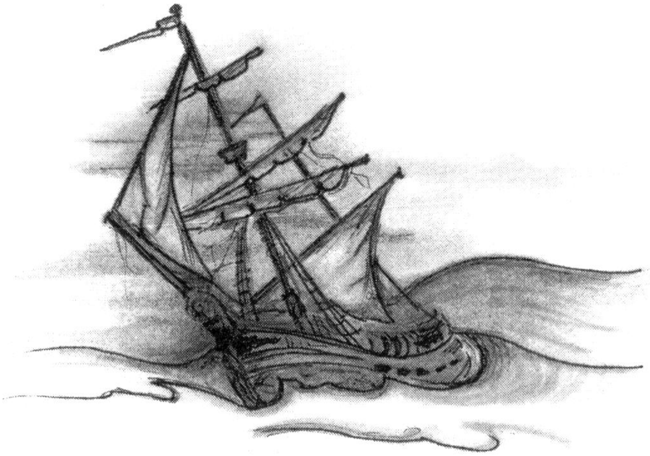

ABOUT THE AUTHOR

I guess I've always been a treasure hunter of sorts. Growing up in rural Indiana I spent countless hours scouring the plowed fields and river bottoms for Native American artifacts. I cherish that collection to this day as every find was a new discovery to me. I would look at the artifact lying on the ground and pause for just a bit before picking it up, wondering about the human whom had last touched it.

I was smitten by the sunken treasure bug very early in life after reading Robert Louis Stevenson's *Treasure Island*. I daydreamed a lot, especially in school when I was supposed to be listening to the lesson being taught that day, which probably explains my poor grades. I finished school and went to work like I was supposed to, so I thought, that is…until one day I realized life was passing me by and I wasn't chasing my dream.

I moved to Florida at the age of thirty-nine so I could get closer to the treasure hunting scene. Eventually, after several years in Florida, I hooked up with Carl Fismer. Carl is one of the most interesting people I know and has unselfishly invited me in to his realm of treasure diving knowledge.

I haven't found a pile of gold or silver yet, but any day now…I will dive down and return to the surface having fulfilled my dream.

PHOTO GALLERY

Jason and Gary Parker

Missy, Joshua, Gary, Bailey and Blake Parker

*Carl "Captain Fizz" Fismer
Missy and Gary Parker*